■

The Goldin Boys

■

Also by Joseph Epstein

A Line Out for a Walk

Partial Payments

Once More Around the Block

Plausible Prejudices

The Middle of My Tether

Familiar Territory

Ambition

Divorced in America

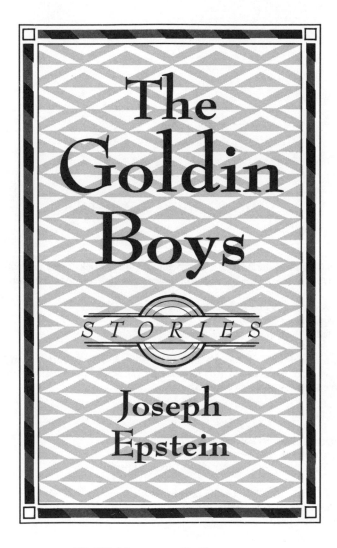

The Goldin Boys

STORIES

Joseph Epstein

W·W·Norton & Company
NEW YORK · LONDON

"The Count and the Princess," and "Schlifkin on My Books" were first published in *The Hudson Review*. The remainder of these stories appeared in *Commentary*.

The text of this book is composed in 10/13 Galliard, with the display set in Bernhard Modern. Composition and manufacturing by The Maple-Vail Manufacturing Group. Book design by Michael Chesworth.

First Edition.

Library of Congress Cataloging-in-Publication Data
Epstein, Joseph, 1937–
    The Goldin boys & other stories / Joseph Epstein.
      p.   cm.
    I. Title.   II. Title: Goldin boys and other stories.
  PS3555.P6527G6   1991
  813'.54—dc20   91–2194

ISBN 0-393-03022-9

W.W. Norton & Company, Inc., 500 Fifth Avenue, New York, N.Y. 10110
W. W. Norton & Company, Ltd., 10 Coptic Street, London WC1A 1PU

1 2 3 4 5 6 7 8 9 0

*For
Carol Houck Smith,
dear friend*

 CONTENTS

The Count and the Princess / *11*

Low Anxiety / *35*

No Pulitzer for Pinsker / *55*

The Goldin Boys / *81*

Kaplan's Big Deal / *106*

Schlifkin on My Books / *135*

Marshall Wexler's
Brilliant Career / *152*

Paula, Dinky, and the Shark / *179*

Another Rare Visit with
Noah Danzig / *198*

The Goldin Boys

The Count and the Princess

C ount Peter Kinski had of course dropped the title from his name when he came to live in the United States at the age of twenty-two. But he had never quite succeeded in dropping the idea of himself as an aristocrat; and while his own stay in America was now more than three decades long, and he had become an American citizen, he continued to think himself a visitor. Perhaps visitor-observer would be more precise, for Count Kinski fancied himself rather in the tradition of those other aristocratic observers of America, Tocqueville and Lord Bryce. (Although he had not yet actually written a line of it, for the past eight years he had been gathering material for a work he had tentatively entitled "America in Her Decline.") Yet unlike either Tocqueville or Bryce, Count Kinski was tossed by circumstances into the churning of local life—in the City of Chicago, of all places—riding buses and subways, shopping for and preparing his own meals, paying bills and earning the money to pay them by teaching political theory at a city college on the northwest side. The Count alternated in his feelings about all this: sometimes he felt an almost unbearable bitterness because he had to undergo such indignities; but sometimes he felt proud because he had been able to survive them.

Certainly he had not been born for such a life. His childhood had been spent on the family estate, seventy kilometers to the south of Lodz, where he was brought up by various French governesses and educated by his tutor, a German Tolstoyan, Herr Kügler, in foreign languages, rudimentary science, and history. Before the Nazis swept through Poland, he had been sent off to school in Switzerland. He returned briefly—oh, so briefly—at the end of the war to the world he had known of large hunting parties, a household staff of more than twenty servants, and his father's, the old Count's, life of leisurely elegance. But no sooner had he begun to settle into the life for which he was intended than the Communists had taken over Poland. Although an aristocrat, the old Count was a liberal in politics and a Westerner in culture—exactly the sort of man the new regime wished to remove. Peter and his mother were packed off to Paris, where they installed themselves in the Ritz, there later to be joined by his father. But before he could join them, his father, under the strain of this, his second reversal of fortune, died of a heart attack. Peter (now Count) Kinski and his mother were left stranded at the Ritz, with very little money and only the jewelry she had managed to smuggle out of Poland at their departure.

Between them Peter and his mother decided upon an academic career for him. He enrolled as a doctoral candidate in political philosophy at the University of Chicago. The plan was for him to go off to America first. His mother would remain in Europe, in the hope of salvaging something from the family's latest disaster. But before she could join her son Countess Kinski suffered a stroke, and died less than two weeks later. One of the Kinski family's agents sent on the money her jewelry had fetched to Peter—some $16,000 in American currency. She was buried in Père Lachaise Cemetery. Peter never knew where his father was buried, or if he was buried at all. An only child, he was the last of his line, the final Count Kinski of a family that traced its descent back to the thirteenth century.

Even at the University of Chicago, that most cosmopolitan of American universities, he was an oddity. In an otherwise bohemian graduate student setting, he wore suits of an English cut, carried a walking stick, read Proust. He lived alone at International House, among students from India and Nigeria and veterans from World War Two on the GI Bill. He studied under Leo Straus, and chose an ambitious dissertation on Thucydides and the origins of totalitarianism in Sparta. It was a dissertation he was never to finish, for before it was really underway his money had all but run out, and he was forced to take a teaching job at the school at which he had now been teaching for more than twenty years.

After leaving the University of Chicago the Count moved to the somewhat rundown Chicago neighborhood called Rogers Park. He rented a one-bedroom apartment in an older building on Pratt Avenue less than a block from Lake Michigan. Slowly he acquired furniture, bought many books, a few good rugs. When his English clothes wore out, he bought American ones that roughly—rather too roughly for his taste—approximated them. His only palpable evidence of his old life was four undershirts, with the Kinski family crest sewn into them by Panushka, an elderly family maid who had helped to raise him as a child; these he kept in the bottom drawer of a mahogany chiffonier he had purchased at a Salvation Army store.

Living among his books and pipes, taking the El and then a bus to the college three days each week, cooking his meals, the ingredients for which he bought at a locally famous German delicatessen called Kuhn's, he somehow reached his fiftieth year. He had grown heavier and lost much of his hair. He still carried his walking stick. He read, attended the Chicago Symphony downtown, went occasionally to art films, kept no television set nor ever learned to drive a car. By carefully husbanding his salary—he taught most summers; what else was there for him to do?—he was able to afford a holiday in Europe once every four or five years, where he could speak the French and German that had never left him. Christmas Eves he took himself, with the aid of the El and two buses, to a Polish restaurant in the suburb of Berwyn, where he ate a traditional meal of duck and dumplings and spoke Polish with the owners.

At the college he made no real friends. When he first arrived there, an attempt had been made to throw him together with a teacher of Russian, also an emigré named Dimitri Suslenko, who spoke Russian with an atrocious Ukrainian accent. To Americans a Slav was a Slav, and how could they know the age-old enmity between Poles and Russians? Suslenko, though rough-cut, doubtless of peasant origins, was a decent enough fellow in his boorish way, but the Count, an admirer of Santayana and Henry Adams, a reader of Schopenhauer and the Duc de Saint-Simon, could not hope to find any common ground with him. To himself he laughed to think of this Suslenko teaching young students to speak Russian with a heavy Ukrainian accent, which was tantamount to teaching English with a heavy Yiddish accent. But no one else at the college could know this, of course, and he was not about to remark upon it.

In his way Count Kinski loved America. He would always be grateful to the country for providing him a safe port after the storms of his last years in Europe. But grateful though he was to this country, there were things about it, small things, to which he could never reconcile himself. Above all, the familiarity of Americans he could not, after all these years, quite manage. The waitresses, for example, who would set a cup of tea before him, then ask, "Anything else, honey?" Or the occasional black student who would address him as Man, as in "You gonna want that term paper typed, Man?" The fellow with whom he shared his office at the college seemed to specialize in such familiarities. Six years ago, when he moved into the Count's office, upon introduction he said, "Nice to know you, Pete." The Count continued to address him as Professor Ginsberg, and only after three years of sharing an office could he bring himself, after insistent pleas, to call him by his first name, Barney. Meanwhile, Barney Ginsberg had advanced to calling him, the Count, "Babes." "How're you making it, babes?" he would say when Count Kinski arrived at the office in the morning.

Ginsberg was a puzzle to the Count. He was a man of the Count's own age; in fact, he was fifty-three, a year older. Yet he seemed to dress like a boy. He taught in blue jeans; he wore a variety of caps, sometimes a baseball cap, sometimes a Greek fisherman's cap, sometimes a tennis visor. He had long grey sideburns and a drooping mustache in the style of the cossacks. He seemed not so much to wear clothes as to sport a number of costumes, disguises. He was a sociologist by training, with a Ph.D. from New York University, but he taught courses with titles that sounded like American magazine articles: Blacks and Jews, The Holocaust and the Suburbs, Sex and the Changing Middle Class. His students called him by his first name. Once, when the Count was in the office, a young girl came to see Ginsberg with tears in her eyes; as the Count was leaving the room, to give his office-mate privacy, he heard the girl say that she was pregnant and ask what he intended to do about it.

Barney Ginsberg was a popular teacher; Count Kinski, as he himself knew, was not. If many of the courses he taught had not been required for a degree in political science, the numbers of students who enrolled for his courses would have been even smaller than they were. And there were sometimes as few as seven or nine students in his courses. He taught the only way he knew how—from on high. He lectured for the full fifty minutes: on Locke, Rousseau, Montesquieu, Marx, his beloved Tocqueville. Sometimes he would close his eyes and imagine himself delivering these lectures at Oxford or the Sorbonne. Then he would open them to note that a few of his students had closed theirs, to dream surely of places far distant from those citadels of learning. He had a reputation as a hard grader. He filled the margins of his students' papers, questioning their inchoate ideas, correcting their English. They must have thought him a little mad.

They, his students, were themselves a strange lot. Most of them worked, and were not students full-time. They wanted, for their various reasons, a degree, perhaps to get a better job. Many were blacks; a few were Mexican. A number of them were housewives whose children were grown, or at least old enough for them to return to school. Count Kinski of course encouraged no intimacy between them and himself. When they came into his office, as one or another occasionally did, to question him about a term paper, he always addressed them as Miss or Mr.; they called him Professor. Over the years he had had a few bright students: a Japanese boy named Bob Anoba, who went on to law school; a Swedish girl named Karen Lingren, who went on to graduate studies at the University of Chicago. But he, the Count, had lost touch with them.

Was Mrs. Sheila Skolnik to be another of his memorable students? It was difficult to say, though it seemed unlikely. This was the second of his courses she had taken; autumn term she had written a quite respectable paper for his course in Political Theory. No power of thought, you understand, but well organized, neatly typed, largely grammatical. Under the current dispensation, such small blessings loomed large. She had made an appointment to discuss her paper for the current semester's course in Continental Political Thinkers. She had told him she wished to write on the subject of Tocqueville and the Ancien Régime. It was late afternoon. She was due for her appointment twenty minutes ago. The Count had given up on her, and had begun to pack his briefcase. Across the room, Barney Ginsberg, feet on his desk, was reading a paperback, a detective story with rather a lurid cover.

A knock on the door. "Enter," said the Count.

"Excuse my being so late," said Mrs. Skolnik. A Jewess, in her early thirties, she was tall, had thick dark hair but blue eyes, was slender but of ample bosom. Ginsberg dropped his feet from the top of his desk at her entrance, set down his detective story, and stared.

"I am very sorry, Professor Kinski," she said. "Is there still time for our meeting?"

"I fear not," said the Count. "My bus leaves in ten minutes. Perhaps on Friday we can meet."

"Can I drive you home, Professor? Maybe we could talk about my paper on the way?"

"Very well, Mrs. Skolnik," said the Count, feeling there was perhaps something slightly irregular about this. "My apartment is on Pratt Avenue, near the lake. Are you certain I shall not be taking you out of your regular way?"

She said not at all. The Count put on his overcoat. As he held the door open for his student, he bade Professor Ginsberg good evening.

"Right on, babes," said Ginsberg, and, though he could not be certain, the Count thought he saw him wink.

Mrs. Skolnik had a red sports car, a Japanese model, and getting into it, his legs stretched straight out, his briefcase on his lap, the Count felt as if he were sitting on the ground. They talked about Mrs. Skolnik's paper. The Count suggested books she might consult;

she asked questions about the paper's length, its deadline, what he expected it to accomplish. The subject was quickly exhausted, and a long ride still lay ahead. The Count would have been perfectly happy to remain silent the remainder of the way, but felt that it would not perhaps be courteous to do so.

"What does your husband do, Mrs. Skolnik, if I may ask?"

"Oh," she said, "Larry was a dentist."

"I am sorry," said the Count, "I did not know you were a widow."

"I'm not," she said.

"But you spoke of your husband in the past tense?"

"I guess I did. I didn't notice. No, Larry and I were divorced four years ago."

"Have you children?" the Count asked.

"Yes, two. A boy and a girl, Ronnie and Melissa. They're both in school now, which makes it possible for me to go back to school myself. I'd like eventually to go to law school. That's why I'm majoring in political science."

"I see," said the Count.

"I live with my parents now. My mother's being able to watch the kids is a great help. Larry still sees them every Sunday. But it was tough on them for a while, not having their father with them."

"I see," said the Count, who felt the conversation getting rather more intimate than he liked. He asked her where her parents lived, and they fell into a general discussion of neighborhoods in Chicago and its suburbs. Her parents lived in the suburb called Northbrook, a relatively new and rather wealthy one. When she pulled up in front of his apartment building, she remarked on how nice it must be to live so close to the lake. The Count agreed that it was, especially in summer, then crept out of the sports car, thanked her, and waved good-by from a crouching position as she drove off.

The day's mail brought a copy of the Zurich monthly *Schweizer Monatshefte,* which he read with his evening meal: herring in aspic, a Hungarian sausage and green beans, with a torte and tea for dessert. After clearing and washing his evening's dishes, he poured himself a digestif, put a Mozart quartet on his phonograph, and read in Santayana's *Dominations and Powers*. Towards eleven o'clock, as was his custom, he retired to bed, there, as was distinctly not his custom, to dream of making unspeakably passionate love to Sheila Skolnik.

When he arrived at his office on Friday morning, Barney Ginsberg was already there. He seemed to be dressed in the outfit of a stevedore. He wore blue jeans, a thick sweater with a high neck, the sleeves pushed up on his hairy forearms, and a blue wool cap which he had on indoors.

"So?" Ginsberg said.

"Pardon?" said the Count.

"So—did you boff her?"

"Sir?" asked the Count.

"Forget it, babes. I already know the answer. No chance. I already know the type, all too well. She's a princess, if ever there was one."

"A princess?" The Count's interest was piqued.

"A Jewish Princess, babes, for Christ sake."

"I see," said the Count, not really seeing at all, but not wishing to carry on the conversation any further.

Sheila Skolnik was not in class that day; nor was she in class again on Monday. Wednesday, when the papers were due, she called the Count on his office phone.

"I'm sorry to have missed class," she said. "I've had the flu. But I've finished my paper. Can I deliver it to you tonight at your apartment?"

"That is not truly necessary, Mrs. Skolnik. If you have it to me in class on Friday, that will be sufficient."

"But I don't really want to be late. Will you be at home tonight?"

"Yes, but . . ."

"Good. I'll be there around eight."

"Yes, but . . ." She had already hung up.

"Most irregular," Count Kinski muttered, "most irregular." He cleared his dishes, poured the remains of the consommé from the small pot into a jar, wrapped the remaining slice of Westphalian ham for the refrigerator, returned the heavy textured Lithuanian bread to his bread box. "Most irregular."

The Count decided to take his tea this evening in his wing chair, the chair in which he sat most evenings to do his reading. It was 7:40; Mrs. Skolnik was to arrive at 8:00. A heavy rain pattered against the metal portion of the air-conditioner that rested on the sill outside his living-room window. He thought, as he perhaps did too often, of his boyhood at his family's estate. Of his life there among the servants. Of Herr Kügler's accounts of Yasnaya Polyana. Of his mother, a fragile woman of artistic temperament, playing Chopin on the grand piano in the drawing room. Of a trip his father took him on to Warsaw, and of their going together, just he and his father, to a puppet opera with a full puppet orchestra. He must have been eight years old at the time.

The Count no longer asked why history had done to him what it had—why it had allowed him to glimpse the old life, to live it long enough to develop a taste for it, and then, like a rug from under a clown, had pulled it roughly away. Still, he often thought, had history not intervened, first in the form of the Nazis and then in that of the Communists, one barbarian horde replacing another, what might his own life have been like? Much, he supposed, like his father's: seeing after the family business, sitting in the provincial assembly, organizing the round of hunts, buying horses, travelling to European capitals for business and pleasure. (His father was an ardent Anglophile, and loved London above all other world cities.) Although his own habits were more bookish than his father's, his responsibilities, and hence his life, would not have been much different. Where his father had improved the family stables, he perhaps, given the chance, would haven enriched the family library. Doubtless by now he would have long been married, have had children, a son of his own to take to the famous puppet opera in Warsaw.

Twenty minutes after eight and still Mrs. Skolnik had not arrived. Outside the rain continued, undiminished in force. It was a grave mistake allowing her to deliver her paper to him at home. Most irregular, and now to irregularity was added tardiness. By this hour the Count had generally settled into his work—grading student papers, going over lecture notes—or his reading for the book on America he hoped one day to write. He did not appreciate his customary schedule being interrupted in this way. He would not permit it to happen again.

At 8:45 the doorbell rang. Having rung the buzzer to let his visitor in, the Count walked to his front door. He lived on the third floor of a walk-up building. Coming out to the hallway he watched Mrs. Skolnik climb the last half flight of steps. She was utterly drenched by the rain.

"Sorry to be so late," she said. "I couldn't find a parking space." She brought a large manila envelope out of an ample leather shoulder bag. "Here is my paper. At least it's dry, even if its author isn't." She stood out in the hall, water dripping off her. Her hair was a great dishevelment. She sneezed, said good night, turned to depart, when the Count heard himself say:

"See here, you are very wet. Please come in to dry off for a bit. Perhaps you will have a cup of tea."

"Thanks. I'd like that." She removed her boots in the hall; also her raincoat, which was soaked through. Underneath the coat her skirt and blouse were greatly blotched with rain.

"Allow me to get you a towel," said the Count, leading the way toward his bathroom. "Will Earl Grey be acceptable? Or is there another tea you prefer?"

"Whatever you have will be fine," she said, the towel under her arm, slowly closing the bathroom door.

The Count put on the water, got out a fresh set of tea things, set out some biscuits and chocolates on a small teak platter. He had inserted two linen tea napkins in small pewter rings, when he heard his bathroom door open. Setting down the tea things in the living room, he turned to see Mrs. Skolnik, barefoot, drying her hair roughly with the towel, and wearing, so far as he could make out, nothing but his yellow terry-cloth robe, which she must have discovered hanging on its place on the back of the bathroom door.

"I hope you don't mind my borrowing this for a while, Professor," she said. "My clothes are soaked through, and I put them on the bathroom radiator to dry."

"I see," said the Count. "I see."

He bent over to pour the tea, but his hands shook. The tea pot made a great clatter against the thin China cup and saucer. Mrs. Skolnik put her hand over his to steady it. He turned and her eyes were only inches from his. He stood, and so did she; her robe had come slightly open. He was about to speak, when she gently covered his mouth with her hand. They embraced and she took him by the hand into the bedroom, where they did things together that the Count hadn't even dared to dream.

When he woke in the morning the Count found a note on the kitchen counter next to her Tocqueville essay, still in its manila envelope.

Dear Professor,
    Excuse my calling you professor but it occurs to me I don't know your first name. For complicated reasons, mostly having to do with my kids, I had to return home late last night. If I had any choice in the matter, I would have liked to stay, so that I could be with you now instead of this note. I hope you do not mind if I call you sometime later this afternoon at your office.

               Truly,
               Sheila S.

The Count felt himself greatly confused. What would he say when next he spoke to her? Before last night, life had seemed so orderly, so simple. No longer. What was the American idiom? In the soup. Yes, he was definitely in the soup now.

In the office Barney Ginsberg was dressed in what the Count considered his mufti. Which for Barney Ginsberg meant jeans, a shirt of flowery pattern, the top three buttons undone, and three neck chains, one with a Star of David, another with an astrological sign, the third with an animal's tooth.

"You've come to the right man, Pete," said Ginsberg, when the Count had most tentatively broached the subject pressing on his mind.

He, the Count, had not mentioned Mrs. Skolnik's name.

"Yep, you've come to the right doctor, kiddo," Ginsberg said. "Since my divorce nine years ago the subject of women is my great subject. If I was twenty years younger, I'd write my dissertation on it. 'Unattached and Attached Women in the Last Quarter of the Twentieth Century: A Field Study' by B. L. Ginsberg. Dissertation hell, we're talking about a god damn best-seller."

"It is not disconcerting to you, Barney, seeing many different women?"

"Not in the least, babes. I ask only two prerequisites: women I go out with must have a job and they must have no sex hang-ups. With my alimony and support payments I'm too broke to help support anyone, and I'm too old to teach the basic course in human sexuality."

"But do you not find yourself in—how to put it?—emotional entanglements?"

"What kind of entanglements? Look, Pete, with me these ladies know up-front what they're getting into. We provide each other a little service. When this loses its interest, we split. No hard, no complicated, feelings. You only go around once."

"But you feel no misgivings?"

"Only when some chick I'm still interested in splits before I do."

"No responsibility accompanies these intimacies?" asked the Count.

"What am I supposed to do, babes, propose marriage because some broad agrees to sleep with me? Come off it. The way I look at it I'm grateful but so should she be. There's no longer any such thing as an innocent women, if ever there was, which I frankly doubt." Ginsberg brought his feet up on his desk. He was wearing red shoes with blue stripes across them.

"I see," said the Count, who was not certain he did.

The Count was gratified that Barney Ginsberg was out of the office when Mrs. Skolnik called. He asked if she had arrived home without any difficulties. He asked after her illness. Was she feeling any better? She said she was but thought it would be better to remain home for a few days.

"Won't you call me Sheila?" she asked.

"Yes," said the Count, failing to do so.

"And what can I call you?"

"My *prenom,*" said the Count, noting a slight quaver in his voice, "is Peter."

"Are you free on Sunday, Peter?"

"Yes," he said. "Yes, I suppose I am."

"That's the day Larry spends with the children. It's sometimes a lonely day for me. Can we spend it together?"

"I think that will be very nice."

"Please call me Sheila."

"Yes," said the Count, "I should like to be with you on Sunday, Sheila. I should like it very much."

"I would too, Peter."

Sunday was a bright day, and a warm one for late March in Chicago. Because the Count did not drive a car—yet another American thing he had failed to learn—she was to come to him. The day before he had bought a pheasant from a Czech butcher on the Near North Side. He planned dinner, and perhaps a walk along the lakefront into Evanston. He was tidying his apartment, putting away books and his pipes, a Bach cantata was playing over the radio, when, a little past noon, the doorbell rang.

She wore grey trousers—did Americans still call them "slacks"?—a white blouse with a small soft collar under a yellow sweater. The yellow of the sweater made her dark hair seem even lusher than he had remembered it; the color also did fine things for her eyes. As he took her coat, she leaned in, touching her cheek to his. His heart jumped.

"Well, Peter," she said. "Here we are."

"Exactly. Just so," he said.

"It's a beautiful day."

"It is indeed. Can I get you a cup of tea," the Count gulped slightly, "Sheila?"

"None for me. I had late breakfast with the children before their father came for them. A shame to waste a day like this. Maybe we ought to be outdoors?"

Not until they reached Evanston, nearly two miles from his apartment, did the Count note that he had forgot his walking stick. They spoke easily together—more easily than he would have thought. She told him of her girlhood in the Chicago suburbs; spoke of her marriage, which had ended after her father had revealed to her that her husband had been cheating on her with other women, many of them his patients. She told him of the effects of the divorce on the children, her love for whom, so evident, touched the Count in its simplicity and strength of feeling. He spoke of his own childhood, so different from hers, of his schooling, of his dead parents. When he talked of his life since arriving in America, he realized, hearing himself describe the routine of his days, that he hadn't had much of a life, at least in any sense that she was likely to understand: he taught, he read, he shopped, he fixed his meals, one day led into another and thirty years had gone by.

Dinner was a great success. She had never eaten pheasant before, and this pheasant, although she could not have known it, was a particularly delicious one. They drank two bottles of wine. She asked him if he had read all the books in his apartment. He said not nearly but was afraid buying books was his great vice. She said her son looked as if he might be a serious reader one day; at any rate, she hoped so. When she asked him, he told her that he spoke four languages and read six. She said she took Spanish in high school but was not very good at it. The Count had bought Napoleons for dessert, but when she looked at her wristwatch she said she was afraid she hadn't time, because she liked to be home when their father brought her children back. He walked her to her car, where before getting in she kissed him lightly on the mouth, telling him she had had a marvelous day.

The Count felt exhilarated. Back in his apartment, he made himself a cup of tea, lit a pipe, and sat down to read dear Sheila's paper on Tocqueville. It began:

Alexis de Tocqueville was born in 1805 and died in 1859. He was a nobleman by birth, his title being that of a Count. His ancestors were also noblemen. The Tocquevilles, like so many other families of aristocrats, did not fare well during the French Revolution of 1789.

He could bring himself to read no further. The paper, in its rudimentariness, its utter lack of intellectual sophistication, depressed him. How could he care so for a woman who wrote such sentences! Yet he did, did he not? He put the paper back in its envelope. He couldn't bear to read further, no, not this evening.

Sundays became their regular day together. They went for walks. Occasionally they would go downtown. She liked movies. Once he took her to the Art Institute, showing her the five or six paintings there that he loved. Less successful was an outing to a concert of Baroque music, during which he noticed her nodding off. She had no interest in serious music. Politics, too, were of no interest to her; not even the woman's liberation, which nowadays seemed to put so many other women into a state of agitation. She had never been to Europe, and showed little curiosity about it. The farthest she had been from Chicago was on a trip to Hawaii, where she had gone to a dental convention with her husband. Once, as a special treat, the Count bought caviar for their hors d'oeuvres; she complained about its saltiness. Most Sundays he prepared their dinner; when she did so the fare was usually plain, steak and fried potatoes, roast chicken and rice. When they went out, the Count noted that other men stared at her, which made him proud but uneasy. Some Sundays they made love, but not every Sunday. In class they pretended scarcely to know each other, though the Count sometimes found himself lecturing to her alone, like a Spanish gentleman serenading his lady on her balcony.

The Count was made nervous by her invitation to meet her parents and children. She arrived to pick him up at 2:00 on the Sunday afternoon of their meeting. He wore an English suit with a waistcoat; something told him not to bring along his walking stick. It was possible, he considered, that Sheila's father and mother were only a few years older than he; they could indeed be his contemporaries. This was one among several things the Count hesitated then chose not to ask her about as they drove along the freeway out to her parents' home in Northbrook.

"Peter Kinski," said Sheila, once they were in the house, "I would like you to meet my parents, Mr. and Mrs. Morris Feinberg."

"It's very nice to make your acquaintance," said Mrs. Feinberg. She struck the Count as being perhaps four or five years older than himself, slightly heavyset with a reddish tint to her hair. She wore an inordinately large diamond ring on her left hand. In the face of the mother, an old Polish proverb held, is written the future of the daughter. The prospect was not at all displeasing to the Count.

"Professor," said Mr. Feinberg, vigorously shaking the Count's hand, "my pleasure, I'm sure." He, too, could not have been more than four or five years older than the Count. He appeared to have lost none of his hair, which was thick and still quite black. He had on plaid trousers and a golf shirt with an alligator over the left breast; his upper arm muscles bulged. He wore one of the new digital watches, very large with a black face and a heavy silver band. The Count himself carried a thin pocket watch of French make.

"Sheila, dear," said Mrs. Feinberg, "maybe the Professor would like to go into the family room with Daddy, while we put the finishing touches on dinner."

"You care at all about baseball, Professor?" asked Mr. Feinberg. They were in a room whose walls were covered with knotty pine. At one end was a bar. At the other a television screen that looked to be five feet wide and four feet high, beneath which was some very complicated-looking equipment. Chairs and couches were placed about the room. A bookcase along one wall had a set of *World Book* encyclopedias, *A History of the Jews* by Abraham Sachar, and a number of trophies with figures swinging golf clubs atop them.

"No," said the Count, "I fear athletics marks yet another gap in my knowledge of America."

"Sure," said Feinberg, "I can understand that." He picked up a small box on a lamp table, which turned on the television set, on which appeared men in pyjama-like outfits, going through movements and motions altogether mysterious to the Count. "I grew up playing the game, and I still love to watch it. Sheila tells me you teach politics."

"Yes," said the Count, vaguely distracted by the darkness of the room and the colors floating about on the large screen.

"I have to tell you that this year was the first time I voted for a Republican for President. That's something I thought I'd never live long enough to see."

"The United States has gone through great turmoil. Perhaps it is not so surprising that your own politics would change."

"Still, in the house I grew up in FDR was like a god. He could do no wrong. Sheila tells me you were born in Poland."

"This is true."

"Our family, as far as we trace it, was from Poland, too. From Galicia. Life was never very good for the Jews in Poland. There are even people who say that under Hitler the Poles were worse even than the Nazis."

"It was less than good" said the Count. "Sometimes, when I brood upon the tortured history of my country, I think it has been so tortured—so deserving of its torturers—because of its treatment of the Jews. It makes a shameful chapter in our history, Mr. Feinberg."

"Let me turn this goddamn thing off." Feinberg picked up the gadget, pressed the button, and the colors on the screen faded softly away. "I'd like it if you'd call me Morry. My guess is we're not that far apart in age."

"I should like to, but only if you will agree to call me Peter."

"So tell me, Pete, what's the story with you and my daughter?"

"The story?" asked the Count.

"You know, where's it headed?"

"Headed?" asked the Count. "I do not know. I do know that I am greatly fond of your daughter."

"Excuse my giving you the third degree. I've no real right. But I hate to see her hurt again. Did she tell you it was me who found her husband cheating on her? I'll spare you the details. But I could've killed him at the time. He made too much money too fast. Couldn't handle it. But it broke my kid's heart. Have you been married before?"

"No," said the Count, "I have not."

A door opened. "Soup's on," said Mrs. Feinberg.

The dinner was chopped liver, a chicken soup with dumplings, a beef tenderloin, broccoli, salad, coffee and ice cream. Much of the conversation was about the Feinberg's grandchildren. The boy, Ronnie, played hockey, which pleased Morris Feinberg. The girl, Melissa, was said to be very shy, and soon, according to her father, she was going to need braces on her teeth, which wasn't going to help her shyness any. Mrs. Feinberg asked the Count to call her Sylvia.

"You know, Peter," she said, "we really are very fortunate to have the children with us. We have friends whose kids have moved to California, or who themselves have moved to Florida, who get to see their grandchildren once, maybe twice a year."

At eight o'clock their father brought the children home. Sheila met them at the door. The Count saw him standing in the foyer; she did not invite him in. He was tall, sun-tanned, expensively dressed, his hair, blondish, combed over his ears. The Count felt awkward looking out at him from his chair in the living room. No, he decided, it was not awkwardness, it was jealousy he felt. He wished this man had never existed.

"Ronnie, Melissa," said Sheila, a hand on each child's shoulder. "I want you to meet a very good friend of your Mommy's. This is Professor Kinski."

The boy shook hands manfully; the little girl looked away bashfully. The Count was pleased to see that both children resembled their mother. He thought the girl dear; he preferred children shy, as he had been when a child. Their grandparents asked them what they had done on their day with their father, and Sheila rose to say that she probably ought to take Professor Kinski home.

On the drive back the Count told Sheila about his conversation with her father. "He wanted to know what was the story between us. What, my dear girl, do you suppose the story is?"

"I don't know, Peter," she said. "What do you want it to be?"

"I shall require some time to think about it," the Count said.

"There is no one hurrying you," she said.

"Let me get this straight," said Barney Ginsberg. He was dressed today as what the Count assumed was a cowboy: boots, jeans, a leather shirt, a red bandana round his neck. "Now let me get this straight. You've dipped your wick a few times and now you're thinking of getting married?"

"Dipped my wick?" asked the Count.

"You know, slept with this chick. Let's get serious, Pete. You're in your fifties, babes, and you don't exactly have a lot of turn-around time. One big mistake now and it's ballgame for you."

"I don't think you quite understand, Barney. I am happy when I am with this woman. My life seems better with her near."

"I see, pal, I see. But tell me, what will you live on? Her annual wardrobe probably equals your salary. I know these kind of Jews. Country club *yidlach*. You're a highly educated man, Pete. Let's face it, what'll you talk to her about—designer clothes? Get serious, friend, get serious."

"But serious is precisely what I am."

"And you say there's two kids thrown into this fine bargain?"

"Yes. Two children. That is correct."

"Get serious, man. I mean, get serious."

Of his own seriousness the Count had no doubt. He had never, he thought, been more serious in his life. Marrying this woman could not but change his life, and in the most radical ways. He might not have known much happiness since arriving in America but he had succeeded in establishing order in his life, and there was a measure of happiness in that. Until Sheila, he had assumed he would end his days a bachelor, among his books, his music, his pipes, his plan for writing his great book on America in her decline. Perhaps it was time to admit that he would never write such a book—that the book, or at any rate the idea of the book, was important to him only so long as there was nothing else in his life. He was, he could tell himself, a man who was planning an important book. But if it was so important why hadn't he by now sat down to the writing of it? It was perhaps time to ask such questions.

Between this book, which was his future, and his early years in Poland, which was his past, the Count realized that until now he had spent almost no time in the present. Sheila Skolnik was the present. She represented life at the quotidian: living, breathing life in its daily aspect. The past, while he could not help but dwell on it, was never to be returned; the future, this book written for the ages, was never to be. Was his life, then, no more than two fantasies, one of the past and one of the future, while the present, life itself, was escaping him?

But did he really want to face the present? He tried to imagine his and Sheila's life together once they were married. An immensity of detail flooded him. Where would they live? Would he have to buy a car, to learn to drive it? What would Sheila's very American children make of his very un-American ways? Would the next Count Kinski, albeit by adoption, turn out to be a hockey player? Would Sheila, who was still young, want more children—his children? Where would the money come from to run this complicated ménage?

No less difficult was it for him to imagine their evenings together. Their Sundays were leisurely and lovely, true enough, but what about, once married, Wednesday nights? He would doubtless not be able to eat the same foods he now ate, but would have to change his diet to accommodate the children. After dinner, which would have to be eaten earlier than he now ate—again as a concession to the children—what would they all do? Would he have to buy a television set, round which they would all sit, *en famille,* jaws agape, watching God knows what inanities? Would he, as now, have his evenings free to read? Doubtless not. And Sheila? What did she do with her evenings now? He didn't know; he couldn't imagine. What, really, did he know about her?

No, it was quite impossible. The risks were simply too great. Barney Ginsberg was correct; it was too late to change his life. He had gained order. Why trade it for chaos, on the slim thread of a hope of happiness. Happiness, that essentially American ideal, what had it to do with him? History had already decreed that happiness was not to be his lot. So be it—it was time, finally, to accept the decree. He would one day die alone but at least he would live in peace. Better to allow his life to continue as it had been before. He would break with Sheila Skolnik, this woman who threatened his order, this—what had Barney Ginsberg called her?—Jewish Princess. It was all quite impossible.

The Sunday on which the Count intended to inform Sheila that things must end between them she arrived at his apartment around one o'clock with Melissa in hand. The little girl was getting over a cold, and was not feeling well enough to go off with her father. The Feinbergs had made plans for the day, so Sheila brought her along to spend the day with them. She had brought crayons and a coloring book from home. The Count set out a glass of milk and a plate of Swedish cookies for her; she worked at her coloring book at his small dining room table. Sheila suggested that they take her to a movie; a nearby theatre, The 400, was showing a rerun of Walt Disney's *Bambi*. The Count had purchased two sea bass for his and Sheila's dinner, but this, as even he recognized, was not child's food, so they decided to go out for dinner after the movie.

The Count took his walking stick, which was a damnable nuisance getting into Sheila's sports car. Melissa sat on his lap. At the movie theatre she sat between him and her mother. Sheila bought her a large plastic cup of Coca-Cola and a box of popcorn; also a box of something called Black Crows. What extraordinary things American children insert into their mouths, thought the Count. The seven-year-old child snuffled at his side. The movie turned out to be quite terrifying, even though done in animation. A forest fire scene in which the little deer loses its mother brought Melissa to tears; as the scene unrolled, she, who had until now scarcely spoken a word to him, clutched at the Count's arm. Later she slipped her hand into his. He was much touched by this.

After the movie they drove to a place called McDonald's for dinner, a restaurant, Sheila told him, that Melissa adored. The Count had seen these McDonald's dotting—scarring?—the cityscape, but of course had never been in one. The one they were in, on Clark

Street in a working-class neighborhood, seemed to be run by children, for of the ten or twelve uniformed workers behind the long counter none seemed older than sixteen. Sheila and Melissa ordered easily enough. But the Count found himself befuddled. He was unable to decipher the menu on the wall behind the counter; the light and din in the place further disoriented him.

"A hamburger, please," he finally said, "and a cup of coffee."

"What kind of hamburger, sir?" the girl taking his order asked.

"What kind?" asked the Count.

"Have a Big Mac, Mr. Kinki," said Melissa.

"Kinski, dear," Sheila corrected her. "Kinski, not Kinki."

"Very well. A Big Mac, then," said the Count.

They found a table, and the three of them began unpacking what seemed to the Count innumerable little plastic and paper packages. Melissa seemed in a state of high delight. The Count removed his sandwich from its plastic crate, and examined it. He had been brought up on European gastronomy, and, insofar as he was able in America, kept to this diet. This was a sandwich, he concluded, that required two hands to manipulate. Thus he lifted it to his mouth, and bit into a melange of condiments and what the Russians call grasses and a simulacrum of bread and meat. *Echt*-ersatz, he thought. As he chewed he felt a sensation akin to listening to Mozart's *Twentieth Piano Concerto* played on a wet tuba.

"How d'ya like the Big Mac, Mr. Kinki?"

"Kinski, darling, Kinski."

"I find it," said the Count, "very splendid. Most delicious." He wondered how he could dispose of the remainder, but, seeing no way to do so without hurting the child's feelings, he managed, with the aid of large draughts of tasteless coffee, to swallow down nearly half the sandwich.

Back at the Count's apartment, Melissa returned to her coloring book in the dining room, while Sheila and the Count settled in the living room.

"Thank you," Sheila said, "for putting up with that restaurant. I saw it wasn't easy for you."

"No, no," said the Count. "Not at all. I found it—how shall I say?—edifying."

"Well, you're nice to have done it."

"Sheila," said the Count, hearing a tremor in his voice, "I have some sad things I must say."

"Sad things?"

"Yes. I fear, though this is not easy for me to say, that there is little point in our continuing to see each other in this way."

"Why do you say that?" She seemed shocked; she hadn't been expecting this.

"Because I have been alone too long. I cannot change my ways. No. Perhaps it is more honest to say that I do not want to change my ways. Not now that I am more than fifty years old."

"Are you sure about this, Peter?"

"I have thought much about it."

"I see."

"I shall always be grateful to you for your friendship."

"I see."

"Do you understand?"

"Yes," she said, "I do." And then she called: "Melissa, it's time for us to go home."

The child had put her coat on. "Thank you for a very nice day, Mr. Kinski," she said, holding her mother's hand at the door. The Count touched the girl's cheek. He would never see her again.

"May I see you down to the car?" he asked.

"I don't think so, Peter. Maybe it's better to say good-by here." She appeared to the Count as if she were holding back tears. She put out her hand. A century ago the Count would have bowed and kissed it. Now he held it, not wishing to relinquish it. And then she and the child were gone.

The Count felt relief. He poured a cognac, put Handel's *Wassermusik* on the phonograph, took down a Pléiade volume of *Les mémoires du Duc de Saint-Simon*. He could go undisturbed back to the old life now. Order and quiet. He sipped his cognac. He read about *le roi soleil*. He closed his eyes, the better to imagine King George in his barge floating down the Thames listening to Handel's lovely music.

The book dropped to his lap when he put his hands to his eyes to stop the flow of tears.

He had made a hideous error. He didn't want to live, nor to die, alone. He had turned away a woman who had loved him, whom he had loved—loved still. But was it too late? Why need it be? He would call Sheila tomorrow. No. Why wait? He would go to her tonight. He would ask forgiveness, propose marriage, give up whatever was required of him to give up of the old life, take on all that was implied in the new. Time was left to him, and he would make it matter. Let chaos come. He would buy a television set for the children; dogs and cats, if need be. Hundreds of details would have to be worked out. He welcomed them. He telephoned for a cab, and, when asked where he was going, announced his destination as Northbrook. At the closet, he put on his coat. He looked at his walking stick, which he picked up, held before him in both hands, and, in a quick motion, over his raised knee broke it in two. As he ran down the stairs to meet his cab, Count Kinski's laughter rang round his empty apartment.

Low Anxiety

■

*H*arry Resnick slipped in behind the steering wheel, drew the seat belt across his lap, tilted the wheel forward, and flicked on the radio. He hadn't slept well the night before, but now, getting into his car to make the trip down to the shop, he felt slightly reinvigorated. This car could do that to him. He always felt a little lift in spirit driving it. It was a Chrysler, a New Yorker, top of the line. It was deep brown, a color the company called Dark Suede, and fully loaded: cushy leather seats, lacquered paneling on the dash and doors, a stereo radio and cassette deck that resounded wonderfully in the enclosed space of the car, a voice that reminded you not to neglect to fasten your seat belt. The windows were tinted, back and front and on the sides. A computer registered voltage, RPMs, how much mileage had elapsed on a trip, when the car would next need fuel, and more. The salesman at Walton Chrysler, in Skokie, a nervous character named Art Feldman, when explaining how the computer worked, told Harry, "No kiddin', it'll practically even tell you when you gotta take a leak."

"My God, honey," said Sharon Resnick the first time she sat in the Chrysler, "it's like sitting in the lobby of the old Saxony Hotel in Miami Beach in 1954." Sharon drove a small BMW, a 325i—a "Beemer," their daughter Deborah called it. Sharon wanted Harry to buy a Mercedes, but didn't push it. The extra twenty grand or so a Mercedes would have cost wasn't the issue. He didn't even mind that it was a German car. Harry liked Chryslers; his father always drove Chryslers, long deluxe ones, Imperials, with tail fins a man could impale himself upon. Besides, it seemed to Harry as if every lawyer, every commodities market guy, every schmuck whose ship had come in nowadays drove a Mercedes, and the rest had Jaguars. There must have been fifteen or twenty Mercedes on his block in Highland Park. Chryslers were good enough for his old man, they were good enough for Harry.

From within, the Chrysler gave a sealed-off, protected feeling that Harry liked. Not long after he bought it, in the moments before drifting off to sleep, he began to think about taking a long trip alone in the car. Lulling himself to sleep, he thought maybe he would head west from Chicago with no particular destination in mind. Maybe he would run up to Vancouver, then shoot down the Pacific coast to Mexico, afterward spend a little time in the Southwest. Traveling light—a few pairs of slacks, five or six golf shirts, a pair of loafers, a windbreaker, pajamas, socks, and underwear would be all he'd need— he would stop at night at Holiday Inns or Ramadas. Evenings he would find a restaurant and eat a steak or roast beef or spaghetti, something a little life-threatening, read the local papers, walk around whatever town he happened to be in, return to his room, watch some television, maybe some night baseball, then take off early the next morning, driving the dark brown Chrysler over mountains and through piney forests and deserts. The trip, as Harry thought about it, had no time limit; it might last a month, but then again it might last four months. He would return when he felt like it—no sooner.

Of course he would never take such a trip. Over the twenty-one years of their marriage, Sharon and he had gone to Acapulco, Hawaii, the Virgin Islands, once on a cruise in the Caribbean, and last year they spent a week each in London and Paris, staying at the Connaught and at the George V; in Paris Sharon bought him five one-hundred-dollar shirts at Charvet. Harry had learned that roughly a week was the extent of his tolerance for a vacation. Each time he went away he was anxious to get back, to open his mail, fall into the old routine, slip back into harness. He probably got this from his father. The old man didn't know anything but work; he died at "the shop," as he always called it, at seventy-four, of a heart attack, alone, just before locking up. The night he died Harry's mother telephoned him at home. It was already eight o'clock and Pa hadn't come home yet and she was worried. Harry drove downtown, opened the place, noticing that the burglar alarms had not been turned on, and found his father face down on the floor of the receiving room, where earlier that day they had taken delivery on a shipment of metal desks. Harry sometimes wondered if he would die in the shop, too. Compared to a hospital bed, tubes stuck in every hole in your body, among strangers and in strange surroundings, the prospect of dying in the shop didn't really seem so bad.

Clicking the automatic door-opener, Harry pulled out of the garage into an early gray March morning. Chicago snow was still on the ground, now turned to black and icy sludge encasing old candy wrappers, cigarette packets, and dog crap, making even the costliest homes in Highland Park seem bleak. The news on the radio wasn't very new. Harry felt that every one could save a lot of time if the station, News Radio 78, would simply insert a tape announcing that the Arabs were still crazy, the situation in Central America horrible, the blacks complaining, and the economy, lousy to begin with, was getting worse. This was Monday. Sunday night's television news— and Harry and Sharon usually went to bed after the ten o'clock news— was the usual prescription for depression. Harry had noticed that, Sunday being a day off for politicians, and hence for stories about foolish promises and scandal, the local television stations filled in with accounts of family homicides, tavern shoot-ups, arson, and infants found abandoned in garbage cans on the West Side. Highland Park was roughly twenty-five miles from downtown Chicago, yet nearly every Sunday night, after the news, before they went to bed, Sharon asked the same question: "Harry, did you double-lock both doors?"

The traffic was light on the freeway at this hour, and Harry pulled into the Lake Street parking lot at 7:20. The old man used to come down at this time, and while his father was alive Harry would come in half an hour later. Harry liked the quiet of the place in the early morning, before Charley, the porter, or Arlene Bernstein, the secretary and bookkeeper, arrived. He used the time to assemble his thoughts, make a list of things he needed to do or people to see, prepare for his various appointments, go over invoices. Resnick & Son, Office Furniture, was a golden business—how golden Harry knew only after his father died. Sam Resnick had played his cards close to the chest. He and Harry's mother lived with no effort at display and very little waste. He gave a lot to Jewish charities, though he never belonged to a synagogue. At the reading of his father's will, in Abe Kaiserman's office on LaSalle Street, Harry learned that, as his father's only child, he had been left more than three-quarters of a million in real estate and other assets and that his mother had been left roughly the same sum. Add his own savings and investments to that figure and Harry was essentially out of the financial wars. That was eight years ago, when Harry was forty-two. His mother was now eighty-three, and eventually he would come into her money. Harry could retire tomorrow without any worry. But to do what? He didn't golf. He wasn't a card player. He certainly wasn't about to move to California or Arizona or Florida, where he would be bored stiff in a warm climate. Besides, he liked his life. He liked Chicago, where he had grown up. He liked the office-furniture business. He liked cutting a serious deal. He liked coming down to the same shop that his father had spent the better part of his life in.

Harry kept the place pretty much as his father had in his time. A scramble of desks, cabinets, chairs, lamps up front in the not very showy showroom. Then, behind a glass partition, which allowed him to see the showroom and the front door, his own office; next to it, the cubicle of Mrs. Bernstein, who had worked for his father and who was now in her late sixties; out back the receiving and storeroom. Not long after Harry went to work for his father, dropping out of college at the end of his second year at the University of Illinois—his father thought he was foolish to be studying business in Champaign when he could be doing business in Chicago—one of his first ideas was to redesign the showroom. He presented the plan to the old man, who glanced at it for maybe ten seconds, then said, "I think we'll just leave things the way they are, Harold. The point isn't to look prosperous; it's to be prosperous." His father explained that their customers weren't looking for elegant surroundings; they were buying price. If the showroom looked too sleek, the customers were likely to think you were doing too well—that you were soaking them. In those days, his father dealt with owners of businesses—not, like now, with decorators hired by them—and would argue and squabble, with aggressive joking and swearing, hammering out a deal, selling things off the books, then getting hit for an additional 2 percent off for cash.

In those early days, Harry didn't get much in the way of advice. Sam Resnick had a floor lady, a woman named Sylvia Spivak, dark, thin, heavily made-up, a divorcée in her early forties, a hard number. She was supposed to break Harry in, to teach him the ropes. She wasn't someone who sucked up to the boss's son; in fact, she seemed to resent Harry's even being on the premises. Perhaps she sensed that he would one day replace her. In the meantime she did what she could to discourage and humiliate him. She kept him working out in the receiving room with the porter; she'd send him for sandwiches and coffee for customers; she looked for mistakes in everything he did, and generally managed to find them. Although Harry was still living with his parents and every night drove his father home in the white Imperial, it was, somehow, understood that he was not to complain about Sylvia Spivak. His father, who missed very little, could hardly have missed Sylvia's treatment of him. The unspoken assumption was that Harry would have to work it out on his own.

After roughly eighteen months, the break came. Late one afternoon, Sylvia had closed a cash deal with an old customer, Irving Medintz, and as she was walking him to the door, she left an envelope with Medintz's $3,300 in it on top of one of the showroom credenzas. Harry noted it. His father was waiting on other customers. Harry slipped the envelope into the inside pocket of his jacket. For the hour or so before closing, while going about his own tasks, he watched Sylvia searching in desk drawers and under chairs, attempting to conceal her panic over the loss of the money. She said nothing about it to Sam Resnick before she left for the night.

On the drive home, Harry took the envelope out of his coat

pocket and handed it over to his father. He explained what it was and how he came by it.

"You let her go home thinking she had lost more than three thousand dollars of the firm's money?" his father asked. "She's going to have quite a night, I'm sure."

"I hope so," said Harry

"That's pretty hard, Harold," said his father.

"Not near hard enough, as far as I'm concerned," said Harry.

Harry arranged for his father to be out of the shop for half an hour the next morning, at which time he called Sylvia Spivak into the office. He was sitting in his father's chair when she came in. She looked surprised, amused, faintly contemptuous of his presumption.

"Missing anything, Sylvia?" Harry began.

"What do you mean?" she said.

Harry slipped the Medintz envelope out of his pocket and dropped it almost languorously on his father's desk.

"Where did you find that?" she snapped.

"Just where you left it." He was tempted to add the word "dummy," but didn't.

He sensed her combined relief and resentment. "What do you want?" she asked.

"You off my back," he said, "and for good."

She left without saying another word. Three weeks later she gave notice. Harry became his father's floor man, a flunkey no longer. He found he had a natural aptitude for making deals and took pleasure in doing so. He oversaw the change in the nature of the business, from dealing with owners to dealing with interior decorators, from customers looking for price to customers looking for tax write-offs. By his late twenties he was making more than a hundred grand a year.

After a decade or so of the usual bachelor hijinks—an apartment on State Parkway on the near North Side, part ownership of a bar on Rush Street, a series of brassy convertibles and brassy young women to go in them—Harry, at thirty, married. Sharon Goldstein, who was four years younger than he, grew up in the same neighborhood,

West Rogers Park, went to the same high school, though she finished college, the University of Illinois, with a certificate to teach grade school. Fourteen months after their marriage, their daughter was born. Over the next five years, Sharon had three miscarriages, and her gynecologist warned her that any further pregnancies could be dangerous. Harry would have liked a son, but he was mad about Deborah, the only child of an only child, who was good at school (she was a sophomore at Northwestern, where she lived in her sorority, ΑΕΦ), and who had her mother's good looks and good heart and, he hoped, some of his own common sense and savvy.

Harry was to meet his daughter, alone, for an early dinner that evening in Evanston. It wasn't a meeting he looked forward to. Last night, before they went to bed, Sharon had told him that, four weeks earlier, his daughter had had an abortion. It stunned him. Deborah had wanted to tell him about it herself. He had a thousand questions. He went to bed churning with confused and violent feelings. He tossed for better than three hours. To calm his nerves, he imagined himself driving, in the Chrysler, a tape of Ella Fitzgerald playing on the cassette deck, along rain-soaked roads in Oregon, large lush trees forming a green canopy overhead; or along the Pacific Highway out of San Francisco headed toward Monterey, the ocean and rocky beaches on his right.

"Dinner with Deb" was the last item on his list of things to do that day. Others were: "Bank deposit," "Richie Melnick—11:00," "Lunch at Mother's," "Shipment from High Point," "Run D & B on Brodsky."

The initials D & B, standing for Dun and Bradstreet, called to mind the initials D & C, which stood for Harry wasn't sure what, except that he recalled them in connection with Sharon's miscarriages and much talk of cervixes and uteruses, and he wondered if his nineteen-year-old daughter didn't have to go through similar horrors for her abortion. He too easily imagined the doctor's office, the stainless-steel instruments, the table and stirrups, the doctor in green operating-room uniform, clear plastic covering his shoes to prevent bloodstains. The picture of his daughter in this setting sickened him, and through the morning he fought to put it out of his mind.

"That is a smart young *faygele,*" his father pronounced upon first meeting Richie Melnick. Richie, who was Harry's age, was then not yet thirty but clearly an operator, clearly an interior decorator who was going to turn a big buck. He was one of the first of the decorators to go after the business of corporations. The money was greater and the aggravation less than in dealing with insecure suburban women, whom he would have to schlep through the Merchandise Mart in search of the exact right lampshade for the bedroom or the perfect tone of grasspaper for the den. Vice presidents of firms like International Harvester didn't want to talk lampshades or grasspaper, which was fine—and profitable—with Richie. He drove a tan Rolls, wore Italian suits that must have cost a grand a throw, had more French wrist watches than most men had neckties. A decade or so ago Richie bought a four story brownstone on Astor Street. Sharon and Harry were once invited to a dinner party there. Among the guests were members of the boards of the Lyric Opera and the Chicago Symphony and the Art Institute—people who had risen and who were on the rise. Richie Melnick, lower-middle-class and Jewish and out-in-the-open-no-bones-about-it homosexual, was one of them. Harry was impressed.

Yet that evening Harry also realized that he did not himself wish to rise. He had no wish to collect art that did not give him pleasure, or to haul himself off to committee meetings and dinners among people with whom he did not feel comfortable. He supposed he had enough money to play, but the game didn't interest him. He was stuck with his own lack of pretensions. He and Sharon talked about it that night on the drive back to Highland Park. They were not in disagreement. She, like Harry, was content to live quietly and well, among their friends and for their daughter.

Deborah again. Harry tried to put her out of his mind when, from his office, he saw Richie walk into the shop. Richie, like Harry, was losing his hair. A stylist did his best to cover this up through the art of the comb and the blow dryer, but the final effect was that of a middle-aged man trying to conceal his baldness. Richie's skin had taken on a pinkness, a too-well-scrubbed look that seemed artifically induced. Harry didn't know about homosexuality much more than a kid in Chicago picks up on the streets, but one look at Richie in his present condition made it plain that he had long since crossed the line from being desirable to being the desirer. Richie rarely talked about his personal life, but he always asked after Sharon and Deborah. He spoke respectfully about Harry's father. When Richie's mother died three or so years ago, Harry went to the funeral chapel. So far as Harry knew, Richie had no permanent lover. Whenever Harry read AIDS stories in the *Trib,* he thought about Richie and hoped he would be spared that horror. They went back twenty years; the "smart *faygele*" his father had first spotted was not only a very clever businessman but, within the limits of business, which could be wider than many people thought, a friend. Twenty years they had done business together; they began as young men and were now themselves on the way toward being the older generation.

Richie was in the shop to nail down the details of a small job he had turned over to Harry. A new advertising agency had hired him to do its reception and conference rooms; also the young president's office. Less than forty grand was involved. Of that sum, Richie and Harry between them figured to profit by roughly eleven grand. There were worse ways to begin the day.

"So how go things at home?" Richie asked, after they had settled their business. "Sharon OK? How's the kid doing at school?"

Harry thought for a second about telling Richie exactly how Deborah was doing at school, and how his thinking about it was driving him nuts, but decided against it. The Resnicks, his father used to say, don't discuss family problems with people outside the family.

"Same old crap—going along," Harry said. "How's by you?"

"I'm thinking of selling the building on Astor Street," Richie said. "The real-estate putzes tell me the price will never be higher.

Besides, I think the neighborhood may be going down. Last week five heterosexual couples moved in on the block. They say I can get a million five for the building as it stands."

"So what would you do with a million five? Retire?"

"Right now, with this little AIDS thingy, I'm not thinking so much about retiring as about staying alive. Every morning I emerge from my shower to do what I call a little death check. I look for splotches, discolorations, swellings, lumps, warts, freckles, you name it. No picnic, friend."

"What a world!" said Harry.

"Brave new world," said Richie, "and it doesn't figure to get better soon. I don't envy kids like Deborah having to grow up in it. In some ways, I'm glad not to have kids but only myself to worry about. You're lucky your daughter is a square kid."

"Yeah," said Harry. "I suppose so."

After Melnick left, Harry made a few business calls, signed some letters, and walked over to the lot to get the car. He drove the few blocks down Lake Street, turned north on Michigan Avenue, passing Saks, Nieman-Marcus, Magnin's, Water Tower Place, and Bloomingdale's, while on the radio he learned that a local rapist had been apprehended in Michigan, a policeman had been wounded in a shoot-out in a currency exchange on the South Side, and the Dow Jones had fallen again. He turned onto the Outer Drive just north of the Drake Hotel. The lake was green on this cold March day, the waves seemed not merely relentless but aggressive.

Not long after her husband's death, Harry's mother had moved into a small two-bedroom apartment on the fourteenth floor of a newer building at Belmont and the Drive. Her friends Pearl Feinstein and Faye Schwartz—like her, widows—lived in the building, though Pearl had since died and Faye's diabetes had so weakened her that she had to hire a Russian woman, a Soviet Jew, to come in to help her bathe, clean the apartment, and prepare her meals. His mother looked in on Mrs. Schwartz two or three times a day, and on four different occasions had had to call an ambulance to get her to a hospital late at night.

The wind coming off the lake as Harry turned into the revolving door lashed his face like an insult. The doorman announced him over the house phone—"Mrs. Resnick, your son is here"—before buzzing him into the inner lobby. When the elevators stopped, three Jewish-looking kids of high-school age—two girls and a boy in punk clothes and haircuts—got off. Not much of a day for purple hair, thought Harry, as he removed his gloves while the elevator climbed to the fourteenth floor.

"On time as always, Harold," his mother said at the door of her apartment. They embraced lightly; he kissed her forehead; looking down upon her head he could see scalp through her thinning hair. She had grown smaller with age. In the lottery of old-age illnesses, she had drawn arthritis, which left her with twisted hands and sore-ness in the hip joints. She gave off an old-fashioned female smell, reminiscent of the sachet she used to keep in her dresser drawers in the bungalow in West Rogers Park.

Not that she had ever seemed young to Harry. When he was born she was already in her thirties. Although she was the wife of a rich man, she had practiced Old World economies: washed and ironed her own sheets, spent entire days baking and preparing heavy meals, worked alongside the cleaning woman who came in twice a week. She was born in Białystok, was brought to the United States by her parents at the age of six. Was it in Poland as a child that she had acquired the worried look that never left her eyes? Harry's father, who was born in Russia, remembered witnessing, as a small boy, a pogrom in his village. Harry's mother looked, for as long as Harry could remember, as if she were always expecting one.

Many of the things from the old West Rogers Park house—the large breakfront, the grand dining-room set with sideboard and buf-fet, the grandfather clock—seemed too bulky for the small low-ceil-inged rooms of this new apartment. The thickness of the drapes darkened what might otherwise have been a light room. His mother was eighty-three and she knew one way of decorating. She also knew one way of cooking, which was heavy food in large portions. Harry came here once a week for lunch, which they ate together in the kitchen, and it was almost always the same lunch: chopped liver over lettuce with a radish, a bowl of soup (either chicken or cabbage), brisket, and potatoes with green beans out of a can, coffee and pastry. Eating these lunches, Harry felt he could practically hear the arteries near his heart creaking to a close. "It's convenient," Sharon said, "that at your mother's you get your calories, your carbohydrates, and your heavy cholesterol all in one sitting."

They talked about what they always talked about at these lunches—the past. Harry's mother recalled the summers they had spent in South Haven, in Michigan, where they rented a cottage and his father drove up on Friday nights to spend the weekend. He recalled his father had no wardrobe for leisure, and would walk down to the beach in his swimming trunks, an undershirt, black business shoes, and silk socks with little clocks or arrows on them. His mother mentioned the wonderful suntans he would get as a child; too much sun nowadays, Harry thought, and you risked skin cancer.

"Kaiserman called yesterday," his mother said. "He says he's putting the tax forms in the mail."

"If you have any questions, Ma, you'll call me. If not, just sign them and send them back."

"How are things at home, Harold?"

"Sharon's well. She sends her love. She says she'll see you at least once before *Pesach*."

"And Deborah?"

"Deborah's fine, Ma."

"She's doing well in college?"

"Just fine, Ma. Deborah's always been a good student. School's not her problem."

"Oh," his mother said, slightly suspicious. "What is?"

"Nothing, Ma. It's just an expression." Harry imagined himself telling his mother, with her permanently worried look that her granddaughter's problem was that she got herself knocked-up and had, consequently, to have her womb scraped or punctured or whatever the hell it is they do in an abortion. But it was all over and done with now. Hey, Ma, no problem!

Harry was able to steer the conversation onto the subject of the business. They talked about the people in this building; about her friend Faye; about the police and fire and ambulance sirens in the night, so many of them; about her doctor, who had a yacht, he must be making a fortune; about people from the old neighborhood. She walked Harry to the door.

"Anything you need before I go, Ma? You got enough milk in the house?"

"Everything's fine, dear. Tell Sharon I'll call her over the telephone tomorrow. Kiss my darling Deborah for me and tell her that grandma loves her."

"I will. Take care of yourself, Ma. You need anything, anything at all, call me, and at any hour."

They embraced again at the door. Harry felt her brittleness, his nostrils filled with the smell of her agedness. Whenever he left her nowadays, he wondered if he'd ever see her again. Eighty-three was eighty-three.

Back at the shop Harry found that a shipment of reception-room items ordered for Florence Shapiro had come in badly fouled up. The chairs were vinyl when they were supposed to have been naugahyde, and one of the couches had a rip, probably made en route. Harry had to call the plant in High Point, North Carolina, make arrangements to ship the goods back, and finally telephone Florence—a decorator who was in her late sixties and whom Richie Melnick always called the wicked witch of the old West Side—who was not easy to deal with in the best of circumstances, to tell her that she would have to inform her client of a delay of another four to six weeks. Harry felt almost glad about the trouble; it filled out the afternoon, relieving him of having to think about his dinner with his daughter.

At a quarter to six, after everyone else had gone, Harry began locking up, as he did every night. He slid the bar over the delivery entrance at the back, setting in place and clamping down the heavy lock. He walked past the spot where he had found his father dead, and wondered, were the old man alive, if he would have discussed Deborah's abortion with him. Probably not. On personal matters they tended, Harry and his father, to keep things to themselves, especially troubles. He turned on the burglar-alarm system, turned off the lights, locked the front door, pulled the iron screen across it, locked that. As he walked along Lake Street to get the car, an El train, headed the other way, rattled overhead.

In the sanctum of the dark brown Chrysler, whose motor was nearly soundless, Harry headed north toward Evanston and the restaurant, a place called Leslee's, where his daughter had made a reservation. The evening news was the standard stuff: terrorist attacks in the Middle East, scandal at city hall, charges of racism against the board of education, a further drop in the Dow Jones. Harry turned it off to think about his dinner with Deborah. On his right the lake seemed black, the waves gray and intimidating.

Harry was making a good living when Deborah was born, and she was brought up in the suburbs. Sharon saw to it that, as a child, she had piano and ballet and tennis lessons. At thirteen, she went to summer camp in Eagle River, Wisconsin, where she was given riding lessons and fell in love with horses; at one point there was talk about buying Deborah her own horse, but Harry put his foot down; it sounded too extravagant (even though he could have easily afforded it). He remembered her crying when he said no, and how it pained him to disappoint her. She was wearing her braces—she wore them from her eleventh through her fifteenth year—and Harry never loved her so much as then: her mouth filled with metal and rubber bands, so damned vulnerable looking.

When Deborah was sixteen, Sharon and he had that painful discussion about whether to put her on birth-control pills. These were fast kids, these suburban kids she ran with; lots of them were given their own cars, and not jalopies either, but serious cars, Corvettes and BMW convertibles and antique MG's. For a while, at parties in Highland Park and Glencoe, Harry kept meeting women who, when he asked them what they did, informed him they were social workers at New Trier or Highland Park High. Sharon explained that this meant they worked with upper-middle-class kids who had drug problems or had attempted suicide. You were considered lucky if your kids confined themselves to pot; cocaine stories were plentiful. Sex was talked about less than drugs.

It came up once in a conversation with his old friend Irwin Stein, who had two sons at New Trier. "You know, Harry, when we were in high school, you had to be a genius to lay a nice girl." (Irwin was a genius, all right, but in real estate.) "Now they're all doin' it—going at it like little minks." It was a topic more comfortable for someone with sons than with daughters. Sharon and Harry went back and forth on the question of Deborah and birth-control pills, and finally decided that to put her on them was to tell her, by implication, that it was all right to sleep with boys, when in fact they didn't feel that it was. If it happened, it happened, but they hoped it wouldn't. As far as Harry knew, in high school it didn't. Deborah and her mother were close; Sharon always said that if her daughter had slept with a boy she, Sharon, would know.

Well, apparently Deborah had waited till college, and then had got herself in this fix. Yet was it a fix? The fix, after all, had been fixed—taken care of by the abortion. Why did Harry still feel such anger about it? Certainly he didn't want his daughter, at nineteen, to raise an illegitimate child. Nor did he fancy her married to some college kid, a union destined for divorce. He couldn't claim, either, that he had any principled objection to abortion as the taking of a human life. He knew the arguments but, try as he might, he could not imagine an embryo or a zygote or whatever the hell it was as a full-blown human being. Was it his daughter's incompetence that enraged him? If you're going to sleep around, for God's sake at least be smart enough to protect yourself. And was Deborah sleeping around? Was there more than one boy? In a time already spoiled by too much phony frankness, Harry felt that a serious man shouldn't be asked to think about the details of his own daughter's sex life, and resented it that he was doing so now.

The traffic was light on the Drive. Harry didn't want to arrive at the restaurant too early, so he turned off at Wilson Avenue and headed north toward Evanston down Sheridan Road. Appalachians, shivering in the Chicago winter, trudged along Wilson Avenue. On

Sheridan, Puerto Ricans and Mexicans predominated. A few buildings were boarded up; many others had been knocked down. Public housing had been erected a few blocks from the old Somerset Hotel; the Somerset itself, once a haven for bachelor lawyers, horse-players, sporty types generally, was now a welfare hotel. Zimring's drugstore, a meeting place for some of Harry's friends in high school, had changed hands; at any rate the name was no longer to be seen. Banners on the windows announced that food stamps were accepted. Everywhere he looked Harry felt things had slipped badly, and there was no good reason to think they would ever be returned to what they once were—certainly not in his lifetime.

Leslee's, the restaurant Deborah had chosen for dinner, was on the rim of downtown Evanston. Despite his slower route, Harry arrived ten minutes early. The restaurant was in the basement floor of a new office building; you took a steep escalator to get down to it. Just off the escalator Harry was met by a young man with pomaded hair and an oversized suit—all the restaurants he seemed to go to nowadays appeared to be run by children—who asked him if he had a reservation. He said he had, in the name of Resnick, and the young man said that his dinner partner was already here and had been seated. He led Harry to his daughter. The place had enormously high ceilings; lots of beige vinyl, glass, and steel. The waiters and waitresses were young men and women in black trousers, white shirts, black bow ties. More children.

Deborah was seated in a narrow booth for two. Across from them, well within hearing range, seated at a banquette-like booth, were two elderly women with blue-rinse hairdos and an old gent, very well dressed, who appeared to be well out of it: either deaf or ga-ga or both. Deborah was wearing a dark gray skirt, a red crew-neck sweater over a white blouse with a small round collar. Like her mother, whose good looks Harry never tired of, she was small and dark and slightly chubby. She put out her hand; Harry squeezed it gently, bent down to kiss her cheek, which he managed to do only grazingly.

Deborah had a diet Coke in front of her; Harry ordered a Chivas from their waitress, who left a card with the evening's specials on it at the table. He wasn't sure who seemed more nervous, he or his daughter. Harry was grateful to her for skipping the small talk.

"Mother tells me that I've upset you terribly, Daddy," she said. "If I did, I'm sorry. It's not what I had in mind."

"The truth is, honey, I was upset, and I'm still upset." His voice sounded tough, more aggressive than he intended, as if he were talking to a manufacturer in North Carolina who had screwed up an order. He had to remember he was talking to his daughter, whom he loved.

"What's got you most upset, Daddy? That it happened or that you weren't told about it till it was over?"

"Both things, Deborah. But not those alone."

She seemed calmer, Harry thought, a little too calm for his liking. A subtle shift had taken place; suddenly he was the one who had to explain himself. Would he have preferred it if she had shown strong signs of feeling guilty? Yes, he had to admit, such signs would have been welcome. At least it would have given him the power of forgiveness; he could have acted fatherly in soothing her, in reassuring her of his love.

Harry was never less interested in food, but he forced himself to listen to the waitress's rather lengthy recitation of the specials. The regular menu seemed quite as elaborate. What the hell ever happened to things like shrimp cocktail, prime rib, broiled chicken? He finally ordered something that turned out to be pieces of chicken mingled among corkscrew noodles. Deborah ordered scallops.

"I felt very bad about it when it first happened, Daddy. I also felt stupid for letting myself get into such a situation. But I don't feel quite so bad anymore. I don't know why, but I don't. I wish it never happened, but it did. Now I mainly feel bad about hurting you."

"What about the boy who got you into this? How does he feel about it?"

"His name is Ted Kastner. He doesn't know about it. I didn't tell him, and I don't plan to. I didn't think he could handle it. Because I decided he couldn't, I've decided to stop seeing him. Besides, there was nothing he could have done to help anyway."

"I'm glad you aren't seeing him anymore, Deborah. It will be a real pleasure never to have to meet him." Ted Kastner, Harry thought, a Jewish name. A nice Jewish boy, no doubt. At least it wasn't a mixed abortion. Why did the mind find jokes at moments like this?

"Daddy, did you really expect me not to sleep with anyone while I was in college?"

"No," he said, "I guess I didn't really expect that, but I wouldn't have minded if you hadn't. I would have minded a hell of a lot less than I do about what has happened."

The waitress set down their food. "Enjoy," she said.

"You still haven't told me why this bugs you so much, Daddy, Do you think your daughter is now, somehow, damaged goods?"

"I don't know as I would put it that way, baby, but maybe I do. But not in the way you might think."

"How then?"

"I think it's a goddamned damaging thing for a girl to have had an abortion at nineteen," he said, more emphatically than he had intended. He looked across the aisle at the two old broads and the expressionless face of the senile old gent, and hoped they hadn't heard him.

"Look, Deb," he said, talking more softly now, "if you've had an abortion at nineteen, what've you got planned for twenty-four, or thirty-one or forty-two?"

"What do you mean?"

"I mean that, for the first time, as a result of what's happened, I can imagine a terrible life for you. A life of confusion and sadness and heartbreak. And it terrifies me."

"Why do you think that?"

"Maybe an abortion is a solution to the problem of a pregnancy, but I suspect that it brings its own problems. It isn't as tidy as it sounds; I suspect that it takes its toll. Once you undergo something like this, your opinion of yourself changes, maybe in small little ways, but it changes. Maybe, because of something like this, you no longer think so well of yourself. Maybe it becomes easier to do more foolish things."

'I don't think that's true, Daddy."

"I hope it isn't, sweetheart, I really do hope it isn't."

"But what could I have done?"

"You probably did all that you could do, but I think you may be making a big mistake if you think you got away with it. An abortion, anyhow one of this kind, is a dreary and common and pretty crummy thing."

"What do you want, Daddy?" She had only been picking at her food, but now she gave up even doing that. Tears were in her eyes. Harry remembered her in braces.

"What I want you can't give me, Deborah. What I want isn't even reasonable. I want you back the way you were before this happened."

"What am I supposed to do?" she asked.

"I don't know what you're supposed to do. The world is slipping away, my sweet girl, and there's evidently not much any of us can do about it. But I don't have to like it. And I especially don't have to like my kid becoming a part of it."

Harry called for the check. Outside the street was deserted. The wind whipped away at them. The icy pavement caused them to walk cautiously, Deborah holding on to her father's arm. Harry drove her the three or four blocks to her sorority house. In front of the sorority, she leaned over to kiss him; he wanted to put his arms around her and hug her, but the gesture was awkward and unsatisfactory in their bulky coats in the front seat of the car. Harry told his daughter to call her grandmother when she had a free moment. As she walked toward the door of the sorority, he pushed the button to lower the window on the passenger side to call out to her. But she turned to wave at the door and went inside.

The heater in the Chrysler worked well, and the leather seats, so cold when they first got into the car, no longer gave off a chill. Heading over to Dempster, from where he could pick up the freeway, Harry turned on the radio, then turned it off. The car gave a fine feeling of snugness. Maybe I should have been easier on her, Harry thought. But then his mind drifted to a picture of himself, alone, driving in the deep brown Chrysler through New England, where he had never been. He was driving through a leafy sunset; in the back seat were the *Wall Street Journal, Newsweek,* some local papers, a small suitcase. He ought to keep an eye out for a motel with a restaurant, get a good dinner, watch a little television, rise early the next day. Maybe he would cross over into Canada, tour Nova Scotia, the Maritime Provinces, have a look at Prince Edward Island.

No Pulitzer for Pinsker

■

*C*haracter is fate, as someone once said, but so is the alphabet, as Melvin A. Rosen has reason to know. I am Melvin A. (for Arnold) Rosen and I have often thought that if my last name were Brodsky or Ginsberg or Singer I would never have gotten as mixed up as I have with Ira L. Pinsker, the novelist. Pinsker and I go all the way back to grammar school. I remember the day he walked into our class, the fifth grade at De Witt Clinton Elementary School in West Rogers Park on the far North Side of Chicago. He was a tall kid, even then, with almost too erect a posture and an odd wandering look in his eyes as if he might have needed glasses, which he didn't.

"Class," announced Miss Schoenie, our very flat-chested teacher who had calves as muscular as those of the University of Illinois halfback Buddy Young, "I should like to introduce Ira Pinsker, who has transferred from the Shakespeare Elementary School. Mr. Pinsker, please take the desk in front of Melvin Rosen. Mr. Rosen, please raise your hand so Mr. Pinsker will know who you are."

Pinsker, then ten years old, headed in my direction, near the end of the fifth row from the door, barely avoiding being tripped by a jolly fat boy named Donnie Olsen. As he dropped himself in the seat in front of mine, I recall looking into the back of his long head, a thing I did a great deal of that fifth-grade year, and thinking, "This is a strange guy."

What can I tell you about Ira Pinsker? What can't I tell you about Ira Pinsker? I can tell you about the time he nearly got me killed on the road out of Memphis. I can tell you about the time he sicked a serious paranoiac on me, causing me to tremble every time I left my apartment. I can tell you about the time I had to depart a Lutheran church in Cicero, Illinois, before he caused me to break down with screaming laughter in the middle of his own wedding ceremony. I can tell you about the hundreds of minor mental contusions that Ira L. (the L stands for Lyle) Pinsker has caused me merely by being his strange self: Pinsker the pretentious, Pinsker the oblivious, Pinsker the tremendously awkward, Pinsker the terrifically irritating, Pinsker the (I sometimes think) completely lunatic.

His first day in school, Pinsker got into a fight. That in itself was not unusual. A new boy in a Chicago grammar school in those days was often teased and tested and called upon to demonstrate his manliness. Only Pinsker had the misfortune to get into a fight with Denny Cook, the son of a janitor, the class clown, and easily the toughest kid in the fifth grade. I don't know how it started. All I know is that toward the end of the afternoon the word was going around that Denny was going to cream the new kid after school.

We gathered on the gravel schoolyard at three o'clock. Denny Cook came out first, and began shadowboxing. He was three or four inches shorter than Pinsker and maybe ten or fifteen pounds lighter, but he was wiry, had a hot temper, and hated losing. "Here's the jerk now," someone yelled, as Pinsker approached. He was wearing a leather jacket of a kind I have never seen before or since: it had a yellowish tint and slash pockets that closed with zippers and buttons at the cuffs. Pinsker retained this strange taste for odd items of apparel. He once owned a pair of football cleats that were suede, and in high school he played basketball at the YMCA in sweat pants held up by a piece of rough twine. In adult life he wore shirts that looked as if they might have been made in iron-curtain countries, and his taste in neckties was not up to the level of atrocious.

"Ready to get your block knocked off?" said Denny. Pinsker

said nothing, but took off his goofy jacket, which he handed to me, who was standing in the circle that had gathered around. Those were the days when Don Dunphy was announcing the Friday night fights over the radio for Gillette, and Denny Cook decided to announce his own fight even while fighting it. "The champ comes out of his corner and cautiously circles the big dope," he said, doing just that. "He leads with two quick jabs to the nose," and—*whap! whap!*— there they were. The blood ran from Pinsker's nostrils. "The champ feints with a left to the body and throws a right cross that lands on the mouth"—and so it did, causing Pinsker's gums to bleed. "The big dope looks dazed," announced Denny, in his Don Dunphy voice, stepping in to throw two more quick left jabs to Pinsker's face and then a smashing right hand—*oomph!*— to the stomach. Pinsker, the wind knocked out of him, fell to one knee, the gravel cutting into his corduroy pants.

"C'mon," I heard myself call out, "he's had enough, Denny. Leave him alone."

Denny Cook shot both arms into the air. "It looks like a TKO for the champ," he yelled, getting something of Dunphy's ringside hysteria into his voice, jumping up and down, dancing around as if he were in the ring at Madison Square Garden.

When the crowd of kids had dispersed, I was still standing over Ira Pinsker, holding his jacket. He was on the ground on all fours now, his nose and mouth bleeding, his pants leg torn, trying to catch his breath. "You going to be all right?" I asked. Not having caught his breath sufficiently to talk, he nodded his head. Funny—he never cried. I walked home with him; he lived two blocks from where I did. All the way home he kept repeating, "My mother is going to kill me for these ripped pants." But still he didn't cry.

That first day in the fifth grade at Clinton was decisive for Ira Pinsker. He was not merely badly beaten, but he became, because of the ease and stylishness with which it was done, the class goat. Everyone called him "Pinky," and much worse. Most of our fathers were men on the way up in the world—doctors and lawyers and owners of their own profitable businesses—while Pinsker's father sold women's cosmetics and, apparently, didn't do all that well at it. I say this because the word got around that Mr. Pinsker was an accordion player with a miserable little band that used to play at weddings and bar-mitzvah parties on weekends. Pinsker's old man's accordion became a big joke.

Ira was a decent enough student, but his early growth made him extremely awkward, and his every screw-up, of which there were many in the classroom, on the playground, at the movies, sent us into wild laughter. He hung in there, trying to compete, but he was a marked man—sent out to the boyhood Siberia of right field in baseball, inserted into the pillory of center on our class football team. Slow on the comeback, he could be teased with impunity. "Hey, Pinky, you futz, how's your old man's accordion?" Kids would call large orders in to local drugstores to be sent to his house: three quarts of hand-packed ice cream, tubes of Ben-Gay, cans of pipe tobacco, boxes of Kotex. Orders from Chinese restaurants mysteriously arrived at the Pinsker home. Girls, knowing he was the class goat, never took him seriously. Once he threw up on a high ride at Riverview Park; this was good for months of laughs. We all of us had our best friends—I must have run through five or six of them— or fell in with little cliques. Not Pinsker. Coming out of grammar-school graduation, Donnie Olsen threw a dime cherry pie at him; it missed his head, but caught him flush on the shirt front and ran down the ridiculous hand-painted tie that must have belonged to his father.

I would like to be able to report that I was the sensitive kid who stood by Pinsker through these years. I wasn't. The best I can say for myself is that I was fairly low on the list of his tormentors. I can't say that I ever tried to establish a friendship with Pinsker, but then intimacy seemed somehow impossible with him. For example, he never called me anything but Melvin, a name I hate. (Mel I can live with.) He didn't have the mental quickness and comic sense I required in a friend. His slowness, his physical awkwardness, made him seem a little—I don't know, maybe a little irregular or less than fully human.

High school wasn't much easier for Pinsker. Ours was a large high school, with some 3,000 students, and very social. Pinsker once again fell into his by-now accustomed role of outsider. His reputation as a goat had followed him. By his sophomore year he had grown to about 6'2", without any notable gain in coordination. Yet you had to grant Ira his determination—maybe doggedness is the better word. He went out for track, and ran the mile. Day after day he would run his laps, chugging and churning and growing red in the face. In city track meets, over three years, he never came close to winning a race. Eventually, in his senior year, he was awarded a minor letter.

In high school something new that would grow greater in later years first began to show up in Pinsker—illusions of grandeur. Its early evidence was to be found in his attempting to court only the most beautiful girls in the school. He would call them for dates; he would hang around them in the school corridors. These girls usually had some refinement—he had good taste in women, Pinsker—and none was ever rude to him. But unrudeness was as far as he got. What is of interest, however, was the element of self-deception. Pinsker apparently hadn't a clue that a man with his lowly status was out of place asking such girls out. Nor was Pinsker above putting down fellow students, at least in conversation, for what he thought was their crudity or stupidity. Insufficient self-esteem was not Ira's problem. He was a goat who was also something of a snob. It's not a combination you run into every day.

Which brings me to Harvey Silvers. Harvey was a foot, maybe more, shorter than Ira Pinsker. Silvers's hair was yellow, wavy, and fine, while Pinsker's was brown, lank, and dull. Pinsker's awkwardness made him always a dangerous guest among the bric-a-brac of any mother's living room; Silvers was a wonderfully smooth dancer. Pinsker struggled for words, usually coming up with the wrong or unintentionally comic ones; Silvers had the quickness of a Catskills comedian. Harvey's father owned three men's clothing stores in Chicago, and his son wore cashmere sweaters, mohair polo coats, elegant loafers. On weekends, and most week nights, he had the use of his father's white Fleetwood Cadillac. His family's money gave Harvey an easy confidence; the world was not in any way a frightening or puzzling place for him but instead a kind of amusement park. And one of the most amusing things in it for Harvey Silvers was Ira L. Pinsker.

When we were kids there was a comic book called *The Fox and the Crow*. The inspiration for it must have come from either Aesop or La Fontaine, I don't know which, but the comic book was a lot funnier than both those guys. What it was about was endless stories in which the Crow inevitably bested the Fox, usually after working out richly detailed schemes for which the Fox would fall. On the final pages of drawings, the long and lankish Fox could be found chased by bees, or felled by a giant tree, or hanging by his fingernails from a cliff. As often as not, x's denoting painful unconsciousness were drawn where the Fox's eyes were, while the compact Crow would be shown cheerfully emptying the Fox's refrigerator of hams, turkeys, aromatic pies, and lavish clumps of grapes. The relationship between Ira Pinsker and Harvey Silvers was essentially that between the Fox and the Crow.

During a dull moment cruising around in his father's Fleetwood one Saturday evening, Harvey remarked that he needed to take a leak. When I proposed a nearby alley, he offered a counterproposal of the floor of the back seat of Pinsker's father's Nash, which, fewer than ten minutes later, his polo coat thrown wide open, grin on face, he was acting upon. Another night, as we were finishing a pizza at Papa Milano's on Rush Street, Harvey suggested that Pinsker might like the four or five slices remaining; and so, when we were back in the neighborhood, we drove over to Pinsker's house, where Harvey deposited the uncovered pieces through the mail slot onto the floor of the Pinsker foyer. Although I wasn't along, one night, around three in the morning, Harvey, unable to sleep and feeling an artistic urge, drove over and painted the Pinskers' small front lawn white. "Actually," I heard him correct someone else who told the story in front of him, "the color was called 'champagne velvet.' "

Anyone with good instincts, hearing these stories, is likely to feel sorry for poor Pinsker, bullied and abused by a vicious rich kid. But to feel this way you would need not only good instincts but absolutely no firsthand dealings with Ira Pinsker. Maybe I am myself unusually sympathetic to Harvey Silvers, who has since had a triple bypass operation and is paying out something like ninety grand a year in alimony to two ex-wives. But I happen to think that Harvey and Ira nicely complemented each other. Through their last years of high school, Pinsker would call Harvey to ask if he could tag along with him on a Friday night; and Harvey often went out of his way to pick up Pinsker at Winnemac Park or Hansen Stadium on the West Side after one or another of Pinsker's hopeless track meets. What, after all, was the Fox without the Crow, the Crow without the Fox?

The night we were about to drive to Kankakee for a visit to one of that town's cat houses, Harvey, who was doing the driving, swung around to pick up Pinsker. When someone asked what the hell do we need Pinsker for, Harvey replied, "Why not, the jerk-off's good for laughs." Pinsker was a virgin, and on the ride up of sixty or so miles, Harvey was full of bogus instructions for him, delivered in the solemn voice of a wise uncle. "Ira, whatever you do, don't let her talk you into taking off your socks." "Ira, don't be alarmed if in the middle of things she reaches under the bed and brings up a dry-cell battery." "Just remember, Ira, at all times keep your legs on the outside of hers."

On the way back we all told stories about our adventures, stories that, if my own little narratives are any measure, were a mixture of exaggerations, added comic touches, and straight-out inventions. All but Pinsker, who was stony silent. "So, Ira," Harvey asked, "how didya like it?" After at least fully ten seconds of silence, Pinsker, sitting erect in the middle of the back seat, said, "Harvey, I hope that there will be no idle chatter about this evening." From my own seat next to Harvey's in the front of the Fleetwood, I saw his eyes come alive, a small smile play on his lips. "Idle chatter, Ira?" he said. "What do you mean?" "You know what I mean, Silvers," Pinsker said. "It would be very bad if there were a lot of loose talk about what went on this evening."

"Idle chatter? Loose talk? Pinsker, may I ask you a question? What freakin' century are you living in?"

For the remainder of his days in high school Ira was known as

I.C. Pinsker, the I.C. standing for idle chatter.

He seemed to have a genius for the wrong phrase—a God-given skill for saying or doing exactly the wrong thing at exactly the wrong time. When years later Pinsker went off to the University of Iowa, where no one knew anything of his past, he returned with an odd, almost but not quite English accent. (Iowa may seem a strange place to acquire such an accent, but then we are talking about Ira L. Pinsker.) Maybe it wasn't quite an accent so much as it was that he now tended to speak in something like italics, every word strongly emphasized and calling attention to itself. To his earlier talent for the inappropriate, he now added certain stiff new phrases. "See here," he would say to the kid cleaning his windshield at a gas station, "do get the back windows as well." Or, addressing a high-school girl bagging groceries in the supermarket: "Indeed, if I may, mightn't I have these groceries placed in two separate bags?" But he really went too far, I thought, when at his own wedding, to a Lutheran girl from South Dakota named Linda Fergusson, he was asked by the minister if he would take this woman to be his lawful wedded wife, Pinsker replied neither "I do" nor "I will," but "I shall." I suppose we were lucky that he didn't say, "I daresay I shall." I was one of four people at his wedding—neither his own nor his wife's parents attended—and when I reported this "I shall" business to Harvey Silvers, he smiled and said, "That Pinsker—what a plu-perfect schmuck!"

Why did I stay in touch with Pinsker after high school? Well, we went back a long way together since that first day he sat in front of me—P before R—in grammar school. Maybe I'm sentimental, but I don't find it easy to break off with people—never have, and I still occasionally see four or five guys I knew in high school. Yet maybe there was something more to it with Pinsker. Although I always knew he was a little nutty, that he was acting a leading part in some play that had a long run in his head alone, despite this I thought that he had a weirdly impressive courage. Running all those losing miles in high school, for instance; or refusing to have any other than the highest opinion of himself, even in the face of ridicule.

I remember a YMCA basketball team he organized during our last year of high school. Pinsker, at 6'3", was our center. He played in sweat pants, often with a rope and sometimes with his street belt holding them up, a torn track jersey, and Chuck Taylor All Stars that his mother must have put in the washer with something very red, for Pinsker's gym shoes were hopelessly pink, the only pair of pink Chuck Taylors I have ever seen. He had still not yet come into his coordination, and there was something almost painfully rigid about his performance on the basketball court. Smaller men ran circles around Pinsker, larger ones beat on him at will, cracking him with elbows in the ribs, knocking him to the floor, cutting him up pretty badly generally. Yet Pinsker kept coming at them. He couldn't win but he wouldn't quit. Doggedly, relentlessly, probably stupidly, Pinsker hung in there. At the end of the season our team—we called ourselves (what else?) the Idle Chatterers—was 4 and 11, and yet, somehow, though we weren't even close to getting into the playoffs, it was a satisfying season and I came away with a certain respect for Ira's tenacity.

I went to college in the city and then to law school at Northwestern University. "Studying torts and chasing tarts," Harvey Silvers used to joke about me in those days. (Harvey went a year to Roosevelt University, where he found himself interested in accounting, until his father asked him why. "You don't study accounting," he told Harvey, "you hire accountants." This caused Harvey to drop out of school and go directly, at nineteen, into his father's business, at which point he began to drive a Cadillac of his own.) I bring up Harvey's torts-and-tarts crack not to brag, but the fact is that I wasn't too bad with women in those days. I had two older sisters at home; I therefore had a good sense of what makes women interested in men; and I had a normal young man's voracious appetite for sex. Above all I understood that in order to have a girl surrender to you, you had to make a respectable show of surrendering to her first. This, for some reason, I never had any trouble doing. The truth is, I grew up a sister's boy; I liked women, and, with a wife now of twenty-five years and a daughter of twenty-two, I still do. I wouldn't carry on about this if my good friend Ira Pinsker, the novelist, hadn't as we shall see made it important that I establish my bona fides in the matter.

By the time I was in my second year of law school, Pinsker had probably decided to become a writer. At any rate, he had begun to work at that series of hopeless jobs ill-performed that he retained until he produced his first novel at age fifty-two: hotel clerk, cab-driver, fundraiser for failing colleges, public-relations consultant for charities devoted to secondary diseases, headhunter for corporations located in out-of-the-way states. It was while he was working as night clerk at the old Commonwealth Hotel, off Diversey Avenue, near Sheridan Road, that he called on me in my capacity as moderately successful seducer of young women. He had met and quickly struck out with a beautiful Southerner who lived in the hotel, and he thought maybe my luck would be better. Pinsker was not known for his generosity, but I nonetheless answered the call.

I once read that it isn't a good idea to sleep with someone who has more problems that you do, but if in those days I had tried to live by that rule, I would have had no sex life whatsoever, for at twenty-four years old, still a law student, I now see that I hadn't any problems at all. Rose Hess, the girl Pinsker introduced me to, on the other hand, did have a problem or two: she was an alcoholic; she had had tuberculosis; she had two kids living with her mother back in Kentucky; and she was running away from her husband, an unemployed coal miner who had followed her here to Chicago. This last, highly anti-aphrodisiacal fact, which Pinsker had failed to report, clinched it. After two drinks taken in a bar on Diversey, during which all this information poured out, I told Rose Hess how nice it was to meet her and wished her the very best of luck in her new life in Chicago. I walked off into the night, thinking myself well out of it and commending myself on my fundamental good sense. When I arrived at my car, a red and black 1957 Plymouth Belvedere with push-button drive, I found a note attached to the windshield wiper, which read:

Friend,
I catch you out again with my wife

I slice off your pecker.

Sincerely,
Richard C. Hess

Richard C. Hess's notes were notable for strong verbs. In the weeks to come, even though I never saw his wife again, I received similar notes informing me that he would "club" my head in, "rip" my heart out, "roast" my eyeballs, and "kick" my ass to the moon if he ever caught me with his wife. Some of these notes were left on my windshield; two—which really gave me the willies—were slipped under the door of my apartment. "I gather he must be a bit paranoid," was Pinsker's considered conclusion when I reported all this to him. The future novelist had begun to arrive at his descriptive powers, for when I asked him if he had ever seen Richard C. Hess, he replied that he had noticed him around the hotel a time or two. "Well, Ira," I asked, "what does he look like?"

"Rather a bruiser," Pinsker replied. "Blond, very sinewy, red-faced, a freshly minted tattoo of a snake and a panther curled round a sword on his right forearm. Overall, I should say that he gives the impression of someone fairly menacing. Otherwise, your standard hillbilly type."

Whether Richard C. and Rose Hess ever got back together, I never discovered. All I can say is that I spent five or six extremely edgy weeks until the notes stopped appearing and I could return to my apartment or go out to my car without my stomach turning over in cold panic fear. Sometime during the middle of this awful period it occurred to me that it must have been Pinsker who told Richard C. Hess who I was and where I lived. A clear case of idle chatter, if ever there was one. Thanks again, Ira, that's another one I owe you.

Yet in the fall of that same year I took a trip down South with Pinsker. I was going into my final year of law school, I had always wanted to see the South and didn't know when I would get another chance, and I didn't care to travel alone. No one else could, or cared to, go. Pinsker, ever the free-lance, suggested himself. What I remember him saying is something like he, too, "would like to take in what Henry Louis Mencken so deftly called 'the Sahara of the Bozart.'" Why did I agree to take Pinsker along? Maybe I didn't want to hurt his feelings by turning him down. Maybe I was attracted by his idea of traveling cheaply by staying at Southern chapters of his fraternity, for during his first year at Iowa Pinsker had become a member of Sigma Alpha Mu, a national Jewish fraternity. "Fools that they are, they will welcome us as brothers in spirit," he told me, with a wink and a nudge. "Melvin, we shall eat like kings and at no cost to ourselves." He rubbed his hands together intensely.

I have not until now mentioned Pinsker's thriftiness. It was extreme. In later years, it was said about him that he was able to save money while living on unemployment insurance. If anyone had ever witnessed him picking up a check, that witness has yet to come forth. On this Southern trip I discovered how extreme his thrift could be. We first stopped in Memphis, at Memphis State University, where it was late at night and we learned that fraternities had no accommodations. I suggested that we sleep cheap by checking into the downtown YMCA. Why not in the car? Pinsker wondered. I preferred not to, but Pinsker, with the obstinacy that led him to run three years' worth of mile races without ever finishing in the money, won out. Large-hearted guy, he gave me the back seat.

Sleeping in the car was damned uncomfortable, but what Pinsker's cheapness led us into next was slightly dangerous. We were sitting on the back veranda of the student union at Southern Methodist University in Dallas, appraising, with heartfelt admiration, the effects of fresh air and physical exercise on that institution's extremely healthy female undergraduate population, when I mentioned that it was nearly time for lunch. At Southern Methodist there was, of course, no SAM chapter, nor any other Jewish fraternity. I thought we might have a sandwich in the student union, and push on. Pinsker had another idea. Why spend good money, he reasoned, when we could pass ourselves off as Sigma Chi's from Iowa and eat on the cuff in the Sigma Chi house at SMU.

It struck me at once as a tremendously bad idea. Neither of us looked remotely like a Sigma Chi. Even then I had to shave twice a day if I was going out in the evening and, as I well remember, I was wearing a white-on-white shirt with French cuffs rolled up to the elbows, a pair of dark gray slacks, and black tassel loafers, and looked every inch the big-city Jewish law student of the late 1950's, which, after all, is what I was. Pinsker, with his rather widely separated eyes, his already receding hairline, and odd clothes—that day he was wearing a shiny maroon windbreaker, a pair of blue corduroys, and black wing-tip shoes—Pinsker looked like someone from another country, or possibly another planet. We were not exactly your two typical Sigma Chi's from Iowa. "Take courage Melvin," Pinsker declared, "these morons will never know the difference." Since college Pinsker, I thought, had developed a foolhardy contempt for the intelligence of almost everyone but himself.

I don't remember much about how we got past the door of the Sigma Chi house, or how Pinsker was able to evade the rigmarole of exchanging fraternity handshakes and passwords. I do remember him telling a tall, rather well-built kid who met us at the door—he, apparently, was a pledge—that we were Sigma Chi's from the University of Iowa, Alpha Eta chapter, and then introduced me as Roy Peters and himself as Chick Nelson (*Chick Nelson!*) Then he said, my friend Chick did, "We're not, I trust, too late for lunch?"

As we walked through the large living room, through the trophy and chapter rooms, into the dining room, I recall feeling as if I were in some old movie in which Laurel and Hardy are Gypsies who have disguised themselves to pass among the palace guard in order to be able to rescue a beautiful young peasant girl from a malevolent aristocrat. But all that we were rescuing was a small lunch check that Pinsker didn't want to pay. The meal was already in progress. Huge platters of meat loaf and mashed potatoes and green beans were being passed around by muscular, mostly blond, crew-cut college boys. We sat at one of the tables near the entrance. Pinsker introduced us as

Sigma Chi's from Alpha Eta chapter. Everyone at the table seemed to be named Bobby or Don or Ray. "What kinda football team you gonna have at Iowa this year, Chick?" one of the Sigma Chi's asked. "I think we are Rose Bowl bound," said Pinsker, "but would you mind passing the meat loaf?"

I had to concede that Pinsker was handling himself fairly well. He was batting small talk around, inventing facts and figures about old Alpha Eta chapter back in Iowa City, and talking up the fraternity's intramural sports success. Meanwhile, he helped himself to seconds of everything, including two slices of cherry pie. I was about to reconsider slightly my opinion of his hopelessness, when one of the Sigma Chi's at the table asked good buddy Chick what kind of pledge class Alpha Eta was anticipating that fall. "Well," said Pinsker, dabbing a bit of cherry pie from the corner of his mouth with his paper napkin, "we'll be looking as always for as many classics majors as we can find. Also art history majors and philosophers. A fraternity like Sigma Chi can use all the philosophers it can get its hands on." That maniac Pinsker, I thought, now he's done it. I looked to the exits in the room, just in case we had to make a run for it. But the Bobbys and the Dons and the Rays seemed transfixed with incomprehension. Before we left, old Chick got them to have the cook make us up some sandwiches for the road.

We stopped at Austin and Houston and pushed on to New Orleans, where we stayed at the Sigma Alpha Mu house at Tulane. We were to be there only for a day, so I offered to treat Pinsker, who claimed that his funds were running low, to a night on the town. We had dinner at Brennan's, listened to Dixieland at Preservation Hall, sang dirty ditties at Perry O'Brien's, and began a round of the jazz bars. Fairly early in the evening, I made a small discovery: when it came to drinking, Pinsker, though a large man, was a short hitter. Two drinks and he became sleepy; three drinks and his speech began to slur and his eyelids to droop. It was still early in the evening, and though we planned to head back to Chicago at five the next morning, hoping to make the run from New Orleans in one long day's drive, I wasn't quite ready to turn in. So it became a matter of have a drink and drag Ira, have a drink and drag Ira. Until, that is, I made the mistake of going to the men's room at Pete Fountain's, leaving Pinsker at the bar, from which, when I returned, he had disappeared.

I searched up and down the French Quarter, from starkly lit Bourbon Street to dark, slightly eerie Chartres Street. I looked into strip joints, jazz bars, restaurants. No Pinsker. I walked along the Mississippi River, wondering if he had fallen in. Was Pinsker lying at this moment beaten up in some dank back alley? Was he in an emergency room somewhere? Or, who knew, a morgue? It was getting late. I decided to make one more patrol of the main streets of the Quarter. Around three in the morning, at a striptease joint that advertised as its headliner a dancer named Reddi Flame, I found Pinsker, his head on the bar. A rather heavy-set woman wearing only a single-feather headdress and a loincloth, and billed as Princess Cherokee, was dancing to "Night Train" on a small stage behind the bar. I shook Pinsker awake. "Melvin," he said, his thinning hair in disarray, his eyeballs glazed, "I appear to have lost my shoe," and his head fell back onto the bar. I shook him again. He raised his head, looked directly at Princess Cherokee, and announced, loudly and in his emphatic accent, "Gawd! Is she ghastly!" The Princess, not missing a beat, one large breast whirling clockwise, the other counterclockwise, silently mouthed the retort, "I am not."

Somehow I was able to get the one-shoed Pinsker into a cab. I set him on the front porch of the Sigma Alpha Mu house and went upstairs, where among sleeping fraternity boys I gathered up our things. I loaded the Plymouth; then I stuffed Pinsker into the back seat. An eight-hundred-mile drive to Chicago, where in thirty or so hours I was to begin my last year of law school, lay ahead. Well, thanks to my old friend Pinsker, we were getting a somewhat early start.

The sun beat down as I drove through Mississippi. Near the border of Tennessee, I began to feel my lack of sleep. I stopped for coffee, for cokes, for gas, during which time I ran cold water over my wrists in gas-station rest rooms. Pinsker snored gently all this while in the back of the Plymouth; there was a hole in the sock on the foot from which he had lost his black wing-tip. I cannot say that

I longed sorely for his company. But neither did I think I could go much farther, for, despite all the coffee, coke, cold water, I began dozing at the wheel. Outside Memphis, I decided to wake Pinsker.

I had not thus far on this long trip asked Pinsker to drive a single mile, and for the good reason that his driving frankly terrified me. He had a natural antipathy to activities calling for normal human coordination. He was the only person I ever saw who, when he shuffled a deck of cards, made you feel rather sorry for the cards. Ira was a youthful Mr. Magoo, but without the cartoon character's terrible eyesight. He had a fine obliviousness, a wildly misplaced confidence, that could be amusing in minor activities. But driving was something else again. I didn't want Pinsker driving my Plymouth, but there wasn't time for me to pull over the side of the road and sleep three or four hours and still get to Chicago for classes the next day. I had no choice.

"Ira," I said, in the most serious tone of voice I could command, "don't drive any more than forty-five, fifty miles an hour—tops! There's no great hurry. Don't take any chances. Don't do anything crazy." Before falling asleep in the front seat beside him, I looked down to the floor on Pinsker's side, where I noted again the missing wingtip. He had brought only the one pair of shoes on this trip.

The next thing I saw was an enormous threshing machine looming up before us—and fast. "Goddamnit, Pinsker!" I shrieked. He was asleep at the wheel, which I grabbed and jerked, hard, to the right, sending the Plymouth skittering off the road, tires screeching. I remember thinking, "I don't want to die with Pinsker so near. Please don't let me die with Pinsker so near." The car turned over, not once but twice, and landed upright. The roof of the Plymouth was ruined, the hood caved in. I had a gash over my right eye that later took nine stitches to close. Pinsker was shaken but uninjured.

Not long after we had extricated ourselves from the car, the man driving the threshing machine, a farmer in overalls and a baseball cap, came running back. Once he saw that neither of us was seriously hurt, he asked which one was doing the driving. I pointed disgustedly to Pinsker. "Well, young man," the farmer said, "that was a mighty fancy piece of driving, mighty fancy indeed." Pinsker's eyes seemed to focus somewhere off in the distance. I saw that he was reinventing what had just happened, with himself in a heroic role. "I gather it was chiefly good instinct and quick reflexes on my part," he replied, "but I thank you all the same."

Then and there, I should have strangled him.

Pinsker totaled my car, scarred my face, and neglected to say a word in apology. I really had had enough of him to last me a lifetime, so, once back in law school in Chicago, I drifted away. Less than a year later, I passed the bar and went to work for the law firm of Liebman, Goldberger, and Meyers. Two years further down the road, I met and not long afterward married my wife Rochelle. We were living in Skokie, Shelley was pregnant with our daughter Shari, when one day, on my way to acquire a deposition from a client on the near North Side, I stepped into a cab outside our office on LaSalle Street and looked straight into the back of a head I recognized from fifth grade.

"So, Melvin," said Pinsker, not letting his current employment cut in the least into his pomposity, "has life been treating you equably?"

"Can't complain, Ira. How about you?"

Pinsker told me that he had spent a year traveling around in Europe (he babbled something about the splendor of Portuguese wines) and a little more than a year in San Francisco (which he referred to as "the Bay Area"). He was driving a cab during the day and writing short stories at night, which he was beginning to send around to magazines. Most important, in less than two weeks he was going to get married. His parents didn't approve of his future wife's not being Jewish, not to mention the added bonus of his marrying in a Lutheran church, so they wouldn't be showing up at the wedding. He would be pleased, he said, if my wife and I would come; the only other people who would be there were a couple who had grown up in the same town in South Dakota as his wife. I said I wasn't sure if we were free that day—it was a Saturday afternoon—but that, if he would give me his phone number, I would get back to him.

I made the mistake of telling Shelley about Pinsker's forthcoming wedding. I love my wife, and one of the reasons is that she has a good heart, but a good heart, if I may say so, can be a terrific pain in the neck. Shelley not only insisted that we go to Pinsker's wedding—after all, she argued, I would be his only old friend present—but she also decided to make a wedding lunch back at our house after the marriage ceremony. I pleaded with her not to do so; I attempted to get her to understand what Pinsker was really like. In exasperation, I pointed to the scar over my right eye, which had faded but was still fairly distinct:

"See this," I said (actually, I was yelling), "here is what you get when you start up with Ira Pinsker."

"Of course, darling," she said. "Now be sure to tell your friend Ira that lunch here will be planned for 1:30. That ought to give everyone plenty of time to drive over from Cicero."

I've already mentioned Pinsker's saying "I shall" when asked if he would take Linda Francine Fergusson for his lawful wedded wife. The new Mrs. Pinsker did not go so far as to say "I shall" when asked a similar question, but back at our place in Skokie for my wife's wedding lunch, she did demonstrate herself well-matched for marriage to Pinsker. She was tall—maybe 5′10″—with auburn-colored hair, wore large round-rimmed glasses, and had thick ankles, which were accentuated by her tall-girl's habit of wearing flat shoes. She had been an English major at the University of Iowa, where Pinsker had first met her, and all she seemed to want to talk about, even at her own wedding lunch, was art. She was clearly mad about Pinsker; and from time to time during lunch she would gaze upon him lovingly and begin a sentence by saying, "As Ira so beautifully put it the other day . . .," or "In Ira's elegant phrase . . .," and then she would say something that didn't seen very beautiful or elegant to me, but then maybe I'm not the best guy to judge. Pinsker himself neither blushed nor corrected her.

I suspect that the former Miss Fergusson, of Mobridge, South Dakota, felt that in Pinsker she had latched on to the real thing, an artist type, a future novelist of great promise, with whom she could ride, well above the crowd, into the stratosphere. Linda Pinsker had as little doubt about Pinsker as Pinsker had about himself, which

was none whatsoever. How does the television commercial for Cha-
nel No. 5 perfume go? Ah, yes: Share the fantasy! Pinsker had found
a wife who apparently completely shared his. At least he wouldn't be
alone any longer. And, I recall thinking at the time, I suppose two
could live as unrealistically as one.

Not long after their marriage, the Pinskers moved to New York,
where Linda was transferred by the public-relations firm she worked
for in Chicago. I had underrated Linda Fergusson Pinsker, for over
the next fifteen or so years she rose in her line of work to be one of
the powerful vice presidents of one of the largest public-relations
firms in Manhattan, and was probably pulling in a couple of hundred
grand a year. I learned this from a client of mine who is a public-
relations man in Chicago. I learned, too, from Harvey Silvers, that
Pinsker's father had died, without father and son patching things up,
and that Ira did not come in for the funeral. How Pinsker himself
was doing was pretty unclear. No one reported hearing about any
books he had written, or seeing his name in magazines, or anything
of the kind.

I would occasionally fly into New York on business, but I never
called him. Then, about three years ago, our firm acquired as a client
the owners of the Chicago franchise of the defunct United States
Football League, and I was put on the case, which involved repre-
senting our clients' interest in the disbanding of the USFL and which
took me into New York for a monthly meeting with other owners
and their attorneys. Generally I would fly in and out the same day,
but then one time, owing to a snowstorm in the Midwest, all flights
to Chicago were canceled. I had a free night in New York on my
hands, and I figured, what the hell, why not call Pinsker?

We met in a small French restaurant on the West Side in the
70's. Linda Pinsker looked much the same; perhaps a bit sleeker and
more confident. She and Ira had had no children and obviously weren't
planning any. I noticed that she no longer remarked on how beautifully or elegantly her husband put things. Pinsker had lost his hair
and replaced it with a thick mustache and beard, which took a little
getting used to; I couldn't quite get over the resemblance of this now

bearded Pinsker to one of those cardboard faces that, when you turned it upside down, became another face. And speaking of face, Pinsker ordered, in French, something that turned out to be the cheek of a young cow. He ate in the continental manner, his fork in his left hand, his knife in his right. His mid-Atlantic accent had become even more emphatic. Yet he was wearing a tweed suit whose jacket had a belt in the back, and his tie had a gravy stain just below the knot.

"So, Melvin," he said, with a slightly condescending smile, "what brings you to Gotham?"

He seemed even a little crazier than I remembered. Eighteen years had passed since he had left Chicago. Near as I could make out, he had accomplished very little. When I asked him what he was doing at present, he chuckled and said, "I currently describe myself as a hack writer. I am at work on a detective story that may or may not have cinematic possibilities. We shall see." And then he said no more about it. Two or three other times during the dinner he similarly hinted at significance, big doings that, he made clear, it wouldn't do to talk further about here.

Meanwhile, he grilled me about his former tormentors in grade and high school. I was able to report to him that Denny Cook, who had beaten him up on his first day at Clinton School, was now a policeman in Chicago. I had heard that Donnie Olsen, who had thrown a pie at him after graduation from grammar school, was doing very well as a plumbing contractor. When he asked about Harvey Silvers, I don't know exactly why, but I decided not to fill him in on Harvey's divorces and medical problems. "You know Harvey," I said, "same old wild man." Not long afterward the check arrived, and was picked up not by Ira but by Linda Pinsker, who paid it, with the authority of long habit, with an American Express card.

I didn't call Pinsker on subsequent trips to New York. A little of him, now as then, went a long way. But about four weeks ago I received from a New York publisher an announcement that they were about to bring out a brilliant new novel entitled *Marvin's Secret Gardens* by Ira Lyle Pinsker. A note accompanying the announcement informed me that Mr. Pinsker would be in the Chicago area promoting his book two weeks hence. A week later Pinsker himself called.

"Melvin," he began, "I trust you received the announcement about my novel." He would be in town the following Thursday and would be autographing copies of his novel at the main Kroch & Brentano's store on Wabash Avenue in the Loop. He'd appreciate it if I would be there. He also asked me to make sure that Harvey Silvers was there. And, oh, yes, he had a favor he wanted to ask me. He then read over the phone a list of names of other people he would like to have show up and whom he asked me to call. The list included a number of people who, when kids, had put him down, as well as some of the more desirable girls from our high school who in those days wouldn't have anything to do with him.

"Ira," I said, "I haven't seen or heard about most of these people in more than thirty years. Some must have left Chicago. For all I know, some may even be dead."

"Try, Melvin," he said. "It's important. Try."

There were thirty or so names on Pinsker's list, and I wasn't about to call even half of them. I did make sure that Harvey would be there; and I called seven or eight others, some of whom said they would try. "So the old Idle Chatterer has really written a book," said Larry Fleischer, who had taken over his father's office-furniture business. "What the hell do you suppose is in it?" I said that I didn't know, never having actually seen a copy.

Kroch's was crowded when I arrived at about a quarter to twelve. Part of the crowd was from the beginning of the lunch rush; but a lot of people were there because that same morning Phil Donahue was autographing copies of a book he had just published. People—most of them women—were on the stairs, clutching copies of Donahue's book, patiently awaiting their turn. Pinsker was on the main floor, sitting at a table on which were piled fifty or sixty copies of *Marvin's Secret Gardens*.

Standing there talking with him was Harvey, in a dark blue velour running suit, a thick gold chain around his neck, his once wavy blond hair now combed to camouflage—not very successfully—his baldness. He must have come directly from the East Bank Club, where he worked out on an exercise regimen since his triple bypass. Pinsker sitting down in his absurdly erect posture was nearly as tall as Harvey standing up. Pinsker was wearing a black knit tie over a plaid shirt and a weirdly light green corduroy jacket over that; half-glasses perched on his nose, his beard seemed to bristle aggressively. Looking at them before they saw me, I smiled and thought, "The old Fox and the old Crow meet once again."

"Ah, Melvin," said the great author as I walked up. "You are here, too. What a pleasing surprise!"

Somehow I didn't have the heart to say, "Come off it, Ira, you horse's ass, you begged me to be here." Instead I picked up a copy of the book, which had a lavender jacket and, on the back, a picture of Ira Lyle Pinsker in a turtleneck sweater and a wide-brimmed Italian-looking hat. As I was shaking Harvey's hand, a woman walked up to the table. She wore butterfly-shaped glasses, her hair was swept up into a high bouffant, and she carried a copy of Phil Donahue's book.

"Are you somebody important?" she asked, looking at Pinsker.

"Perhaps one day I shall be much more important than your friend Mr. Donahue, Madame," Pinsker replied, without a trace of irony. "But just now I am a writer, merely, a novelist by trade, who works at his craft to the best of his ability."

"Oh, yeah," said the woman, completely puzzled by what she had just heard, and walked away.

Two or three other people from our high school came in during the forty or so minutes I hung around. During that time Pinsker may have autographed ten or twelve books, which he did with great courtliness and flourish. This was Ira Pinsker's shining hour, Ira had come marching home, Pinsker victorious. Well, let him have joy in it, I thought, when, during a flurry of activity at the table, Harvey pulled me over to the side.

"Thirty-one years later," Harvey said, "and he's still a schmuck. When I first walked in here, you know what he said? He said, 'Harvey Silvers, I had no idea that you were interested in the much-neglected fictive art. How endless are the world's surprises!' Can you believe that yutz? I only wish his old man's Nash were at the curb now, so I could step outside and take another leak in it."

"Are you going to buy the book?" I asked.

"Whaddaya, kiddin' me?" Harvey said.

Before I left, I decided that I probably ought to buy a copy of Pinsker's novel. With his famous cheapness, he was not about to give me one. So I shelled out $22.95, plus tax, and brought my copy of *Marvin's Secret Gardens*, along with my receipt, up to Pinsker to sign.

He opened the book to the first clear page, brushed away a few imaginary flecks of dust, and in a bold hand, in brown ink, wrote,

To Melvin Rosen,

Without whom none of
this would have been possible,

Best wishes,
Ira Lyle Pinsker

What in the hell could that mean? Was Pinsker up to his new trick of hinting at significance where none was to be found? That night, reading his book straight through until I finished it at 2:45 in the morning, I found out.

The full name of the character Marvin in *Marvin's Secret Gardens* is Marvin Rabin. He is roughly my age. He has dark hair, two sisters, grew up in West Rogers Park in a building strikingly like my own, is something of a braggart when it comes to women. He did not, it turns out, go to law but to dental school. He is married and has a daughter. He lived in Skokie during the early years of his marriage, and toward the book's close lives in Highland Park, which as it happens is where my wife and I now live. When Marvin Rabin talks in *Marvin's Secret Gardens* he doesn't, to my ear, sound so much like me as he does like a certain goat with whom I went to grammar and high school, and who went on to write a novel in his early fifties. One more little item about Marvin Rabin—he's homosexual, very very homosexual; is now, was then. The secret gardens of Ira Lyle Pinsker's title refer to Marvin Rabin's—I almost wrote Melvin Rosen's—duplicitous homosexual life.

I'm not about to recount the entire goddamn novel, which is narrated by a tall, amazingly suave fellow named Nicholas Pinter,

who is a kind of (not very) Jewish Somerset Maugham, but a few
scenes might give you something of the book's flavor.

Nick Pinter, whose good looks and urbanity make him naturally
successful with women, throws a good-looking Southern girl his old
friend Marvin Rabin's way while Rabin is still in dental school. Despite
his bragging, Rabin is made out to be a pitiful bumbler, nervous and
distracted around women. It turns out that the Southern girl is married, to a Kentucky coal miner who has followed her to Chicago.
Rabin, whose taste runs to rough trade, comes on strong with the
husband. When the husband beats hell out of Rabin, Nick Pinter
knows for the first time that his old school chum is "gay" (the word
Pinsker uses throughout the novel).

It's pretty hard not to admire Nick Pinter's tolerance and general
strength of character. He's a good friend. He takes his pathetic pal
Marvin Rabin on a trip not to the South but through Europe. There's
a lot of boring description of architecture and cities. They drink a
good deal of wine together, especially in Portugal. One night in Lis-
bon, Marvin comes on to Nick. Tears flow and a lengthy confession
follows, detailing the falsity of Marvin's entire life and ending with
his said proclamation of a long-time love for—right, you got it—the
elegant Nicholas Pinter.

This crap goes on for more than 350 pages. Marvin, struggling
to lead a straight life once he knows he cannot "have" (Pinsker's
word) Nick, marries a woman who I had no trouble telling is meant
to be modeled on my own wife. He is forced to live a life of complete
deception, wearing disguises to gay bars, picking up rough trade, all
the while, as far as anyone (except Nick) knows, conducting the
straight middle-class life of a Midwestern dentist. Let me ruin the
ending for anyone who might care to read the novel by saying that
Marvin Rabin eventually commits suicide, leaving a long letter
declaring his love for Nicholas Pinter and giving Pinter power of
attorney (my God, can you imagine me doing that?) to watch over
the future of his, Rabin's, sadly deceived family. The novel closes
with the gallant Pinter ruminating on the unfathomable design of
the gods when it comes to human destiny.

I don't read much fiction, but I don't think you have to to know that *Marvin's Secret Gardens* is no Pulitzer Prize-winner. Nor, with all of Pinsker's snobbery, would I guess that it had much chance of becoming a big seller. Still, so ticked off was I when I read it that I had it checked by an expert in our firm to determine if the author of the book couldn't be sued for libel. Nothing I would have liked better than to sue the beard off my old friend Ira.

When I calmed down, which took a few weeks, I began to wonder. Why did Pinsker do it? One possible answer is that he really does think I am queer, despite what I take to be strongly persuasive evidence to the contrary. People these days, as we all know, believe anything. Or it could be that Pinsker didn't think I was queer at all, but thought that making me so would provide him with a good story, and one that would show off the character of Nick Pinter, Pinsker's almost insanely self-deceived picture of himself. Probably the main reason for Pinsker's writing his novel was sheer preening, along with getting in a few good licks at the middle class while demonstrating his own superiority. Another possibility—the one, I admit, I least like to consider—is that Pinsker hates me, has hated me for years, and the writing of *Marvin's Secret Gardens* is nothing more than a long delayed act of revenge.

But revenge for what? Maybe for not protecting him more when we were both boys? Maybe for adding to his humiliation when he was an adolescent? Maybe for not taking him altogether seriously as a man after he had radically changed himself into Ira Lyle Pinsker, the writer? In all these cases, though, there were worse offenders than I. Why didn't Pinsker go after them? Could it be that Pinsker felt I should have known better?

Yet what could I have done? As a boy, Ira Pinsker was awkward and out of it; as a man, he forged a style that led him into a life that was wildly delusional. When you press me on it, yes, I believe I am my brother's keeper. But being Pinsker's keeper? What would that involve? Maybe a good friend would have tried, gently, to divest him of some of his delusions. But even if I had been able to do this, would it have been the correct thing to do? Because of his delusions, Pinsker is, I think, goofy; without them, he would be, I am sure, nothing.

During the few weeks of anger I went through after first reading *Marvin's Secret Gardens,* I thought about calling Pinsker and asking him straight out why he had portrayed me in his novel as he did. But then I thought better of it. If he didn't deny it altogether, I was sure he would only hit me with something like, "Melvin, I am afraid that I am not at liberty to say, at least not just now," or "Melvin, the ways of art are complicated and strange, and, if it is all the same to you, I would rather not go into it."

I try not to think about it. At my age, a man could have a heart attack. There is stress enough in the world. I must remain calm. By now I should know that with Pinsker you can't win. No way—not in this world. Not with Ira L. Pinsker. No way.

The Goldin Boys

*E*ven though the coffin was closed, I couldn't bring myself to walk in front of it and greet the Goldin family in condolence. I thought about it on the drive over to the Piser Funeral Home, but given the circumstances of Buddy Goldin's death, I could think of nothing condoling to say. I signed the visitors' book on my way in, so that, in a week or so, the family would see that Dr. Philip Hirsh had been among the mourners, but that was the best I could do.

I took a seat twenty or so rows behind the family—Buddy's parents, his wife who was still in her thirties, his two young daughters. Staring at their backs, I considered how sorrow destroyed posture. Sid Goldin wore his *yarmulke* at an odd angle at the back of his head, and his expensive suit seemed, in his grief, a poor fit, riding up on his shoulders. Jean Goldin seemed to have shrunk with age and the year-round suntan that she always had now gave her a leathery look that came across as hard and unsympathetic. Sid and Jean Goldin, whom life seemed so singularly to have favored, now drew this most bitter of life's cards: the death of a son as they were approaching old age.

The rabbi, a small man a little too pleased with his powers of enunciation, was sermonizing not very convincingly upon the mercifulness of death. He referred to Buddy, whom he had pretty clearly never met, as Bernard, with a strong accent on the second syllable, which made it feel as if those of us who were Buddy's old friends had never met the man the rabbi was talking about, either. Of course, at no point during this sermon, or during the entire service, did he mention that Buddy Goldin was a suicide.

The other item that went unmentioned in the rabbi's sermon was the absence of Buddy's twin brother Eddie. Twins though they were, Buddy and Eddie Goldin were very different in temperament and, even though unmistakably brothers, also in looks. Both were dark, but Buddy's hair was straight and Eddie's curly. Buddy, at 6'2", grew to be two inches taller than Eddie, who was stockier, more muscular than his brother. As kids, Buddy had had bad skin and Eddie a chipped front tooth (later capped). Buddy always seemed cool and a little detached, while Eddie was hot-tempered, a battler. Yet they always got on well together, at least as far as anyone knew. I never saw them argue, or heard either brother ever say anything against the other—and I used to see a lot of them. Their junior year in high school their father bought them a two-tone Oldsmobile convertible—a Starfire, I think it was called—with a dramatic red and white paint job and leather seats, and they shared the car without argument or any kind of quibbling whatsoever.

I knew that there had been a serious falling out between Eddie Goldin and his parents, and that Eddie had broken with them. He was variously reported as teaching in Thailand, Taiwan, or Zimbabwe—nobody seemed to know for sure. Nor was it clear if he even knew about Buddy's leap from his twenty-third-floor law office at One North LaSalle two days before, late on a sunny Tuesday afternoon. My own guess is that, had he known, despite his trouble with his parents, Eddie would have managed to be here.

I went to grammar school with the Goldin boys at Daniel Boone School, in West Rogers Park, and afterward the three of us were the only kids from Boone to cross the line at Howard Street separating Chicago from Evanston and go to Evanston Township High School. Buddy and Eddie Goldin were sent to Evanston because they had already established themselves as extraordinary athletes and E.T.H.S. offered coaching of a kind not available in the Chicago public high schools. My father, who was a pharmacist, sent me to E.T.H.S. because he was intent on my becoming the physician—which I am today, an internist—that he would have been had the Depression not intervened. It cost six hundred bucks a year in those days to send a kid from Chicago to E.T.H.S. I knew this represented a serious expenditure for my father, who ran his drugstore on Devon Avenue with a careful eye for small economies. Even now I can remember him carting the bundles of newspapers into the store at seven on deathly cold Chicago winter mornings. For the Goldins the extra twelve hundred to send both their sons to high school was of no real concern. Money, for them, was never a problem.

We lived in a six-flat building on Washtenaw Avenue, less than a block from the drugstore, which made it easier for my father to open at seven o'clock seven mornings a week and close at nine-thirty every night but Sunday, when he closed at five, and still be able to slip home for a half-hour at lunch and a full hour or so at dinner. We ate in the kitchen, except for Friday night and Jewish holidays. I had my own bedroom and so did my sister Sheila, who is two years older than I, and so of course did our parents. We all shared one bathroom. We had in our living room, among other furniture, a white couch covered in plastic; we went into the living room only when we had company, which, given my father's work schedule, was rarely.

The Goldins lived only six or seven blocks away, on Lunt, between Francisco and Sacramento, but in what seemed to me another world. Theirs was an eleven-room house, built since the war, red face brick all the way around, with two large bay windows and a connected garage, set out on a triple lot. A crew of Mexicans took care of the lawns and shrubbery. A black woman named Jessie, who lived in a maid's room off the kitchen, did the cooking, and did it extremely well. The double garage held Sid Goldin's blue Fleetwood and his wife's cream-colored Chrysler Town & Country convertible with wood paneling on the sides. Along the inside walls of the garage were golf bags with pastel-colored covers for the woods, tennis and badminton racquets, an archery target, and other sports equipment, all of it of the best quality.

Inside, the Goldins' house gave off a feeling of elegant, expensive, yet somehow casual comfort. Had it belonged to us, my mother, I am sure, would have had all the furniture in the house covered in plastic, or else had herself and her family laminated, and I know for a certainty that none of us would have been allowed to walk on the plush white carpeting with our shoes on. The largest portion of the basement, painted a cool white, was a den and trophy room. Green leather couches and chairs were set around the room. A bar was at one end, a large television set at the other; off in a corner was a juke box. Glass cases were arranged around the walls at various points in the room. These contained athletic trophies. Some had been won by Sid Goldin, who lettered in both football and basketball at the University of Illinois in the 1930's; above one of the cases there was a picture of him, posed with a football in one hand and with the other arm in what passed in such corny photos of the day for a stiff arm, and another photo of him, the lone Jewish face, seated among the members of the 1934 University of Illinois basketball team. Most of the trophies in the room, though, belonged to Jean Goldin, who was a serious amateur golfer—serious enough, I was told, to have had a national ranking when in her twenties. One glass case was given over to the athletic achievements of the boys, Buddy and Eddie, who were then only fourteen. Before they were through, they would need several more cases to hold all their trophies.

The Goldin boys were not merely good but spectacularly good athletes. They had both come into their full growth fairly early, but even before that their athletic precocity was marked. By the age of thirteen they were already playing in the Sunday morning men's softball games at the Boone schoolyard, and not just filling in, either, but playing significant positions: Eddie at shortstop, letting damn little get by him; Buddy in centerfield, racing back to catch fly balls over his shoulder or up to make shoestring catches, but somehow making it all look easy. Did they inherit their athletic ability from their parents? I don't know what the best scientific opinion on the subject is, but if they didn't I wish someone would explain how they came to be such wonderful athletes.

And yet they were very different kinds of athlete. Eddie Goldin

seemed to come by his accomplishments through fierce hard work—
unrelenting hustle, in the old sports cliché—and considerable courage. I have never known anyone physically more fearless. If the occasion called for it, Eddie would slide head first on a gravel field, would
take a brutal charge on the basketball court, and cross-body block a
man twice his size without the least hesitation. Questions of hustle
or courage didn't seem to come into play for Buddy Goldin. He was
what we used in those days to call "unconscious." On a court or a
field everything seemed to come so naturally to him. Even when
running very fast he appeared to lope. Like his brother, he had innate
athletic intelligence; he seemed instinctively to know what to do and
always made what he did look easy. Neither of the Goldin boys ever
fumbled or bobbled or dropped the ball; neither seemed to be affected
by pressure; neither ever made a mistake in a game, at least none that
I ever saw. They were—how else describe it?—gifted, early and richly
gifted.

But then there was something gifted and blessed about the entire
Goldin family, or so it seemed to me when I was a kid. Food looked
and tasted better at their table. Handsome cars seemed always to be
backing out of their driveway on the way to immensely interesting
places. Such surprises as their lives contained all seemed pleasant ones.
What for the Goldins was an everyday matter often tended to knock
me off my feet. One day I came home from school with Buddy, and
followed him down to the cool white and green room of the basement, where his father was playing gin with three other men. Buddy
quickly introduced me to the three men, one of whom was Sid Luckman, the recently retired quarterback of the Chicago Bears. "Nice to
meetcha, Phillie," he said in a high, slightly whiny voice with a New
York accent, not looking up from his cards. Another time, glancing
out from Eddie's room down onto the driveway, I noticed Sid and
Jean Goldin getting into the blue Fleetwood with a woman who
looked very familiar. "Is that woman who I think she is?" I asked
Eddie, who came over to the window. "Yeah," he said, "that's Myrna
Loy. She's a client of my Dad's."

Sid Goldin was a lawyer, the senior partner in the firm of Goldin, O'Connor, and Corzinowski. But he was a lawyer of a particular

kind. As I later learned, he scarcely ever entered a courtroom and he certainly didn't waste his time or eyesight composing or studying legal documents. He was instead a fixer and a smoother, a man with connections and clout, who knew everyone and so was regularly called in to bring together otherwise distant parties for the mutual profit of all. He was the man who knew the man who knew the man who could do what was needed: get you points in a sure-hit Broadway play, have a large parcel of real estate rezoned, call off the unions from organizing your shop. His clientele was generously studded with celebrities, including many former athletes, show-business characters, and Chicago politicians. His own name would on occasion appear in the local columns as "powerhouse attorney Sidney Goldin."

After the University of Illinois, Sid Goldin had gone to law school nights, at John Marshall, and worked days selling furniture for his mother's brother, who had a store on the western rim of the Loop. While working for his uncle and going to law school, he met, courted, and married Jean Goldstein, the only child of Judge Irving Goldstein. It was the middle of the 1930's, a time when local judges were powerful figures in Chicago. Sid remembered once getting caught in a traffic jam on the way to a Bears game with his then future father-in-law, who called over a motorcycle cop, announced that he was "Judge Goldstein, goddammit," and demanded a police escort to Wrigley Field so that he wouldn't be late for the game. Without any hesitation, the cop said, "Follow me, sir," turned his siren on full blast, and Sid and the Judge, following the cop on the wrong side of the street, drove directly to the game without even stopping for red lights.

The Judge loved his daughter and approved of her choice of a husband. He liked having a son-in-law who had been a Big Ten athlete; he recognized that this young man was ambitious and no dope. Sid Goldin's marriage enabled him to avoid the time-wasting error of starting at the bottom. Right out of law school, he was put on to a number of good things by his father-in-law. That he was connected with as powerful a man as the Judge brought him clients without any effort on his part. The Judge looked after his own. In

1942, with America in the war, he arranged to get his son-in-law commission as a major and a job in the Judge Advocate's office at Fort Sheridan, twenty miles north of Chicago. Sid Goldin slept at home every night and emerged from the war a full-bird colonel. The Judge, it sometimes seemed, could arrange anything, except to avoid choking to death, in his sixty-seventh year, on a piece of porterhouse steak at a restaurant in the Loop called Fritzel's. A tough columnist on the Chicago *Daily News,* writing about the passing (and good riddance, he seemed to feel) of types like Judge Irving Goldstein remarked that he died of good living. A widower, he left his only daughter an estate estimated at roughly $1.5 million, and this was in 1957.

The Goldins were never money mad. As Judge Goldstein's daughter, Jean Goldin had grown up with lots of money around. Sid Goldin, even though he came of age smack in the middle of the Depression, earned big money early enough in life not to be nervous about it. No, the Goldins assumed that they would always have enough money not to have to worry about the absence of it interfering with their going through life absolutely first-class. And this they did, with an ease and sportiness that flabbergasted me, a boy whose father worked seven days a week and worried about kids stealing gum and candy from him and a mother who was apparently attempting to save a white couch for eternity.

It was at the Goldins that I first ate a club sandwich, rare roast beef, a salad served after the main course, strawberry shortcake. I don't think they ever had a bad, or even a mediocre, meal, at least not in their own home. It was through being around Jean Goldin that I, then a boy of fifteen, first arrived at the extraordinary insight that someone's mother could be sexy. All other mothers I knew seemed to be receptacles for anxiety who went about for the better part of the day in something called housecoats. Jean Goldin was not a beautiful woman; her teeth were rather too prominent and her features were neither delicate nor refined. But she wore her straight black hair short, in a European cut, always had a deep tan, and dressed in expensive clothes of dazzling colors. She moved wonderfully well and had the shapely, slightly muscular body of a woman who had spent vast amounts of time on golf courses and tennis courts at the best clubs. As their sons' guest at the Royal Oaks Country Club in Winnetka, I recall once watching her in her one-piece black bathing suit poised in concentration on the diving board at the club pool about to execute a complicated dive; Sid Goldin was at the same time applying suntan oil to his large former athlete's body while stretched out on a chaise longue listening to a Cubs game on a portable radio. At that moment the thought struck me, as it had never before struck me about any other parents I knew, that, my God, these two people must have terrific sex together.

I may have gone with the Goldins to Royal Oaks five, maybe six times during the four years I went to high school with Buddy and Eddie, but those times remain among the most vivid memories of my adolescence. I recall the ride down Sheridan Road, Buddy and Eddie sitting up front and I alone in the back, the top down on the Olds Starfire, the leaf-heavy elm trees meeting to form a high tunnel across Sheridan, the mansions along the lake whirling by, the power of the Olds's engine humming, the breeze in my hair. The easy opulence of the country club freshly astonished me each time we drove into the large parking lot with not an old or modest car in sight. I recall the thickness and fine smell of the towels in the locker room; the young Filipino men in white shirts and blue trousers with two thin gold stripes running down the outer leg, whose job it was to fetch drinks, cards, fruit, or sherbert, and anything else members might desire, and to shine the members' shoes while they were out on the golf course or having a swim or in the steam bath; the whap-whap-whap of balls being hit off the practice tees mingling with the slower tempi of the pock, pock, pock of balls being hit on the tennis courts; the slender gray-haired mulatto maître d' whose excellent posture lent him an impressive dignity and a slight distance that always made me a touch nervous; and the food, the largeness of the shrimps and the crispness of the beautiful vegetables and the perfection with which the roast beef was cooked and the lusciousness of the desserts, the ice creams and raspberries and rich yet somehow delicate cakes and custards. The Goldins usually dined at seven-thirty—everyone I knew in West Rogers Park had supper at six—and I remember once rising from the table at Royal Oaks with them at nine-thirty and thinking, with a vague sense of betrayal, that my Dad, dead tired, was just then checking the back door and getting ready to lock up the drugstore.

Neither Buddy nor Eddie Goldin played golf in those days, though Buddy, I learned, would later in life play in high-stakes match games. (Someone was always organizing a "Nassau" or "skins" game at Royal Oaks in which thousands of dollars changed hands, and dollar-a-point gin games were available in the card rooms for those with a taste for serious indoor action.) When they took me to the club, we swam, sunned ourselves, ate, and played half-court basketball, three on a side, against the caddies who had come in after finishing a round or were waiting to go out on a second round. When your team lost, you gave up the court, which we three, since we always won, never had to do. I was the least of the reasons for our never having to relinquish the court. Eddie Goldin, though not that tall, was well-built, a rugged defender, an intelligent rebounder, and a tireless hustler all over the court. And Buddy, Buddy could do everything. He was beautiful to watch. His performance on the court was pure, sure instinct, he didn't have to think about what he did; his body knew what was required and seemed automatically to supply the fakes, the cuts, the quick swoops to the basket, the effortless, perfectly timed leaps, the pull-up dead-on jump shots. "Next," Buddy would call out, after having scored the eleventh basket for our side and thus eliminated yet another threesome of caddies.

In basketball, Buddy Goldin, that great natural athlete, had found his natural sport. At Evanston Township High School he was second-team all-state in his senior year, and later started as a guard at the University of Iowa. Eddie played baseball at E.T.H.S.—he was a ninth-round draft pick of the St. Louis Cardinals as a shortstop—and junior and senior years started at quarterback on the football team. In those years—the middle 1950's—E.T.H.S. was regularly featured in polls as among the top ten schools in the country, often as the very top school. My father read and believed in such polls; they must have comforted him, for he had to sell a lot of newspapers and gum and fill a lot of prescriptions to send his son there. Insofar as one can tell about these things, I guess it was a pretty good school: it gave me a solid grounding in math and chemistry that was later useful in helping me get into medical school. It was a large and competitive place, E.T.H.S., full of bright kids and with a serious atmosphere.

In its sports program, though, the school was really impressive. Its athletic department resembled that of a middle-sized college and one with a winning tradition. All equipment, no matter how minor the sport, was superior; great expense was lavished on facilities, and a modern new fieldhouse was built during my last year there. The contracts of losing coaches were not renewed. Basketball and football games drew thousands; a few college scouts were always in the stands. I remember one afternoon after school watching Eddie Goldin being taught how to execute the bootleg play under the eye of the backfield coach and three assistants who were physical-education majors from Big Ten schools doing their practice teaching at E.T.H.S. (The last E.T.H.S. quarterback before Eddie was now starting at the University of Michigan, where Eddie himself would go on a football scholarship.) Over and over they ran Eddie through this relatively simple play, each time making some small refinement in their instruction. (I never had such careful teaching in med school.) Buddy Goldin told me that the basketball couch would shrink the nets on the game baskets to slow down visiting teams with effective fast breaks. The Goldin boys not only came through the intense pressure of such competition intact; they took it all in easy stride, flourishing under it, starring in it.

I admired Buddy and Eddie Goldin and was proud to be thought of around school as their friend. What they saw in me, I really don't know. I don't think they ever gave much thought to other people's standing, so secure were they in their own, but instead took people as they found them. I was a neighborhood guy; we were all growing up together, however wildly different the circumstances. I was, by the standard of the day, "a good guy," which is to say not a liar or a prig or vicious or mean. That I wasn't in any other way outstanding wasn't a problem for the Goldins or their parents. They weren't, in any sense, snobs. If they had been in the least snobbish, they would have excluded me.

For my own part, I don't think I hung around the Goldins for snobbish reasons, though God knows I was excited by the luxury of their lives and the ease with which everything seemed to be taken care of for them. Then there was the glamor. I never saw Sid Luckman, not to mention Myrna Loy, emerge from a six-flat, or any other building on Washtenaw Avenue. But beyond all this I know I was in awe of the Goldins, all of them, but especially Buddy and Eddie, for their talent. Despite my father's best efforts—he was always supplying me with information about Albert Einstein and other great Jewish scientists—I grew up with no real appreciation for intellectual talent; and among the crowd of kids I ran around with, artistic talent, if any existed, hadn't shown up and I'm pretty sure I wouldn't have recognized it if it had. But athletic talent of the kind the Goldin boys had was not only unmistakable but admired by nearly everyone. I know I admired it. A part of me, even though I am now in my middle forties, still does.

Buddy and Eddie Goldin may have inherited much of the means of their prowess—their coordination, their reflexes, their musculature—from their athletic parents. But where did Buddy come by the ability, which he possessed at sixteen, to pop in two free throws in the last seconds of an overtime to win a game in a state tournament with some 12,000 people screaming at him to miss—and pop them in authoritatively, with no doubt or hesitation about it? Where did Eddie acquire the knack for throwing a football with perfect accuracy into the hands of a receiver forty yards away while freezing rain was blowing in his face and six or seven bruisers going at full speed were trying to crush him? The Goldin boys could do such things because they had talent, and it's called that because few people have it, and if you don't have it to begin with you aren't likely to get it. I knew I didn't have it, and I knew that I never would—I knew that everything I would get in life would come from plodding and from hard work, which was fair enough. But this put me in a different category from the Goldins, who were, for me, extraordinary characters.

Christmas vacation of our senior year in high school, Sid Goldin took his family off for a week's holiday in Barbados, and Jean Goldin asked if I would mind coming in twice a day to walk and feed her dog, a white standard poodle named Francesca, whom she didn't want to put in a kennel. Jessie, the cook, had been given the week off and I let myself in at eight in the morning and then returned at seven at night to walk and feed Francesca again. Under the pretense of keeping the dog company, I would remain in that wondrous house for an hour or so in the evening, feeling the thick carpeting under my feet, drinking in the soft and subtle coloring of the furniture and the draperies. Sometimes I would sit in the white basement, with its green leather furniture and glass trophy cases, turn on the television, pour myself a ginger ale from the bar, and wish I had a room of my own here—wish, guiltily, that my own last name was Goldin and that I was a member of this family.

After they returned from Barbados, Jean Goldin called my mother to tell her that she had a fine and responsible young man for a son. When I next came over, Sid Goldin said, "Good job with the dog, Phillie. We're grateful." He shook my hand, and when he had removed his hand, a crisp new fifty-dollar bill was in my own.

Senior year was a good one for us all. Eddie got his offer from the Cardinals and a football scholarship from the University of Michigan; Buddy made all-state and had some thirty-odd offers of basketball scholarships, from which he chose the University of Iowa; and I was accepted by Yale, though because of the tight money situation at home (my sister was going into her junior year at Wisconsin), I decided instead to do my pre-med at the University of Illinois at Champaign-Urbana.

The Saturday night after graduation, Sid and Jean Goldin threw a party in honor of their sons. An enormous yellow-and-white striped tent went up on their ample back lawn. In one corner of the tent the Ramsey Lewis trio played; in the corner across the way, a black man in a white jacket and a chef's hat stood with a large carving knife and fork before a huge prime-rib roast, a turkey, and a ham. Three small bars were working, two in the tent and a third in the basement of the house. I noticed Sid Luckman in the crowd and, later, Ernie

Banks, the Cubs' shortstop, showed up. There were a few local columnists, the guy who did the evening news on Channel 5, and the wife of the man who was the head of Standard Oil of Indiana. Buddy Goldin pointed out a somewhat withdrawn looking man who turned out to be Burr Tilstrom, the puppeteer; he was talking to a man who had been in prison for allegedly kidnapping a syndicate figure named Jake (The Barber) Factor. Waiters brought around trays of champagne in wide-rimmed glasses. The women seemed light and dazzling in their summer dresses. I found myself at one point talking to one of them, a beautiful young woman who asked me who the Goldins were. She was with a touring company playing *My Fair Lady* at the Blackstone Theater and had been brought here by a man who the year before had won twenty games for the Chicago White Sox.

Whether any speeches were made, or gifts given, or how or at what time the evening ended, I have no idea. For me it was over around ten o'clock, when, I was later told by Eddie Goldin, I passed out after what must have been eleven or twelve glasses of champagne, while singing the Whiffenpoof song to Jean Goldin and a man named Grolnik who was a big real-estate operator on the Near North Side. At their mother's bidding, Eddie and Buddy carried me to the guest room upstairs, where I slept in my clothes until six-thirty the next morning. Rumpled, grubby, foggy-brained, walking up the stairs to our apartment, I met my Dad coming down, on his way to open the store. "You okay, Phillie?" he asked, placing the back of his hand lightly across my forehead. I mumbled something about its having been a long night. In my small dark bedroom, standing over the beige chenille spread on my bed, I peeled off my clothes, letting them fall to the floor, thinking, sadly, that a crucial chapter in my life was finished.

That summer marked the beginning of the end of my friendship with the Goldin boys. Nothing went wrong; there was no falling out. It was just the natural drifting apart that takes place when boys turn eighteen and must act on the pretense that they are now young men. Two days after graduation, Eddie Goldin reported to a Cardinals' farm club in Sarasota, Florida, where he learned the hard but undeniable lesson that he couldn't hit curve balls, which forced him to decide that he had to put his energies into football in the fall at the University of Michigan. Buddy Goldin became a counselor at Ray Meyer's summer basketball camp, where he was able to work out with the guys who played for DePaul, Loyola, Illinois, and other major Midwest basketball schools before he went off to Iowa in the fall. As for me, I worked a forty-hour week at the drugstore, handling the front register, doing stock work, making deliveries, and listening to my father tell me how good life was going to be once I became a physician.

Looking back on my friendship with Eddie and Buddy Goldin, I am a bit amazed at how little intimacy there was in it. For three of the four years we went to high school, we drove there together every morning. What did we talk about? About sports we talked a good deal. About girls a certain amount. Friday nights we often went to the movies together. Sometimes they would take me along with them to some major sports event, for tickets were never a problem for Sid Goldin. None of us dated much. As Jews we were a minority at E.T.H.S., which we wouldn't have been had we gone either to Senn or Sullivan high schools in Chicago. Neither of the Goldin boys talked much about his parents, and I'm not at all sure that they did when they were alone. What I took to be the glamor of their life at home, they took as perfectly natural, and why not, since they hadn't ever known anything else.

Eddie was second-string quarterback his freshman year at Michigan, and he ran back punts and kickoffs and did both very well. Buddy started as a freshman on the Iowa basketball team. He was not yet the star he showed signs of becoming in his sophomore year, but from the beginning he made his presence felt—he averaged something like fourteen points a game—and was completely at ease playing Big Ten basketball. I went to the Iowa-Illinois game at Champaign that year and felt real pride at Buddy's poise on the floor. He looked to have put on ten or so pounds, all of it muscle, which made him seem sleek and more in possession of himself than ever. Both he and Eddie always looked born for the athletic uniforms they wore, so much so that, like certain high-ranking military officers, they sometimes seemed a little disappointing out of uniform. Iowa beat Illinois that night when, at the buzzer, Buddy popped in an eighteen-foot jump shot from the top of the key. All that was missing, I thought at the time, was for him to call out "Next," as he used to do with the caddies. I had hoped to spend an hour or so after the game with him, but it turned out that the Iowa team was getting back on its bus to Iowa City that night and that there would be no spare time. I was sorry to have missed him. Michigan went to the Rose Bowl that year and the Iowa basketball team was playing in a holiday tournament in North Carolina, so I didn't get to see either Eddie or Buddy that Christmas vacation.

Games and glory and expensive travel somehow seemed natural to the Goldins. It was what Buddy and Eddie were born into and grew up with. I always assumed that once spikes and cleats, helmets and balls were set aside, they would settle into a life of easy comfort, with powerful contacts and beautiful wives and children who were themselves splendid athletes. Short of a major illness or some inconceivable financial reversal, how could it ever be otherwise? Or so I believed, until one day in my sophomore year—I recall I was studying for a big midterm exam in organic chemistry—when I called home and my father asked if I had read about the fix my friends Eddie and Buddy Goldin's dad had gotten himself into. I never read the newspapers in Champaign, and told my father I had no idea what he was talking about.

"Apparently Sidney Goldin is connected with some kind of black-market baby ring," my father said. "It looks like pretty serious stuff."

"Is it getting a big play in the press, Dad?"

"Front-page headlines in both the *Trib* and the *Sun-Times*," my father said, "with photos of Mrs. Goldin and your friends Buddy and Eddie. It's also the lead story on the evening television news."

My father went on to ask if I was prepared for my organic chemistry exam, and my mother got on the phone to give me some bits of family and neighborhood news, but my mind was elsewhere and I couldn't wait to get hold of that day's Chicago newspapers. When I did, I found that it was every bit as bad as my father had suggested.

The *Sun-Times* headline read, "CELEB ATTORNEY SELLS INFANTS"; the Chicago *Tribune* ran, "POWERFUL LAWYER BABY BLACK MARKETEER" and beneath that, "Sidney Goldin, Former Illinois Athlete, Counselor to Famous, Linked to Baby Ranch." On page three, the *Sun-Times* had photos of Sid and Jean Goldin in evening clothes at a fund-raising dinner for Adlai Stevenson; lower down on the page were blurry photos of the Goldin boys, Buddy in his University of Iowa jersey, Eddie in his Michigan football helmet. The *Trib* ran a smaller picture of Sid Goldin alone, a head shot in which he looked dark and prosperous and rather beaky. Staring at this photograph, which appeared on the front page, I found myself muttering a line I had often heard my father use, "This doesn't look good for the Jews."

What I was able to gather from the newspaper stories—which held the front page for three days—was that Sid Goldin had operated here in his familiar role of middleman. An OB-GYN man on the Northwest Side named Dr. Howard Peterson was really the main figure. Peterson placed unmarried pregnant girls in homes during their pregnancies, paying their room and board and giving them an additional $3,000 at the termination of their pregnancy, for which they signed their child over to him—or at least they believed they did, since the deal was obviously illegal. Working through lawyers around the city, Peterson turned infants over to couples wishing to adopt children but unable to do so through the ordinary, and in those days extremely rigorous, child-adoption procedures. To obtain a baby in this way cost $20,000, with $15,000 going to Peterson and the remainder to the lawyer.

Sid Goldin had evidently brokered at least seven of these illegal adoptions. The last of them was arranged for a prominent Irish politician, an alderman married to a Jewish woman who was unable to have children. The politician had enemies, and one of them turned the press loose on the story of how the politician, with his mixed marriage, was able to adopt a child when state-run agencies at the time all but categorically refused children to homes where parents did not share the same religion. One thing led to another—or perhaps it would be better to say that one thing led to another which led to Sidney Goldin which led to scandal.

Why did Sid Goldin get mixed up in such stuff? He couldn't have needed the money—though, true enough, lots of people who don't need it will still pick up an easy five grand if they don't have to do much work for it. Apart from the money, my guess is that it gave Sid Goldin pleasure to be the swing man on something so crucial to important people—and all of his clients in these adoptions were important people—as their getting a child. Arranging, after all, is what Sid Goldin did—was what he was famous for—and arranging to get someone a child, a live human being, was in some sense the ultimate arrangement. I'm not sure that Sid Goldin thought about it in this way. He probably viewed it more simply. Some couples needed a child; he knew a man who had children; the people who got the child would be happy; the children would go to prosperous and, as far as anyone could tell, good homes; he, Sidney Goldin, would be the man who made it all possible; and there was an easy five grand in it besides. What was so wrong?

The Illinois Bar Association felt there was enough wrong to disbar Sidney Goldin for a minimum of ten years; and since he was in his late forties at the time, this just about finished him as a lawyer. His law partners bought him out and removed his name from the firm. His rich and famous clients almost uniformly deserted him as a friend. He didn't have to go to trial, and thus risk jail, and he still had all the money he would need to get him through the rest of his life, but the humiliations, small and large, continued for some time. In neighborhood gossip, he was known as the man who sold babies. When it came time to pay his annual dues at the Royal Oaks Country Club, where he and Jean Goldin chose not to show their faces for nearly a year, his check was returned to him by the executive secretary with a curt note saying that the club was cutting back its membership, especially among people who hadn't been making much use of the facilities in recent months, and therefore could not accept his dues; a second check, this one for his original membership fee, was included in the envelope. I currently belong to Royal Oaks, am in fact on the club's board of directors, and I pulled the old Goldin file where I found this letter. I don't like to think about his wife's reaction when Sid Goldin showed it to her.

As for the Goldin boys, both of them soon developed troubles of their own. Buddy was having a brilliant season at Iowa, averaging twenty-one points a game and leading the Big Ten in assists, when, in a game at Purdue, he felt the ball getting away from him and the floor rushing up to meet him, and the next thing he knew he was on a stretcher on the way to the hospital in West Lafayette. His left knee had given out, ligaments had been torn, and, more significant, cartilage had been destroyed. Buddy was through for the season. When he came back for his junior year, he played with his left leg in an awkward harness of tape and plastic braces. He was never again the same athlete. His former quickness was gone; his instincts, built upon absolute confidence in that quickness, were shot. He lost his place as a starter; and sensing that he would never again play big-time basketball, he chose not to return to the University of Iowa for his senior year. He went back to Chicago, finishing his schooling at Loyola University and after that at the Loyola Law School.

Buddy lived at home when he returned from Iowa, and continued to live there until his last year of law school. He took up golf, at which—no surprise—he was marvelous right off, shooting in the middle seventies by the second year he played. He and Sid Goldin played together at public courses. A few years later, when the scandal had been pretty much forgotten, the Goldins joined another country club, Twin Orchards, whose pro told Sid Goldin that, if Buddy really gave golf his full attention, he could be good enough to play on the pro tour. If his father's scandal threw Buddy in any serious way, there was no obvious evidence of it.

As for Eddie Goldin, I heard that, though he stayed at the University of Michigan, he had dropped off the football team, giving no other explanation than that the sport now bored him. I also heard that he had become very earnest about his studies. Eddie was always a better student in high school than Buddy; I don't recall his being in any way exceptional, but then their athletic ability cast everything else about Eddie and Buddy Goldin into the shade. In any case, Eddie, I heard, was no longer a business but now a philosophy major.

When I ran into Eddie on Devon Avenue in the summer between our junior and senior years, I'm not sure I would have recognized him if he hadn't spoken to me first. His dark, curly hair, usually cut short, had grown out and was uncombed. Where before he had been a tidy dresser, there was now something fundamentally rumpled about him: his flannel shirt was unironed, his Levis soiled, his Frye boots caked with mud. In later years he would top off some variant of this standard outfit with a parrot named Crackers who, from his perch on Eddie's shoulder, croaked out political slogans mixed with rich obscenities. Just now he was accompanied by a thin, rather drab-looking girl whom he introduced to me as "Reb." When she shyly said she was pleased to meet me, I detected an Appalachian accent. The three of us walked up the block to a corner restaurant, run by Greeks, called Kofield's.

"My mother's fine," Eddie answered, when I asked about his parents, "and my dad is the same asshole he has always been."

The use of that word rocked me. I used my share of profanity as a kid, and I find enough occasions to use it nowadays, but the word Eddie used to describe his father is one I have always hated. The shock of hearing it from Eddie was compounded by the fact that, among their other qualities as All-American kid athletes, the Goldin boys, neither one of them, ever swore. Meanwhile, that word lay there between us.

"What's the problem with your dad?" I asked.

"There's no big problem," Eddie said, "except that he's a phony, a complete fraud."

"Are you referring to his troubles of a few years ago?"

"Tip of the fuckin' iceberg," he said. "The way we live, the way Buddy and I were brought up, the whole thing through and through is rotten. And of course the fuckin' joke is my old man hasn't any notion how rotten it all is. Like all real immoralists, he hasn't a clue that there's anything wrong with the way he lives."

Nor could Eddie's friend Reb have had the least clue about what he was saying. I noticed she had a small, homemade heart tattooed on her thin upper-arm. She said nothing, but sipped a Coke through her small, gray, somehow immensely sad teeth. I was sure that Eddie had already brought her home to meet Sid and Jean Goldin—just to let them know that his days of adding to the trophy cases were over for good.

What do you do when an old friend sitting across the table from you attacks his own father? I mumbled something about Sid Goldin's always having been nice to me, but it was pointless. Eddie wasn't really interested in hearing any defense of his father. He was still in the early stages of formulating his own distaste for him, convincing himself of the righteousness of his anger, building his case. When it was completed it must have been some case, for more than twenty-five years later Eddie was still relentless in his hatred of his father.

We graduated in the summer of 1961, and that autumn I began medical school at the University of Illinois in Chicago; Buddy started law school at Loyola; and Eddie, who was among the first round of people accepted for the Peace Corps, went off to teach rudimentary construction techniques to villagers in Central Africa. It was in Africa that he acquired the parrot. He liked Africa, for all its heat and insects and desolation, and when his Peace Corps tour was finished he visited Albert Schweitzer, in the hope of staying on and working for him at his hospital mission at Lambaréné on the forested banks of the Ogooué River. Eddie was apparently able to get a personal interview with Dr. Schweitzer, though he was not offered a job. I later heard that, when someone asked him what Dr. Schweitzer was like, Eddie answered that he, too, was an "asshole." At least no one could say that Albert Schweitzer and Sidney Goldin had nothing in common.

After his return from Africa, Eddie went back to Ann Arbor to begin work on a doctorate in philosophy. It took him eleven years to get it. The 60's intervened. Ann Arbor in those days was Berkeley Midwest, and Eddie Goldin was in the thick of it. The boy athlete who had been so fearless at ten and twelve wasn't likely to go in for halfway measures at twenty-five. He was SDS; there was talk of his leaving the United States for Sweden in support of those who fled the country to avoid the draft. As Eddie's friend, even though I scarcely saw him, I was glad it never came to that.

"My son Eddie," said Sid Goldin, seated across from me on the green leather couch in my office in Wilmette at the Plaza del Lago, "has wasted his entire life hating his father. It makes me sick to think about it."

Perhaps Sid Goldin was so openly dour because I had just given him the depressing if far from disastrous news that he would need a gall-bladder operation. He had come into my office for a second opinion, which all the insurance companies nowadays require before they will pay for major surgery. My name had been recommended to him by his regular internist, Howie Kantor—with whom I had gone to medical school and whom I see socially—chiefly because my office is located close to the Goldins' current home in Winnetka. (Once they turned sixty, Jean and Sid Goldin began to spend their winters near Palm Springs, in a condominium they owned at Rancho Mirage.) I was a bit disappointed but not surprised to discover that he didn't remember, until I reminded him of it, that I was the same Philip Hirsh who had run around with his sons in high school. Why, after all, should a man who had had movie stars and professional athletes for clients, who had played in the fast track long before that phrase was even coined, remember a not very interesting boy of sixteen whom he hadn't seen for more than twenty-five years?

I, on the other hand, would have recognized Sid Goldin anywhere. He still had the look of the high roller: the deep sun tan, the expensive clothes comfortably worn, the general air of a man for whom all the more trivial details and little bothers of life—from shoeshines to shopping and tax worries—have always been looked after by hired hands. He had kept his satiny black wavy hair, which now had only touches of gray at the temples. Apart from his gall-bladder problem, his health was good. At sixty-four he wasn't carrying around any extra weight, his heart was sound, his muscle tone was extraordinary.

"Eddie never really took hold," he continued. "By the time he got his Ph.D. degree, he was in his middle thirties. His *meshuggena* politics took up most of his time and energy, at least as far as his mother and I could tell. Anyhow, he never got a permanent teaching post. One year, he's teaching at Geneseo, New York, the next year he's at Irvine, California, one year his brother gets a card from him in Taiwan. The kind of life he leads, he might as well have stayed in minor-league baseball. He never married, you know, and my guess is that he never will."

I wondered if Eddie ever thought of himself as locked forever into the academic equivalent of minor-league baseball. Having once been a first-rate athlete, he could not have found it easy to reconcile himself to being a fourth-rate philosophy teacher. At least I don't think such a thing would have been easy for me. But then I wasn't Eddie Goldin.

"We never hear from Eddie directly," Sid Goldin said. "All we know of his whereabouts is from his brother, whom he calls once or twice a year. The last time Eddie and I were together—it's almost twenty years now—he told me off. Called me a phony and a four-flusher and living a lie. Said that everything I had was built on cheating and deceit. His mother, he said, was no better, since she lived so comfortably with my corruption. But he was damned if he was going to. He wasn't going to take another penny from me, and some day he hoped to pay back every cent I had ever spent on him so that he would be free from any contamination from my crummy life. That's what he called it, you know, 'my crummy life.' My own son."

There was an unbearable silence. "How are things going with Buddy?" I asked, hoping to get the conversation on to a less painful subject.

"Buddy's got his own troubles," Sid Goldin said. He shifted his weight, resting an arm along the back of the green couch. I noticed dangling from his wrist, beyond his cashmere sport jacket and the monogram that showed on the cuff of his shirt, a thin gold chain bracelet. Odd little touch of foppery, I thought, in a man his age. "Your old friend Buddy has a serious gambling problem. It started about fifteen years ago. He wasn't making his nut as a lawyer, so he tried to make up his personal and business expenses through betting on ball games, cards, his own golf games. Twice now he's enrolled himself in Gamblers' Anonymous. His wife threatened to leave him if he didn't go into therapy, which he's in currently. It's a damn mess."

"How bad does it get?"

"All I know is what he's come to me for to bail him out. Whether he's into other people also, I don't know. At first he came for small dips—five and ten grand. Then he jumped it up to twenty, twenty-five, once forty. 'Buddy boy,' I said to him, 'you're going through your inheritance mighty quick.' After each time he comes to me, there is a quiet period, lasting maybe three or four months. But it's waiting for a bomb to go off. The last time he came to me it was for ninety grand. He was into heavy juice with the boys, if you know what I mean. He told me they would kill him if he didn't come up with the money. He wept, my beautiful All-State son, he put his head on my shoulder and clung to me and said, 'Dad, you got to help me, you got to.' Of course I did. I'm his father."

I don't know why Sid Goldin chose to talk so openly about his sons with me. Maybe it was because I was a stranger who nonetheless had known him and his sons in their glory days. I wouldn't be at all surprised to learn that he couldn't talk to old friends with the same candor that he used in talking to me that afternoon, sitting on my green leather couch—a couch that, when I came to pick furniture for my office, I chose because it reminded me of the green leather furniture from his own house on Lunt.

"Dr. Hirsh," he said (and to have him, at whose home I was once introduced to Sid Luckman, address me as doctor seemed very strange), "were my sons once really extraordinary boys, or have I just dreamed it? Wasn't there a time, Doc, when the world seemed to belong to Eddie and Buddy? Or is it all something I imagined? They were such wonderful kids. Respectful. Disciplined. Never in trouble."

"Mr. Goldin," I said, "your sons were the best. They were great kids, gifted and decent and without any meanness of any kind. Being their friend was one of the nicest things about my boyhood."

"What do you suppose went wrong, Doc? Was it my fault? Was it the way we brought the boys up? To this day my wife and I, when we talk about it together, don't really know how to account for what happened. Did we spoil them? You probably don't remember, but I had a little trouble with the press when they were in college, a little scandal—could that have been the problem? What has to happen, Doc, to turn two swell kids into a rebel and a weakling? The more my wife and I talk about it, the less we understand. Beats me," he said with a sigh and rose from the couch.

It beat me, too, and I had no solacing platitudes to offer. I could provide a clear second opinion on Sid Goldin's gall bladder but not on what had happened to his sons. Instead I told him that I would send along my report to the Blue Cross and that a man in his general good health really had little to worry about from this operation. I asked to be remembered to Mrs. Goldin. He thanked me, we shook hands, and the next time I saw him was at Buddy's funeral service in the Piser chapel in Skokie.

That was roughly six months after Sid Goldin had sat in my office. Buddy, I learned from his friend Lloyd Brodsky in the Piser parking lot after the service, had gone into the tank for more than a hundred grand and was being threatened by syndicate collection men. In the suicide note he left in his office, he wrote that he was too ashamed of himself to go back to his father for more money and too ashamed to go on living. He thanked his parents for standing by him as long and as well as they had, and asked that they look after his wife and young daughters, to whom he apologized for what he was about to do—which was to hurl himself from his office window twenty-three floors above LaSalle Street—and whom he asked to try always to remember that he loved them dearly.

I had appointments lined up in the office that afternoon, and so didn't drive out to the Waldheim Cemetery on the West Side. On the fifteen-minute drive back to Wilmette I thought further about the Goldin boys, but with no better results than Sid and Jean Goldin. Buddy and Eddie were blessed with talent—of a small and limited kind, agreed, but real talent nonetheless—and it set them apart, made them different. At least to me, who was without talent, it made them seem radiant and even a little magical. Were their sad endings—Buddy's on the pavement in downtown Chicago, Eddie's to wander all his life unattached and without consequence—somehow connected to their brilliant beginnings? Did the blessing of talent always carry its own inexplicable curse? These were deeper waters than I was accustomed to sail, and it was probably best that I clear my mind, for awaiting me in my office were people who wanted my authoritative assurance that they need not fear death by stroke, heart attack, or cancer, at least not for the present, and from every indication could go on living for years to come, which all of them would be perfectly happy to do without any thought of talent whatsoever.

Kaplan's Big Deal

■

*I*n those days Kaplan had an ambitious pompadour, kept aloft by Wildroot Cream Oil and a comb that he carried in his back pocket. In the other back pocket he kept a shoehorn. Working after school and on Monday and Thursday evenings and all day Saturday, he was, at seventeen, the ace part-time salesman at Maling Brothers Shoes on South State Street. It was at Maling Brothers that he first discovered he had this knack, ability, gift—call it what you like—for persuasion. His customers at Maling Brothers were thick-ankled Polish women and Irish girls, who worked in the Loop as secretaries, file clerks, saleswomen at Carson's, Goldblatts, and The Fair Store. He flattered them, pretended their feet were smaller than they were, quickly sensed their susceptibilities, and usually sent them home with two or three pairs of shoes when they had come in to buy only one. "Shelly," said Sam Margolis, the old shoe dog who managed the South State Street store, "you are a natural, a born salesman."

When his father, in his fifty-first year, died of a heart attack, Kaplan dropped out of the University of Wisconsin, where he was in his third year, majoring in marketing, to return to Chicago. He acquired a real-estate license, began selling what were known as "starter" homes to young Jewish couples then moving to Skokie. He was very good at it. He followed up on even the flimsiest leads, spent tedious hours on the telephone in the attempt to get new listings, worked twelve- and fourteen-hour days, often seven days a week. He could enter into the dreams of these young couples—they came from much the same background that he did—and play to them in a quiet but efficient way. Ruth Rosenzweig, the broker out of whose office he worked, marveled at his ability to close a sale, and on occasion she brought him in to help her on her own deals, splitting the fees. "Sheldon," she once told him, "some day you are going to be a very rich man."

Kaplan's mother died, after a horrendous two-year bout with leukemia, when he was twenty-five. He had been living with her in the two-flat building his father had bought on Rockwell Avenue in West Rogers Park a few years after World War II. An only child, he was his mother's sole heir; the estate, including the building, came to roughly eighty grand. Kaplan put most of the money into real-estate deals of his own on the near North Side that in later years would pay off handsomely. Like him, his father had been an only child. His mother had a brother in the printing business on the West Coast, but there had been a falling out. Kaplan was alone in the world, unconnected, responsible for himself only.

He rather liked the arrangement. He had loved his parents; he knew they had loved him, that he could count on them if he needed them. But beyond the age of fifteen or so he didn't really need them. Theirs was not a family in which one brought one's troubles to the dinner table to chew over along with the brisket. His father, he knew, kept most of his business dealings from his mother; if his mother was unhappy, she apparently never said anything about it to her husband and certainly never did to her son. Sheldon's upbringing had emphasized self-sufficiency—learn to stand on your own two feet, work out your own problems, don't leave a mess, be a man.

After his mother's death, Sheldon sold off the furniture, her jewelry, her Persian lamb coat and mink jacket, the silver, the china— the works. All he kept was a shoe box of old photographs, many of them sepia-colored, from the 20's and 30's, of his long deccased grandparents, of his parents posed on beaches or in front of cars, of himself as a child in sailor or cowboy suits or sitting cross-legged in the front row of class photos in grade school. He moved into a furnished studio apartment in the recently rehabilitated Pratt-Lane Hotel, off Sheridan Road, ate all his meals out. With long hours of work and the easy freedom of the young bachelor life—all-night poker games, out-of-town sports events, the pursuit of women—all he really needed was a place to sleep, shower, and change clothes.

Kaplan was thirty-two when he bought Mid-City Pontiac. All evidence of his pompadour was gone, his hair having thinned out and receded. He had moved from his studio apartment at the Pratt-Lane to a one-bedroom suite at the Belden-Stratford Hotel across from Lincoln Park. Colonel Jacob Arvey, the man who helped win the presidential nomination for Adlai Stevenson and was the most powerful Jew in Chicago politics, lived on the same floor. An old man now, the Colonel one day introduced himself and ever after, always the politician, remembered Kaplan's name, addressing him as Sheldon. A number of well-off, older Jewish bachelors and widowers lived at the Belden. Most of Kaplan's friends had married and by now had young children. He felt no such yearning. He liked living in hotels, owning nothing but his clothes, his real estate, his business—staying loose, liquid, alone. "So tell me, Shelly," his friend Morty Siegel once joked about his preference for remaining as unencumbered as possible, "where do you rent your cuff links?"

Kaplan enjoyed the car business, at least for now. That he knew next to nothing about cars—didn't, technically, own one himself— proved no impediment. What he liked was the action, deals every day. At Mid-City Pontiac he was the sales manager as well as the owner. In more than half the sales, he was called in to help close. At that crucial moment, when the customer and salesmen were a few hundred bucks apart, the salesmen were instructed to say, "Look, why don't we go in and talk with the boss, Mr. Kaplan, maybe he can do better for you than I can?" In they would come, the customers, nervous women, angry men, middle-aged middle-class couples, young guys with tattoos and duck's-ass hairdos interested in buying the hot car in his line, the GTO—all with one thing in common: the certainty that they were in danger of getting cheated and the determination not to let it happen.

Kaplan would come around his large desk to greet them. On the desk was a photograph in a double silver frame of his friend Bert Schwartz's two young daughters; if someone assumed that these were his own children and that he was a family man, this was fine with Kaplan. He had taken to wearing Hickey-Freeman suits, expensive and of a conservative cut, to make himself look older and more substantial. After having been introduced to the customers, he would sit down with them in front of his desk, and he would usually begin by asking his salesman, "Larry, are the Gombergs happy with the car they've chosen? If they are, then all we have to negotiate is the best deal, and I am confident we can, from both our points of view."

Then his reading of character would come into play. What was at stake here for the customer? Money? Pride? Fear of seeming a fool? Some customers needed soothing, others bullying. Everyone came in with the firm idea that car dealers were thieves. That was a given. Some people needed to emerge feeling that they had stolen from thieves and thus were themselves extremely clever. Others needed to feel that he, Sheldon Kaplan, president, Mid-City Pontiac, was an exception, a gentleman and not a monster, a sensible businessman looking for repeat sales and not a pig out to gobble up all he could every time out. The trick was to know what they needed. Whatever they needed, Kaplan gave them, and in the bargain made out very well for himself.

In Kaplan's nine years in the car business, he must have run through something close to a hundred and fifty salesmen. Some stayed a few years, but the more normal tenure was four or five months; a few didn't make it through a month. Something better came along, to hear them tell it, or an ex-wife was after them for alimony, or the Chicago winters got them down. They left without much ceremony. Usually they would call to announce they wouldn't be coming in and provide an address to which any owed commissions were to be sent. A strange crowd, Kaplan thought, men whose only skill was for making other people say yes.

A few years before Kaplan sold Mid-City he hired a salesman named Sy Bourget, a fabled figure, a salesman's salesman. Bourget—he didn't pronounce the *t* in his name—was so good, it used to be said, that he could sell aluminum siding to people who lived in high-rise buildings. Shortly after World War II, Bourget was supposed to have sold a man a two-door Buick and convinced him that, if he brought it back in·three months, they could convert it into a four-door. For more than three years the man kept coming back, and for more than three years Bourget was able to hold him at bay with explanations for the delay, wild promises, and general hot air, and then, when the man's patience was finally worn out, Bourget took in the two-door on a trade for a new Buick Roadmaster station wagon, loaded with extras, for which the man, being a bachelor, had absolutely no use.

Sy Bourget's real name was Seymour Bernstein. He was in his mid-fifties but looked older, especially around his eyes, which were gray and cold. His hair was white yet his pencil-thin mustache was still dark. He wore expensive shoes, flashy shirts, good suits well-pressed; he had a blue sapphire pinkie ring and was never without a manicure. Bourget had four ex-wives and, when working at Mid-City, was living with a girl in her twenties from Kentucky. Women were his weakness, he told Kaplan one night after a closing, over a steak sandwich and a double Scotch at the Black Angus. "What's your weakness, kid?"

Kaplan joked that he hadn't found it yet, though he was still awaiting X-ray results from the Mayo Clinic. Bourget made him slightly edgy. Despite all the differences between them—in age, in style, in success—Kaplan saw in Sy Bourget a quality he felt growing in himself: a deadening boredom with life that came from endlessly repeated examination of human motives toward the end of manipulating others to say yes. Such examination revealed everyone to have an angle, induced general distrust, gave a low view of life and its possibilities. Everyone, one discovered, was an operator, or at least wanted to be, and the only difference between people was that there were those who operated successfully and those who didn't. Winners and losers, the old story.

And women, Kaplan had begun to believe, were the most relentless operators of all. At forty-five, he had never for one day seriously considered marrying. Many of his friends were on second wives; had begun what they called—with a straight face—"second families." Perhaps it was the women Kaplan went out with. These tended to be what he thought of as high-maintenance women, the female equivalent of Mercedes and Jaguars. All were good-looking—what would be the point of going out with an unattractive woman?—and all assumed a certain high level of expenditure. These women, Kaplan decided, were essentially in business for themselves. He took them to musical comedies and expensive restaurants; sometimes he took one or another of them for a three-day weekend in Vegas, or for a week in winter to Acapulco, where he had a share in a large condominium complex. They brought along two and three suitcases filled with jars and three changes of clothes for each day; he usually had a small carry-on bag. Apart from the sex, for which his appetite had not greatly slackened, Kaplan tended to find women an encumbrance and an inconvenience.

The truth was that Kaplan didn't find women very interesting. How women found him was not a question he found very pressing. He no longer looked young. Most of the hair on his head was gone, and hair had begun to show up in dark aggressive patches on his upper back and shoulders. His stomach was still flat—he did sit-ups and played racquet ball a couple of times a week—but his body had begun to thicken, and without gaining any weight he went from a 32″ to a 34″ waist. He wore glasses for reading when he hit forty, but now he needed bifocals. Such sexiness as he possessed was owing, he knew, to his money and the power it conferred. This, it turned out, made him sexy enough. Being the operators that they were, women were usually ready enough to go to bed with him, hoping to establish their indispensability in his life. None ever did. Go close a closer. What he really sought was a woman with a man's mind and a woman's body. He never found her.

Kaplan left the car business just before his fiftieth birthday, four years after acquiring a second dealership, Mid-City Datsun, with which he had done extremely well. He was making somewhere in the neighborhood of three-quarters of a million a year, much of which he pumped into real-estate deals. But the car business had begun to bore him, so he sold his two agencies and opened a two-room office in the John Hancock Building on Michigan Avenue; the office was listed on the directory as S.K. Development. He soon became known around town as a money man, a source of venture capital. Inventors and would-be entrepreneurs wrote to him in the hope that he would back their dreams and schemes: for a geriatric dog food, a male genital deodorant, a serious cultural magazine. Each day's mail brought fresh evidence, if any were still needed, that the number of operators in the country was very close to equaling the population itself.

On the serious side, Kaplan was one of a syndicate of seventeen businessmen who bought and three years later sold the Chicago White Sox. With five other men he put up a fifty-three-story condo building on Sheridan Road. He was in on hotel deals in Puerto Rico, resorts on the west coast of Mexico, private-home development for wealthy Americans in the Dominican Republic. Putting together a complex deal excited him like nothing else he had known. He loved the action.

Kaplan had paid $150 a month for his studio apartment at the Pratt-Lane; he was now paying $9,000 a month for his two-room suite at the Drake Hotel. He still didn't own a car but took cabs and, on occasion, rented limousines. He owned five suits and three pairs of shoes. He recently had had to buy a tuxedo, because, as a money man around town, he was invited to many black-tie dinners, to some of which he went. He gave impressive sums to Jewish charities, usually in honor of his mother and father, but refused all awards and public recognition of the kind that was really intended to get more money out of him. He continued to see the same kind of women, though many of them, in their late thirties and early forties, had some mileage on them and were divorced with children. In his midfifties, he found he had nothing to say to women in their twenties. Marriage with a woman of any age was not a serious possibility.

Kaplan lived in the world of money and deals, and lived there happily enough. Introspection was not his specialty. Yet even so, sometimes he imagined himself in his seventies—an old guy with a younger broad in tow. Less often he thought of death, of dying by himself, alone in a private room at Michael Reese or Northwestern Hospital, no next of kin, in fact no kin at all on the scene, dependent in the end on the kindness of black or Filipino nurses. Dark thoughts, best blocked out. Better to concentrate on the luxury condominium complex at Boca Raton in which he was a heavy investor, a deal that he had worked on for better than two years and that finally looked to be coming together.

It was to meet with the other major investors in the Boca Raton deal that Kaplan found himself one rainy Thursday afternoon at Midway Airport awaiting a flight to New York. The rain had caused delays. Flights were backed up. Midway, normally so much calmer than O'Hare, now took on the frenzied feel of the larger airport. Kaplan carried a small carry-on bag; it contained a fresh shirt, socks, underwear, tie, his toothbrush and shaving things, some papers he needed to go over for the deal, that day's *Wall Street Journal,* which he hadn't yet had a chance to read, and a Robert Ludlum paperback spy thriller, a hedge against the possibility of insomnia which he sometimes suffered when staying out of town.

After checking in at the counter, Kaplan found a seat and unfurled his *Wall Street Journal.* He had begun reading when he noticed a slightly bedraggled young woman, perhaps in her middle thirties, struggling with a suitcase and a large Crate & Barrel shopping bag; at her side was a boy of seven or eight. Kaplan, sitting between two empty seats, moved over one seat to his left, allowing the woman and the boy to sit together. "Thank you," she said, a French lilt to her English. The boy slipped the backpack he was wearing off his slender shoulders. "Read your book, Philippe," the woman said gently, "or go over your lessons. *Maman* will see about our seats."

From behind his newspaper, Kaplan looked down at the boy, who was seated next to him. He was shuffling through his small backpack. From it he took a school workbook; it had to do with math. On its cover was printed University of Chicago Laboratory School. The boy began working through math problems with impressive concentration. When his mother returned, she said something to him in French, which Kaplan did not understand, though the boy answered in clear American English. He held his pencil oddly; he pressed down on the page with great intensity. The expression on his face was one of the utmost seriousness.

He had black hair and blue eyes. His small features were delicate yet in no way effeminate; refined is how Kaplan would have described them. His hands were well-formed, nails clean. As Kaplan was staring at the boy's hands, the pencil point broke on the math workbook. He searched in his backpack for another, but with no luck.

"Care to borrow mine?" Kaplan asked, removing a gold Cross pencil from his shirt pocket and handing it to the boy.

"Thank you, sir," said Philippe. The boy smiled up at him as he took the mechanical pencil. It was a smile that stopped Kaplan's heart—a smile of intelligence and gratitude and natural sweetness. As the boy went back to his workbook, Kaplan wondered what he could do to make that smile reappear.

"Excuse my disturbing you," Kaplan said, touching the boy lightly on the arm, "but do you happen to have any interest in magic?"

The boy nodded yes. "Philippe adores magic," his mother said.

Kaplan took a quarter out of his pants pocket and performed a sleight-of-hand trick that called for the boy to guess in which hand the quarter ended up. Three times in a row the boy guessed the wrong hand. Kaplan next rolled a quarter across the knuckles on the back of his hand. Finally, he placed a quarter on the outer part of his forearm, just below the elbow, straightened his arm, and caught the quarter before it fell to the floor. The boy was dazzled.

"Would you by any chance be interested in learning any of these tricks?" Kaplan asked him.

"Very much," said the boy, in a voice of great earnestness. "I would love it."

As Kaplan explained the first trick, the boy's attention was complete. Kaplan held Philippe's small hand in his own, palm up, showing him how to conceal the quarter between and slightly underneath the middle and index fingers. Rolling the quarter across his knuckles the boy couldn't do. Kaplan assured him he would get the hang of it with practice. The quarter-below-the-elbow trick he got on the seventh or eighth try. His victory smile—a mixture of surprise and delight—blew Kaplan away.

"Philippe loves four things," his mother, leaning across her son's seat, said, "magic, soccer, his computer, and playing the trumpet." Just then the quarter got away from the boy, rolling along the floor out in the aisle of pedestrian traffic.

"He's a great kid," Kaplan said to the woman.

When the plane was ready for boarding, Philippe held out the quarter to Kaplan. But Kaplan told him to keep it to practice with, and took another quarter out of his pocket, putting that into the boy's hand, too, just in case he lost the first one.

"Thank you for being so nice to my son," the woman said. As she walked away, Kaplan noted that her slip was showing beneath the back of her skirt and that the tennis shoes she wore—Nikes, the same brand as her son's—made her ankles look a bit thick. An old line from Kaplan's shoe-selling days on State Street popped into his head: "May I show you something in a nice pump, or maybe an evening shoe?" Now where the hell did that come from, he wondered.

It was a flight without first-class seats. Philippe and his mother must have been seated toward the middle of the plane. Kaplan was on the aisle near the front. He had intended to work on the flight, but the crowded plane and the darkened rainy sky caused him to forget about work. He tilted back his seat and soon was asleep, dreaming of being with Philippe at a Cubs game at Wrigley Field. In his dream it was a sunny day; they had very good seats, and Kaplan explained everything he knew about baseball to the formal little boy who had a French mother. A pop foul bounced off the roof of the Cubs' dugout and landed in Kaplan's hands. He could read the clear print on the ball, felt the texture of the red threads that held it together. Kaplan handed the baseball to Philippe, who for some reason was wearing his backpack and a down jacket, even though it was a warm day. "Thank you, father," the boy said, and leaned over in his seat to kiss Kaplan's cheek.

At LaGuardia, Kaplan, who deplaned before the boy and his mother, waited in the gate area, thinking he might offer them a ride into Manhattan in the limousine he had ordered. He hung back among people who were waiting for passengers on his flight, and then he saw them. He was about to wave when a tall man with a beard, wire-rimmed glasses, wearing jeans and a leather jacket with a fur collar called out, "Philippe, Phil, over here." The boy saw the man and ran to him. They hugged; the man lifted the boy up, a slight affront to his dignity, though he was clearly pleased to be held. This man, Kaplan decided, must be Philippe's father. From the fact that he shook hands rather coldly with Philippe's mother, Kaplan also decided that they must be divorced and that maybe she was bringing the boy to New York for a visit.

"This," said Kaplan to himself sitting behind the wheel of the rented Lincoln Town Car, "is crazy." He was parked on the 59th Street side of the University of Chicago Lab School, along the Midway. It was nearly three o'clock. He had been there since two-thirty, and to pass the time he had been counting beards on students and teachers on their way to and from the university campus; thirty-six had passed in less than half an hour. Kaplan was hoping to meet Philippe Glicksman. Kaplan's secretary had been able to find out that Glicksman was the boy's last name by calling the school; there weren't, after all, that many boys named Philippe. His secretary had also been able to discover that Philippe's mother's name was Françoise Berger, pronounced, like his old salesman Sy Bourget, without the last letter and with an accented *e*. Kaplan was right: there must have been a divorce, with Philippe retaining his father's name and his mother returning to her maiden name.

All of which was interesting but none of which explained what Sheldon Kaplan, former car dealer, venture capitalist, Jewish philanthropist, was doing sitting in a rented car on a gray Chicago day waiting for a third-grade boy whom he had met and talked with briefly in an airport two weeks ago. "This," Kaplan repeated to himself, "is crazy, nuts, completely *meshugah*."

And yet since meeting with the child, Kaplan couldn't get him out of his mind. If things had turned out differently, if he, Kaplan, had had a son, this boy, intelligent and handsome, a boy-man really, earnest and well-mannered, was exactly what he would have wanted. Kaplan, not generally much given to daydreaming, now regularly found his mind wandering to various scenes featuring Philippe and himself: explaining the infield-fly rule to the boy; presenting him with his first car, a red convertible; driving him off to begin his freshman year at Harvard or maybe Stanford, some such joint; finally, taking him into the business. Kaplan found he liked to linger over these daydreams, to fill in the details, replay them before falling asleep at night in his suite at the Drake. Sheldon Kaplan, who all his life had traveled light and loose, wanting both nothing and for nothing, now wanted this boy for a son, wanted him more than he had ever wanted anything in his life, ached for the want of him.

As the kids began streaming from the school, Kaplan kept on the lookout. He finally spotted Philippe coming out of the entrance with a black kid who seemed to be a mulatto and was Philippe's size. Kaplan opened the heavy door of the Lincoln.

"Philippe," he called, the French pronunciation of the name sounding strange to his ears. Kaplan spoke no foreign languages, had in fact never been to Europe, and had no curiosity about it.

The boy saw Kaplan and walked over. He was in his down coat, wearing his backpack. He was carrying a musical-instrument case in his left hand. When Kaplan asked if he remembered him, he merely said, "Watch," and setting down his trumpet case, took a quarter from his pocket, placed it just below his elbow, and perfectly executed the trick Kaplan had taught him at the airport.

"That's terrific, Philippe, terrific," said Kaplan. "Did you have to practice long to master it?"

"Pretty long," the boy said, then remembered his friend. "Excuse me," he said to Kaplan "but I guess I don't even remember your name." Told, he turned first to his friend, then back to Kaplan, and said, "Mr. Kaplan, may I present my friend Andrew Wilson?" Kaplan, charmed, shook the other boy's hand. He had seen nothing like such manners from any of the children of his friends, who were at best cute and at worst whiny or wild. But this Philippe was in another league, another class entirely.

Driving the boy home, Kaplan learned that his mother taught something called comparative literature at the University of Chicago and that his father, who lived in Manhattan, taught psychology at a place called Stony Brook on Long Island. Philippe and his mother lived on a dark block on Woodlawn Avenue between 53rd and 54th Streets, in a two-bedroom, third-floor apartment. The carpet in the hallway was worn, many of the doors had two and three locks. It was a building that had seen better days. Philippe had let himself in with his own key. Kaplan was carrying a large package under his arm. "*Maman,*" he called out, "I am home and I have Mr. Kaplan with me."

"And who is Mr. Kaplan?" Françoise Berger called out from the kitchen. When she came into the room in which Kaplan and her son were standing she was wearing jeans, the same tennis shoes she wore at the airport, and a sweatshirt with Mickey Mouse across the front. Recognizing Kaplan, she smiled and held out her hand. "So nice to see you again," she said in her French-accented English.

"Forgive this intrusion," Kaplan said, "but I saw something the other day at Marshall Field's that I thought your son might like, but I didn't want to give it to him without your permission. Is it all right?"

She looked dubiously at the large package wrapped in Field's dark green paper under his arm, but Kaplan, consummate salesman, knew she couldn't refuse, not with the boy in the room. "I'm sure it will be fine," she said, and Kaplan handed the package to Philippe.

It was a magic set, the best they had, costing $119. If there had been one for $3,000 that came with a girl to be sawed in half, Kaplan would have bought it. Philippe, on the floor tearing the paper from the box, was tremendously pleased. Inside were coins, rings, a collapsible top hat, a trick water glass, rubber rabbits, colored scarfs, two wands, a cape with secret pockets, a miniature guillotine, ropes, false-bottomed Chinese boxes, a pair of white gloves. The boy's eyes shone. With his extraordinary manner of shifting suddenly from child to grown-up, he got to his feet, extended his hand to Kaplan, and said, "I am very grateful for this generous gift. Thank you very much."

"If it makes you happy," said Kaplan, "then it makes me happy."

"It clearly does make Philippe happy," said his mother. "Perhaps, Mr. Kaplan, you will stay to have dinner with us?"

Kaplan had in fact planned on being asked to stay to dinner. During the meal—omelettes, salad course served afterward, good bread, a white table wine (which the boy also drank, in a watered-down version), cheese and fruit and coffee—Kaplan gently pumped Françoise Berger for information. He learned that she had met her husband, Bernard Glicksman, a Jew like herself, during his Fulbright year in Rouen, where she was a student. They married not long afterward. She was his second wife; he was now on his third. She followed him back to the United States. While he taught at the University of Pennsylvania, she worked on a Ph.D. in comparative literature there. Philippe was born when she was twenty-nine; she was thirty-seven now, eighteen years younger than Kaplan. She received neither alimony nor child-support payments from her former husband, though he was supposed to be putting money away to pay for their son's college education. For the two of them, mother and son, living on her assistant-professor's salary was a tight stretch, but by being careful she was able to get by.

"But why do I tell you all these things?" she said "You are very easy to talk to. Now you must tell me something about yourself."

Kaplan didn't give away much. He told her that he was in business for himself. He said that he had never married and lived downtown. He said that he lived all his life in Chicago. He said nothing about his current net worth being somewhere in the neighborhood of $60 million. He also neglected to mention to her that he intended to marry her because he wanted to help raise her son. Before the evening was over, she had accepted his invitation to dinner on the weekend and had agreed to call him Shelly, which in her French accent came out closer to "Jelly."

This was maybe the biggest deal of Kaplan's life and he felt it needed to be handled with the greatest care. He mustn't move too quickly—and yet not too slowly either. The pressure must be there, faintly, not oppressively, but quietly constant. Things were damned complicated, of course, by his not really knowing what Françoise Berger was like, which for him reduced itself to the question of what she wanted from life. With his salesmanly instincts, he would have to feel his way. These same instincts would tell him how and when to close.

He took her to dinner the following Saturday evening at the Cape Cod Room of the Drake Hotel, where he was well-known. The headwaiter, after seating them at a small table in the back near a window overlooking the Outer Drive, said, "The turbot is very fine tonight, Mr. Kaplan." Their waiter, a man named Mario who had worked at the restaurant for many years, made a great fuss, anticipating his preference in wine, soup, salad, potato.

"Do you come here often, Jelly?" Françoise asked.

"Actually," he said, "I live here, have for a number of years." Kaplan couldn't be sure if she found this information impressive or odd.

"It must be very costly. Are you a rich man, Jelly?"

"Next to some people, I am," he said. "Next to others, I'm a piker."

"Piker? What is a piker?" she asked, smiling. She was not beautiful, Kaplan thought, but she did have a fine smile. She was wearing a white silk blouse, not too carefully pressed, under a red cardigan sweater with a black skirt. Coming into the restaurant, walking behind her to their table, he noticed that she had a run in her stocking.

After explaining what a piker was, he made a mental note to be more careful with his language around her. During dinner, he used the old salesman's trick of asking questions and letting the customer do all the talking. He asked her about her work at the university, and understood practically nothing of what she told him—many names were mentioned he had never heard of, several words ending in "ism" were equally lost on him—though he kept his gaze steady, nodded regularly, and from time to time murmured, "Interesting."

Then Kaplan asked Françoise about Philippe. He seemed a happy child. Was he? Did he see his father often? Was the divorce hard on the boy? What did he think he wanted to do when he was older? But

Kaplan sensed that he must not show too much interest in the kid. It was the mother he was supposed to be chiefly interested in.

After dinner, they crossed the street to the lobby of the Knickerbocker Hotel to have a drink and listen to the pianist play and sing Gershwin, Cole Porter, and Rodgers and Hart. At about eleven-thirty, Kaplan took Françoise back to Hyde Park in a cab. At her door, she said she had enjoyed herself. He suggested he might call her during the week. He knew the man who owned the Chicago indoor soccer team; if the team were in town, maybe he could get tickets to take her and Philippe to see a game, if she thought the boy would enjoy it. "I am sure he would, Jelly," she said, and kissed him lightly on the cheek before turning and closing the door behind her.

Over the next month, Kaplan put what he thought of as a three-quarter court press on Françoise. He saw her and the boy not every evening, but usually at least twice a week. He took them to the theater and to movies and once to the Chicago Symphony, where he struggled—and finally failed—to stay awake. They always had the best seats and, at restaurants, the best tables. On a Saturday afternoon, he took Philippe alone to Wrigley Field, where he had tickets in the first row behind the Cubs dugout and through a connection was able to get the boy a ball signed by all the players. Living alone with a European mother in the setting of the University of Chicago, Philippe knew next to nothing about baseball, or about any of the other American sports. Kaplan hoped one day to rectify that.

The first night Kaplan and Françoise slept together it was her idea. Kaplan wasn't pushing it. They were to go to a movie, and when he arrived at the Woodlawn Avenue apartment she told him she had arranged for Philippe to spend the night at the home of one of his classmates. Kaplan felt slightly odd making love in a small bedroom with prints of abstract art on the walls and filled with paperback books in foreign languages. He was also used to women rather more accomplished in these matters, who tended to organize activities around his not their pleasure. (Cut it any way you like, it was he who finally picked up all the tabs.) It was otherwise with Françoise. Adjustments would have to be made.

The following Saturday night Kaplan accompanied Françoise to a party given by one of the senior professors in her department. Everyone there was connected with the university. He was worried beforehand that he would have nothing to say to such people, nor they to him, and he turned out to be right. Twenty or so people were in the living room of the book-lined apartment. Many beards in the room; also much baldness. ("I know," Kaplan could hear his friend Morty Siegel's jokey reply, "and the men were even homelier.") Kaplan was no beauty himself, but he had never seen so strong an air of confidence among people who seemed, somehow, slightly deformed. The women seemed dimmer and more disheveled than the men. Most were married couples, and in order for them to come together, Kaplan imagined, they must have arrived at some mutual agreement to overestimate each other.

Their host, who greeted them at the door, was a large man, red-faced, with an aggressive white beard. He clearly never caught Kaplan's name when Françoise introduced him. Seated on a couch near the fireplace, a short man, bald, with long grizzly white sideburns, wearing a rumpled tweed jacket, mud-spattered shoes, and a turtleneck sweater that looked as if it weighed eighteen or twenty pounds was holding forth with great animation in a heavy German accent. A squat man with a red goatee and a hairdo intended to disguise his baldness, which it only accentuated, seemed bored almost to anger by the German's performance. These were all teachers, Kaplan reminded himself, more accustomed to talking than to listening, and there was, it seemed to him, a lot more talking than listening going on in the room. When their host, the guy in the fierce white beard, brought them their drinks he asked Kaplan what he did, and after Kaplan said that he was in business, he never asked him in what business. Instead he turned to Françoise and began what sounded to Kaplan like a lecture on the subject of a writer with a strongly foreign name.

Kaplan found himself with a glass of white wine in his hand on a couch next to a woman with large earrings who was smoking a cigarette and who began talking to him about her strong desire to stop smoking. She went on and on about it; obviously it was one of her great subjects. Kaplan, the old salesman, put himself on automatic pilot, pretending to listen while looking around the room. None of the men had shoeshines; all of the women wore glasses. No one in this room, he imagined, had been much of an athlete or dancer when a kid, or had trouble with the IRS, or was likely ever to call him to ask if he could get them tickets to a Bears game. No, this was not his room.

Françoise, however, seemed happy enough here. The scruffy German had captured her and another woman and had begun yet another lecture. Some day, if she played her cards right, she would be able to deliver the lectures at such parties. This, in any case, was her scene; Kaplan could at least sense that much, and in doing so he also sensed how unlikely it was that he would ever feel comfortable among these people. Not that he was much for social life—his closest friends were still those fellows he went to high school with and who were now lawyers or dentists or accountants or ran small businesses. As a bachelor, he was not a regular part of their crowd and only saw them and their wives on the occasion of their children's weddings or a twenty-fifth anniversary party or at the funerals of their parents. The women in this circle talked about travel and clothes and their children (now grandchildren) and dieting, lots about dieting. Françoise would have felt just as awkward among them as he was in her circle. Not that he felt all that comfortable in either place. French writers or Italian designers, it was all pretty much the same to him.

"Jelly," Françoise said, in the car on the way back to her apartment, "I hope that the evening was not too terrible for you."

"Not at all," he lied, "it was very interesting. Some very intelligent people were in that room. An impressive group. Only I was thinking about Philippe."

"What about him?"

"I was thinking maybe it would be healthier if he grew up in a more normal setting."

"Healthier and more normal? What can that mean, Jelly?"

Kaplan's salesman's antennae warned him that he was in dangerous waters and to proceed cautiously. "I guess I really meant 'more regular,'" he said. "By which I mean more in the workaday world, where fathers go off to regular jobs, most mothers stay home to look after their children, and not everything is intellectualized and talked to death."

"I see," Françoise said, "such as you find in your own healthy and normal neighborhood on the twelfth floor of the Drake Hotel."

Kaplan had not expected that arrow in his forehead. "The Drake Hotel and the University of Chicago aren't the only alternatives, Françoise," he shot back. "There are suburbs, nice neighborhoods in the city. If Philippe were my son, I would find a place for him to grow up in a more ordinary way. The boy is extraordinary enough in his own right."

"But he is not your son, Jelly. So why do you worry so about him? Sometimes I think you think more about Philippe than you do about me."

"I care about you both," Kaplan replied, rather unconvincingly he thought.

No more was said, and when Kaplan drove up in front of Françoise's apartment, she told him not to bother parking. She was tired and preferred to go directly to bed.

Kaplan realized that he had made a serious mistake. He had told a divorced woman that she was raising her child badly. Dumb. And, besides, not even true in Françoise's case, for she was careful and completely responsible about everything having to do with her son. What was true was that he, Kaplan, wished the boy to have a more American upbringing. At the Cubs game, for example, he discovered that Philippe didn't know what he wanted on his hot dog because he had never had a hot dog before. Kaplan found that astonishing. The kid never used slang, for the good reason that he knew none. Everyone, even his classmates, called him by his full name, Philippe, never Phil or any nickname. It was as if the boy were being raised in another country.

Nor, even though both his parents were Jews, was there anything especially Jewish about him. Bernie Glicksman, the boy's father, had been brought up in New York in something called Ethical Culture, which, as Françoise once explained, attempted to instill the ideas of religion without allowing God into the discussion. As for Françoise, her parents, both of whom died in their fifties, though themselves much more French than Jewish, had never got over the shock at having to escape to Switzerland (money easing the way) when the Nazis occupied France. So Philippe grew up with a Jewish name and a Jewish face but nothing else. Kaplan was very far from an observant Jew himself, but one of his recurring daydreams was standing behind Philippe on the altar stage at Temple Sholom on Lake Shore Drive at the boy's bar mitzvah.

Kaplan's stock of daydreams seemed to increase, and he enjoyed plugging them in, like cassettes, when he had a free moment: He and Philippe at a Bulls game (Kaplan had done business with the owner of the Bulls, a real-estate operator named Reinsdorf). Taking Philippe shopping for school clothes. Fishing with Philippe in hip boots in a mountain stream in Canada (Kaplan had never fished in his life). Driving the boy around Chicago, showing him the neighborhood he grew up in, taking him to the restaurants he liked, instructing him in the dangers and pleasures awaiting a young man of adventurous spirit in a modern big city. Kaplan sometimes wondered what, apart from business deals, he had thought about before meeting this boy.

Kaplan figured that maybe the bad effects of his last meeting with Françoise had worn off. The three of them had eaten an Italian dinner on Taylor Street, and gone to see *The Last Emperor,* toward the end of which Philippe fell asleep. He was in his bed now. Françoise and Kaplan were in the small living room of her apartment, and he was about to leave when she said, "Jelly, I should like it if you would please read the story I have marked in this book and the whole of this novel."

Kaplan took the two paperback books she handed him, and he sat up late that night reading, with some difficulty, the story "Death in Venice." The novel, *Lolita,* he couldn't get through, but felt he didn't have to. He got the point. Fortunately, he planned to be in Boca Raton for five days next week and wouldn't see Françoise till the weekend. It would give him time to think things through.

In Florida, Kaplan felt he had botched things badly. In a business deal, he would have been much sharper. In business, his mind searched for the other party's desires, and hence his weaknesses, and once he knew those he knew how to play the game. Tax questions his accountants handled; loopholes his lawyers closed up. Kaplan alone knew the stakes, was aware of the higher plan; his specialty was minimizing risk while maximizing potential gain. Keep your head clear and your heart out of it and nine times out of ten you win. But with Françoise and Philippe, he was the one with the desire, and hence the weakness; his heart, far from being out of it, was thoroughly engaged. So much so that he failed to ask the most fundamental questions: why should Françoise want him? He would be getting a son out of the deal. What would she be getting? A very rich husband, yet she seemed unimpressed by, almost completely uninterested in, Kaplan's money. (He had developed a very good nose for people who were interested in it.)

Kaplan had not pursued her ardently enough. He had let his love of her son show through too clearly. Why else had she given him that story and that novel? Did she actually suspect him of being some kind of pervert: Gustave Humbert von Kaplan? He wouldn't put it past her. From his admittedly limited experience, Kaplan knew that nothing was quite real to an intellectual, a person who lived so completely in her mind as Françoise, that she could not relate to a book. Kaplan's problem was now to convince her otherwise.

But the larger problem was to convince her that his feelings were genuine. Successful salesmen, Kaplan knew, always sold themselves first. Could Kaplan sell himself on this young French academic woman? She was not beautiful, at least not by the standards he used, though she had a good smile and a certain natural refinement, which was partially what attracted him to her son, who must have got it from his mother. She was obviously intelligent—a high IQ type—but hers was not an intelligence that was much stimulated by the reality of everyday life. Kaplan recalled one evening explaining to her the subtleties of purchasing political influence in the city of Chicago, but the subject seemed to leave her bored. He would never be able to discuss the books that interested her, nor she the deals that interested him. Her friends were not his idea of a swell bunch—he hoped to

God Philippe would never turn out to be like them—and his friends would no doubt leave her equally cold. Such thinking yielded quite a balance sheet: all debits.

On the credit side was the large item of love for Philippe. This they both had in common. Kaplan had no doubts about the genuineness of his feeling for the boy; Françoise, of course, had proved hers—proved it every day. There was something very impressive about a woman trying to raise a boy on her own. When Kaplan thought about Françoise, a foreigner alone in the world but for her son, he was moved, his heart was touched, he could forgive her everything. She might be a little screwy—imagine giving him those books to read—with poor taste in people and not very good instincts about what was real and what wasn't. But all that disappeared when placed next to her devotion to Philippe. When he saw this in action—when she put food before the boy, or tucked in the shirt that sometimes came out of his pants, or inquired if he had brushed his teeth before he went off to bed—at such moments, yes, Kaplan loved her.

Coming out of the Drake on the Drive side that Saturday morning, Kaplan greeted Julius, the black doorman on the day shift, and stepped into the large Winnebago camper he had rented for the weekend. He had promised to take Philippe and his friend Andrew camping in Kenosha, Wisconsin. The man from the rental agency showed Kaplan how to hook up the water and the portable gas tank, which supplied the energy for the two-burner range and the hot water heater. A television set and refrigerator were also included. The camper slept four. Kaplan arranged to have it stocked with groceries. The rental for two days, insurance included, came to a little more than six hundred bucks. A case-hardened city type, Kaplan knew diddly about camping, the country, or the outdoors generally. If he hadn't thought that it would rob some of the fun from the weekend, Kaplan would have hired a driver and a chef to come along. As it was, he had to buy some tan pants, a couple of golf shirts, a windbreaker, and tennis shoes for the outing. All he owned was business clothes.

Françoise and the two boys boarded the camper on Woodlawn

Avenue, she carrying a small suitcase with clothes for the weekend. The boys were excited by the gadgetry and plushness of the camper's interior.

"It's really splendid, isn't it, Mr. Kaplan?" said Philippe, in his oddly stiff adult manner. He always referred to Kaplan as "Mr. Kaplan," a slightly awkward situation for which Kaplan had no good remedy. It seemed wrong for the boy to call him by his first name, and wrong, too, to suggest "Uncle Sheldon." He himself would have liked to call the boy "Phil," or to find some winning nickname for him. For now, though, they remained "Mr. Kaplan" and "Philippe."

"Neat wheels, man," said Andrew, cutting through complications. Maybe, thought Kaplan, he ought to pursue Andrew's mother. It would be a hell of a lot simpler.

While the boys roamed around in the back of the Winnebago, Françoise sat up front next to Kaplan. They scarcely spoke, for driving this machine was like driving a truck and took most of Kaplan's concentration. He had to laugh to himself—here he was, the man who organized his life to travel light and unencumbered, maneuvering this buslike vehicle whose cargo included a French woman and two young boys, off to spend a weekend doing nothing he particularly cared to do. Life had its little surprises, no doubt about it.

It was only when they arrived at the camp grounds and Kaplan, with a good deal of confusion, hooked up the water and electricity and the boys went off to inspect the large park nearby that they had a chance to talk. They were sitting on red canvas directors' chairs by the side of the camper.

"It is very kind of you Jelly," she said, "to go to all this trouble and expense for us in this way."

"I have a motive. It's that it really pleases me to see your son happy. But speaking of kindness, it wasn't, you know, very kind of you to give me those stories to read. What was your motive there?"

"Mixed motives, I suppose," she said. " I felt—I still feel—that your affection for my son is, well, it is unusual. And perhaps I feel, too, a bit jealous, thinking that you care more for Philippe than you do for me. I know you have tried to hide this, but it comes through nevertheless. Perhaps in giving you those books to read I was striking out a little at you."

"You say my feeling for Philippe is unusual, but do you really mean 'unnatural,' like in those stories?"

"I am not sure what I think, Jelly."

"Well, let me clear things up for you. I love your son. I loved him when I first saw him. And everything I now know about him causes me to love him more. I love him for himself and I love him for myself, for purely selfish reasons. I love him because I think I can be useful to him, both with my money and with what I know about life. What I know about life is very different from what you know. Naturally, I tend to think what I know may be more important. Maybe it is; maybe not. But with what we know together we can do a lot for him. You, I realize, already have done a lot for him—make that *everything* for him. But I think I can help out, and I want to. For him and for you and for myself. It would make me feel that my life was a little more worthwhile, that it made a little more sense."

"And where do I fit in all this?"

"You are the boy's mother, and though maybe you don't think about it in the way I do, in my view he is a great achievement, one that does you real honor. Raising this boy by yourself alone from the age of three took guts, and raising him to be so kind-hearted and likable a kid took character. I didn't realize it at first, but in fact I love you for what you have done for your child. It may not be the thing you want most to be loved for, but it seems to me that it's every bit as legitimate as loving someone for her mind or her looks or stylishness—at my age, and from my point of view, it seems to me even more legitimate."

Listening to himself, in the way all good salesmen train themselves to do, Kaplan sensed that he was doing well (he wasn't sure that he was really even selling), that he was convincing, that he was on a roll, that he was—as how many hundreds of times in the past—closing.

But just then Philippe and Andrew returned, said they were starved, and conversation came to an end as Françoise began preparations for lunch. The discussion was never picked up, and the weekend went by in a blur. The boys seemed to be having a great time. Saturday afternoon they rented a boat and tackle, and all four fished, catching a large number of small rock bass which, against Andrew's protests, they threw back. That night they cooked hot dogs and hamburgers on a portable barbeque and walked into town to see a movie. They slept in the four fold-out beds in the Winnebago.

Out for a walk early Sunday morning, Kaplan noticed a riding stable nearby, and when he returned to the camper asked if anyone cared to join him for a ride. Françoise declined. Andrew begged off, saying that he didn't like horses close up. If Philippe was also afraid, he pretended not to be, and after breakfast he and Kaplan walked off to the stable together.

It was Philippe's first time on a horse. Kaplan had not ridden since summer camp in Eagle River, Wisconsin, as a thirteen-year-old. Philippe looked small and brave sitting upon the large horse, his hands stiffly gripping the reins. Kaplan told him he was doing fine and that he would be with him all the way. At a narrow place on the bridle path, Philippe's horse walked in front, seeming especially huge under so light a cargo. When the path widened, Kaplan rode up alongside Philippe and asked him how he felt about trotting a little. The boy gulped and said yes, he would like to try. The two of them trotted along side by side for a hundred yards or so, until Kaplan grabbed the reins of the boy's horse to bring him to a stop. Philippe was breathless and his face was flushed and he began to laugh.

"That was wonderful," he said.

"I thought so, too," Kaplan said. "We'll let the horses rest a moment and then we'll try it again."

And they did. And then, after another while, they did it again and then again and again. Alone on the bridle path, just the two of them, Kaplan listened to the boy's laughter ring out, light and silvery, above the trees.

After they had returned the horses to the stable, Philippe said, "I loved that, Mr. Kaplan. May we do it again some day?"

"Of course we can," Kaplan said. "And by the way, we ought to find something for you to call me besides 'Mr. Kaplan.' "

"What?"

"How about 'Jelly,' like your mother calls me? And what about if I call you, instead of Philippe, which is a bit formal, what if I call you Jam? Then we could be Jelly and Jam."

The boy's small serious face broke into wrinkles as he giggled. Jelly and Jam, they walked down the side of the road back to the camper and along the way the boy slipped his hand into Kaplan's. Squeezing lightly, the ace salesman, multimillionaire, venture capitalist felt his heart melt.

After an early evening dinner of steaks and potatoes cooked on the grill and a salad, Françoise loaded up the Winnebago, Kaplan disconnected the water hook-up, and they drove home to Chicago. On the way home, Kaplan quizzed the boys about the names of the capitals of the states and taught them to sing "A Hundred Bottles of Beer on the Wall." It was ten o'clock when they dropped off Andrew at his mother's apartment. Philippe was asleep when they pulled up before Françoise's apartment, and Kaplan carried him up the three flights of stairs.

"It has been a lovely weekend, Jelly," said Françoise, "thank you so very much."

"I have to be in New York for a few days on business," he said, "but I'll call you when I get back."

At the Drake he turned the camper over to the night doorman, to whom he slipped two twenties to make sure it was returned the next morning. Undressing in his suite, he felt it had been a fine, successful weekend, and fell asleep thinking of himself as husband and father, Sheldon Kaplan, family man.

When he returned from New York, at nine o'clock on a rainy Wednesday night, there was a letter from Françoise at his hotel. It was on University of Chicago stationery and was typed. It was the first written communication he had had from her, and he found it a bit strange to be addressed by her as "Dear Shelly" instead of as "Jelly." The letter got right down to business.

"I'm writing this letter at eleven o'clock on Sunday night, after our lovely weekend in Wisconsin. Philippe is now in his pajamas, asleep, and it has been a little less than an hour since you left here to return to your hotel. Philippe and his friend Andrew enjoyed themselves immensely and I did, too, though I have been able to think about little else than the points you raised in our interrupted conversation on Saturday morning. Before I go on to say what I feel I must say, I want you to know how honored I am by your regard for my son—honored and pleased that a man of your experience thinks my little boy so extraordinary."

Kaplan didn't like the sound of that last sentence. To the eye and ear of the experienced salesman, it had the ring of Thanks But or No Sale about it. The letter continued:

"I am also honored by what you said about your feelings for me developing out of your admiration for the way I have raised Philippe. At a time when everyone is so nervous about whether or not she is doing the right things for her children, it is very good to be told that one is not the failure one is almost certain one is. And, if it is not vain of me to say so, I think your are correct when you say that it is better to be loved for having raised a child well than for having written a fine book or for just about any other reason. You put that very well on Saturday morning, I thought, and it reminded me how clear-minded and penetrating you can be.

"And how persuasive, too. Without setting it out in detail, you have made plain how much you could do for my son, both through worldly experience and through your wealth. I may be an academic woman, with what seems to you her head in the clouds, but I am also French and middle-class and therefore not without respect for money and what it can do. Although I have never spoken to you about it, I have been living with an almost continual anxiety about money since my divorce. How splendid it would be, married to you, simply never to have to worry ever again for the rest of my life about rent and clothes and dental bills and dozens of other things! To have all that settled and solved and out of my mind would be a great luxury in itself."

Kaplan didn't like those "woulds"; they made him very edgy.

"Being married to you would give my son a father he could

admire and whose love for him isn't in doubt. Financially, it would make possible for Philippe many advantages he does not now possess. As for me, marriage would end my loneliness, which, despite the busyness of trying to manage a career and raise a son, has at times been considerable. We have little in the way of common interests, I realize; in fact, I know almost nothing about what it is you do. But I admire the mastery you seem to have attained in your own world. It seems to me manly and impressive, and it is something that I should like Philippe, whatever he does later in life, to appreciate and emulate."

Still alive? Kaplan wondered. Maybe not yet knocked out of the box?

"I suspect you do not credit me with an overdeveloped sense of reality, but about my own life and that of my son I try to make as few mistakes as possible. I have already made one mistake in marriage and I do not wish to make another, which, as I approach forty, could be my last. So much about us makes me nervous: we come from very different worlds, live in very different worlds, have very different views about what matters in the world. What we share is love for Philippe. And even here I wish things were otherwise. I wish that you had discovered my son through me rather than the other way around. A question you have to ask yourself—it is a question I have been asking myself for a while now—is, would you have cared at all for me if I had not been the mother of Philippe? If there had been no Philippe, would you have attempted to see me again? I do not like to think about the answers to those questions."

Kaplan, setting down the letter, didn't in the least mind thinking about them. The answer to both was no. But he considered them both purely theoretical—she was the boy's mother, through the boy he learned of her quality—and Kaplan had little interest in theoretical questions. Life in practice offered complications enough.

Two lengthy single-spaced paragraphs followed, expressing doubts, hesitations, fears. Kaplan read with impatience, skimming over the paragraphs as he might over the boiler-plate language in a legal contract. He skipped down to the final paragraph.

"If your feeling for me comes through your admiration for my love for Philippe, then you should know that much of my feeling for you is also in good part owing to your love for him. In a way, we are both putting a lot of pressure on a little boy, making him responsible for the love between two adults. Philippe, you should know, adores you, but then he has chiefly known you as someone who has brought him gifts, taken him places, made life more exciting for him. I wish he could know you in a more everyday way—see you angry or bored or depressed. I would myself like to see you in these states. (I assume you lapse into them like the rest of us.) If I were not so thoroughly bourgeois a woman, I would suggest that we live together, but, however useful that might be for us, I do not think our doing so would be the best thing for Philippe. So instead I propose that, before we do anything final, we put each other on a year's trial: that we take a full year to see how we truly feel about each other and how Philippe feels about us as a couple. I hope you will agree that this makes good sense. But we can talk about all this—and much more— when you return from New York." She signed the letter, "With love."

Kaplan took the No Sale sign down in his mind. He had apparently closed again—though for a brief moment he wondered just who was closing whom. He realized, too, that once married, he would have to live with more clutter and less freedom in his life. A flash of doubt intruded on his triumph. But then he remembered that he would now be on hand as Philippe grew up, he would live with an interesting woman whose intelligence he had underestimated, he would not die alone, he would not be entirely forgotten after he was gone. Could a man ask for more? Well, thought Kaplan, maybe a little more, and he began to plan how he could sell Françoise on reducing the year's trial to six months, settling and finally closing out the deal, his instincts told him, at not more than eight months, tops.

Schlifkin on My Books

■

ortunately, I happened to be in the room when the police called to inform my wife that my body had been dragged from Lake Michigan. "There must be some mistake, officer," I heard my wife say, "but Samuel Kravitz, my husband, is right here with me now, and very much alive." I picked up the phone, identified myself, and asked what the hell was going on. The police officer, a man named Howard Levine, told me that they had fished a corpse out of the lake roughly four hours before, and the corpse was a man wearing a grey tweed overcoat, a Hickey–Freeman by make, with the name S. S. Kravitz sewn into the lining. I was S. S. Kravitz, no question about it; there was no question either about who was wearing the overcoat. Schlifkin was wearing the overcoat, Louis Schlifkin, my customer, crazy Louie. I know because I gave the coat to him. "Officer," I said, "the name of the man you found in the lake is Louis Schlifkin. I would be grateful if you'd see to it that he got a decent Jewish burial. I'll take care of any expenses involved."

I first met Schlifkin some three years ago. I was in my office, going through the orders that had come in that morning's mail, when Cora, the black gal who was then my floor lady, came in to say that a new customer was making a terrible mess of the stock and that she didn't seem to be able to stop him. I strode out of my office, Cora following, and in our sales room saw a small man, my own size, rummaging through our stock, breaking open boxes, going into cartons, digging in where he didn't belong, and leaving, as Cora said, a terrible mess. He was wearing a navy pea coat and a woolen watch cap. He was stocky, and when he turned to face me I noted that one of the temple pieces of his glasses was held together by electrician's tape. One of his bottom teeth was missing; his nails were ragged and filthy.

"Look here," I said, "if you plan to be a customer of ours, you'd better behave like it. I won't have you handling our merchandise as if it were garbage."

"So what's the matter with you?" he said. "Didn't *yentz* your wife last night?"

I don't think I have been spoken to that way in forty years. And with my employees standing about, I don't think I have been spoken to that way ever.

"All right," I found myself saying, pointing to the door. "You— out! And I don't want to see you in here again until you're ready to handle yourself like a gentleman."

"Go screw yourself!" he said, picked up two shopping bags he had brought in with him, and walked out. As he left, it occurred to me to wonder if he had put any merchandise in those shopping bags.

Back at my desk I thought, Do I need this aggravation? I concluded, fairly quickly, that, yes, I do. I was then sixty-eight years old. Believe me, I'm not bragging when I say I don't need the money. My kids aren't in the business. My daughter Sharon is married to a dentist who does very well. My son, Marvin, is a professor of philosophy in California. The philosophy he teaches doesn't sound like philosophy to me; he says he is interested in something called "the problem of language." What exactly is the problem, I have asked him, but I've never been able to understand his explanation. In any case, like his sister, he appears to be settled in life and, from all I can tell, reasonably happy. My wife's sister's oldest boy, Norman, works for me. Two years ago I made him a minor partner. Like me, he never went to college, but he's a go-getter. Not yet thirty, he drives a little Mercedes convertible that I'm told costs upward of fifty grand.

I've asked him not to park it in front of the place. It sends off wrong signals. It might give our customers the idea that we are doing very well—which, between you and me and the lamp post, we are. I myself drive a Pontiac, two years old. I'm not sure I could tell you what color it is. It's good enough. I'm too old to show off.

But I spoke of needing the aggravation. The truth is I love this business. I love to come down in the morning—I usually arrive forty-five or so minutes before everyone else—and straighten up the stock, go through the mail, page through the *Wall Street Journal*, get myself set for the day ahead. The name of our place is Bonnie Beth Enterprises. People ask me, Who's Bonnie Beth? My wife? My daughter? I tell them it's a long story. In fact, it's a short one. When, thirty-odd years ago, I first went into this business, I had a partner. Bonnie and Beth were the names of his two daughters. We were together less than five years and I caught him cheating. Petty cash, postage money, nickel and dime stuff, maybe it came to a lousy two, three thousand a year. Still, once you catch someone, trust is shot. I told him, either you buy me out or I buy you out, but I don't think we can go on together anymore. He cried like a baby. He took the money I bought him out with and bought eleven laundromats, none of which did any good. He was a diabetic, and died four years ago—a horrible death. Life isn't easy.

We started out in costume jewelry. We were jobbers. Bought most of our stuff from Providence, Rhode Island. Before long, though, that dried up. So we began importing from Hong Kong and Taiwan. In recent years, I've been buying close-outs—the left-overs from failed businesses. Earrings, cufflinks, pendants, wires, you name it, if the price is right I buy it and can find a way to unload it. I'll let you in on a little secret: buying is where you make your money. We buy in volume, hundreds of dozens, even, if the item can be had at the right price, hundreds of grosses. We pay our bills; we have cash on hand; if the deal looks right, we move. At the moment, for example, I am sitting on two hundred dozen neckties that I bought for eight cents a piece. I'm told that the neckties are too wide, they're out of fashion. Fashion, smashion—at eight cents a piece, how can you go wrong? Eventually, I'll unload them.

Some three weeks later Cora came in to say that that man who had caused the trouble was back. I had told her to alert me if he returned. "O.K., Cora," I said, "I'll handle him."

I picked up an order book and walked into our sales room. There he was, still in the pea coat and wool cap, still the electrician's tape on his glasses, still with the two shopping bags.

"I'm ready to be nice," he said, the missing lower tooth showing in his smile.

"Good," I said. "Now what can we do for you?"

Filling out his order I learned that his name was Louis Schlifkin and that he lived on Milwaukee Avenue, about three blocks from our place of business, in a Polish working-class neighborhood that was beginning to go Mexican. I also learned that this Schlifkin was a man in love with merchandise. He shopped with such excitement, such abandon, that at least twice—once when he ripped open a box of cheap Japanese binoculars and another time when he nearly destroyed the display card for a grouping of friendship rings—I had to tell him to take it easy.

"How much I got?" he wanted to know. "How much it come to?"

"So far, $183.75."

"Whaddya got good for another twenty bucks?" He was obviously going to spend every cent he had on him. At the close, when he paid his bill, mostly in greasy fives and singles, he had maybe three or four dollars left. I walked him to the door.

"Thank you for your business, Mr. Schlifkin."

He picked up his shopping bags, and, as he pushed through the door, over his shoulder said, "*Abi gesunt, Shmuel.*"

Soon Schlifkin began coming in two and three times a week. Sometimes he would buy eighty or ninety dollars worth of merchandise, sometimes forty or fifty. Once he came in for an order totaling $18.62. I learned that he was selling it on Maxwell Street—"Jewtown," as the blacks called it. He had no car, so he would schlep a card table and his shopping bags on the bus, and set up shop there on the street. Did he show a profit? Maybe a small one. I could of course tell Louie Schlifkin's holdings almost to the penny by the size of his orders. I always waited on him myself.

How old was Schlifkin? I'm not so sure. I made him out to be in his late fifties. He could have been younger. He still had a full head of hair, and it was black. But his face was sallow; it showed all the traces of having lived a hard life. He wore gym shoes even in the winter. I learned that he came from Cleveland and that he had a brother there in the furniture business. He talked horribly about him. "A miserable prick, my brother," he once said to me. "He wouldn't give you the time of day." He also had a sister in Cleveland, who was married to a lawyer. Schlifkin, obviously, was the family black sheep. Later I learned that his sister used to send him a monthly check to cover his living expenses. My guess is that this was done partly out of charity, partly to keep him out of Cleveland, where he might prove an embarrassment to the family.

One day, in the middle of a bitter winter week, Schlifkin came once more to buy. He seemed hesitant, a little nervous. "Shmuel," he said, "I have a favor to ask." He called me Shmuel, I called him Schlifkin. "Shmuel," he said, "how about carrying me on the books for a hundred dollars credit? This past week, with the terrible lousy weather, has been a disaster. Whaddya say? Jew to Jew. I won't crap out on you. You know I won't screw you. I need you too much."

"Schlifkin," I said, "I give a man like you credit, I lose a customer. I make an enemy. You'll never come back. It's a big mistake. Believe me, I've seen it happen time and again."

"Look Shmuel, without the credit, I'm done for. Tapped out. *Kaput.*"

I thought a moment about it.

"All right. I'm putting you on the books for seventy-five dollars. But don't disappoint me."

"Shmuel," he said, 'you're a *mensch*. I won't forget it."

Now you might wonder, Why did I say seventy-five dollars and not give Schlifkin the hundred dollars he asked for? I don't know. Maybe I've been out on the street too long. I mean, what is twenty-five dollars to me. Between you and me, I give more than twenty thousand dollars a year to charity, forty thousand if you count Israeli bonds. Maybe I was only trying to show Schlifkin I wasn't a complete soft touch. Maybe I didn't want to lose him as a customer, not that his trade with us came to all that much. The truth is I had come to like Schlifkin—"Crazy Louie," as my nephew had now begun to call him. Maybe he reminded me of what, if my luck had been different, I myself might have been. I don't know.

What happened I could have predicted. He paid back fifty of the seventy-five, and then the next week was back into us for the full seventy-five. Eventually I let his credit creep up to $200 and carried him pretty much permanently on the books for that. I set the ceiling at two hundred. What the hell! Did it really matter so much? Besides, by now I had made much more than that in profit in dealing with him.

And then, in November, Schlifkin didn't show up for two weeks. This was unusual. Was he, I wondered, in trouble? Had he skipped out? Was he dead? Schlifkin had no phone, so there was no way of getting in touch with him. One morning when it was quiet in the place I decided to walk the three blocks to his apartment to see for myself. It was a grey day and we had had an early snow, and the streets were covered with that combination of frozen snow and filth that sometimes stays on the ground from November through April in Chicago. Walking over I thought, if Schlifkin had died, who would even know about it?

His place was above a discount shoe store on Milwaukee Avenue. The hallway was dark, the stairway from the ground to the second floor was steep. I imagined Schlifkin schlepping his card table and shopping bags up and down it. There were no bells for tenants, so I walked up the stairs. The doors on the second floor had names scribbled on index cards taped to them: Rodriguez, Strazewski, Morales, and, at the end of the hall in the back, Schlifkin. I knocked on the door, waited, then knocked louder.

"Hold your goddam horses." It was Schlifkin. He came to the door in his pea coat, under which he had on a ripped sweatshirt and a pair of jockey shorts on which the elastic around the legs had long given out. As for his room, mess doesn't begin to describe it. Pipes

ran around its low ceiling, from one of which Schlifkin had hung
out to dry two tired looking pair of underwear pants and a flannel
shirt. On a small table was a can of Heinz Vegetarian Beans with a
spoon in it and the package from something called Twinkies. A milky
film clung to a jelly jar. In the way of furniture the room had a bed—
where Schlifkin, having taken off his pea coat, now lay—an arm
chair with the stuffing coming out of the seat cushion, and a small
television set with a hanger for an antenna. There was a small sink, a
hot plate, but no refrigerator. The bathroom must have been somewhere down the hall. Schlifkin pulled a grimy blanket around him;
his pillow had no pillow case.

"Where've you been?" I asked.

"I had an angina attack," he said.

"You have angina?"

"For the last four years, yeah."

"What do you do for it?"

"I go to Cook County Hospital. They give me pills. I lay low
for a week or two and it goes away."

This awful room couldn't be helping much. How long had
Schlifkin lived here? How many places like it had he lived in before?
Something had to be done about this. This was no way for a man to
live.

"How's business?" he asked. "What're the hot items?"

"Business could be better. Nothing much new. My import guy
tells me he's holding four cases of mini-cameras, with the film, for
me. Also lighters, a pretty good imitation of the old Ronsons. Otherwise, same old crap, what can I tell you?"

"What're you getting on the cameras?"

"To you," I said, "fifteen dollars a dozen."

"Sure—to everyone else probably twelve dollars a dozen."

"I'll hold back four dozen for you when they come in. The lighters you'll look at when you're back on your feet. I also have a deal
upcoming on scatter pins that may be for you. Meanwhile, Schlifkin,
can I do anything for you? You need money, food, what?"

"What I need's a new engraver. The old one's on the bum. Lock-
ets, bracelets, lighters, it's scratching up everything it touches, though

most of the time my high-class customers don't seem to notice."

"I'll get you an engraver, don't worry."

"I'll be in early next week. Hold the cameras, and don't forget the engraver, which I expect you to throw in for nothing."

When I got back to my place, I put in a call to Schlifkin's sister, Mrs. Jacob Rabin, in Shaker Heights, Ohio. I had her name and number from the credit form Schlifkin had filled out for us; she was his only reference.

A maid answered, then Mrs. Rabin came to the phone.

"Mrs. Rabin, my name is Samuel Kravitz. I'm a–er–business associate of your brother Louis Schlifkin. Please forgive my calling you, but your brother is ill. What's more, he's living in terrible conditions, and I am wondering if there isn't anything to be done about it."

"What's wrong with Louis?" she said.

"He's had an angina attack. Did you know he had heart trouble?"

"I did, Mr. Kravitz, but I'm afraid I don't know what can be done. His brother and I send Louis a regular check every month, you know. Louis is a problem, Mr. Kravitz, a problem with no solution. I've asked him to come back to Cleveland, but he wants no part of it."

"Mrs. Rabin, he's living in a rat hole. He's a sick man. Something's got to be done."

"Mr. Kravitz, believe me when I say that there is nothing to be done. Louis is Louis. He's a terribly self-destructive man."

"Self-destructive?"

"Louis was my mother's favorite, you should know, Mr. Kravitz. But from the very beginning he was trouble to her and to the rest of us. She left him more than thirty-thousand dollars in her will. Louis went through it in less than a year. I sometimes think Louis is in competition with his older brother, to whom he doesn't even speak. No, Mr. Kravitz, I'm afraid that Louis is Louis, and there's nothing to be done about him but let him live his life the way he wants to."

"I see," I said.

"It's been very nice of you to call, Mr. Kravitz. And if Louis becomes very ill or needs more money for special care, I hope you'll let me know."

After hanging up, I thought about what Schlifkin's sister had said. Schlifkin was self-destructive? What could that mean? That he had had a long record of failure, I suppose. Or maybe that he worked against his own best interests. So we take bad luck and poor reasoning and put a label on it—self-destructive—and feel a little smarter? Or, in Schlifkin's sister's case, it gives a little heart's ease. But who made Schlifkin self-destructive? His mother, who maybe loved him too much? My own mother died when I was ten. Do I owe my success in life to that? Other men who have had mother love have gone on to great triumphs, I'm certain. What else did his sister say? Schlifkin was in competition with his brother. What did that explain? Who set up this competition? Who gave Schlifkin a brother he couldn't hope to compete with, let alone defeat? Where was it fixed that Schlifkin was to be one of life's losers? The only thing that his sister said that made any sense to me was that Louis was Louis. Schlifkin was Schlifkin. But how did Schlifkin get to be Schlifkin? It's a serious question.

Schlifkin had recovered from his bout with angina and was coming in again regularly. One morning on my way out of our apartment, I noticed my wife had set aside a pile of clothes to give to Good Will. From it I fished my old grey tweed overcoat, a blue pinstripe suit, and two of my shirts, frayed a bit round the collars and with my monogram, S.S.K., over the pockets. Why not give these to Schlifkin? He was roughly my size. God knows he could use them. I put the clothes in a shopping bag and took off for the place.

Driving down I wondered if Schlifkin might not resent these clothes as charity. He thought of himself, comic as it may seem, as a businessman. Ours was a business relationship. One businessman doesn't, after all, give another businessman his used clothes. Still, Schlifkin could use these things. If he didn't want them, or if he resented them, he could tell me to go screw myself. It wouldn't be the first time he had done so.

Schlifkin didn't come in that day but the day after. It was early in December, a real honey of a Chicago day, somewhere around zero with plenty of wind. Working out of doors in such weather couldn't have done Schlifkins's heart any good.

"So Shmuel," he said, his face still red from the wind, "whaddya got that's hot?" With his usual delicacy, he rifled through our stock, buying maybe eighty or so bucks' worth.

"Oh, by the way, Schlifkin, I brought from home a few things, a suit, an overcoat, a few shirts, my wife thought maybe you could use them. I've got more clothes at home than I know what to do with."

"Sure. Throw 'em in my bag. Shmuel, what's your best price on these bolo ties a dozen. I want your best price, Shmuel, no bullshit now."

That morning Schlifkin left wearing my Hickey-Freeman overcoat over his pea coat, his woolen cap pulled down over his ears.

In the months that followed it was an odd feeling seeing him in my clothes. He didn't own a belt, so he used a piece of rope through the loops of the trousers. He continued to wear his black gym shoes. He wore the shirts, which he must have washed out in the small sink in his room, but of course he didn't know from ironing. SSK, my monogram, remained over his pockets. Sometimes he would wear the suitcoat over a flannel shirt and a pair of grey washpants. The temple piece held on by electrician's tape had fallen off his glasses and he never bothered to replace it. Meanwhile, I let him go up another hundred bucks, and was now carrying him on the books for three hundred.

What did Schlifkin, who worked like a dog, do with his money? For one thing, I don't think he made very much. My nephew once went down to Maxwell Street to deliver a package of merchandise to him, and came back to report that Schlifkin was selling our stuff at criminally low prices, marking things up only fifteen and twenty-five percent when his mark-up should have been more on the order of a hundred percent. Then there was the *schmear* he had to pay to get a decent location on the street. A good share of his customers proba-

Schlifkin on My Books

bly stole from him. I used to plead with him to raise his prices, I used to argue that with such a low mark-up there was no way he could hope to make out, but there was no talking to him. Schlifkin loved the action.

"Shmuel," he'd say, after I'd read him one of these lectures about getting a decent mark-up, "Shmuel, I'm like you—I work on volume."

Schlifkin was all business, oblivious to clothes, to the way he lived, even to his heart trouble. He was also, unfortunately, oblivious to what went on around him, and I wasn't all that surprised when one day he walked in with a gash under his eye, his hand bandaged, and two of his upper front teeth chipped. I was surprised, when I came to think about it, that it hadn't happened before. While he was closing up on Maxwell Street, after dark, three young thugs robbed him and beat the hell out of him. They took his money and his merchandise, leaving him only his card table. For good measure, one of them stepped on his glasses. Without glasses, Schlifkin looked like some sort of small burrowing animal, prey to every other animal, who didn't see well in the sunlight.

"The thing is, Shmuel, I haven't got a dime to give you on account. And I haven't got any stock. Those *mumsers* took everything. New glasses are going to cost me sixty-five bucks and Friday my rent is due."

"So what do you want from me, Schlifkin?" As if I didn't know.

"Look Shmuel, I'm into you now for nearly three hundred. Let me go to five. Shmuel, put me back in business. Give me a break."

"Schlifkin, maybe now's the time to go back to Cleveland."

"Screw Cleveland. I like it here."

"Schlifkin, if I put you on the books for another two hundred, I'm going to set out certain conditions."

"These are?"

"First, that you stop giving merchandise away. That you begin to get a decent mark-up. Second, that at the first chance you get a checking account, so that you're not carrying around every penny you own on you. Third, that you don't hang around Maxwell Street after dark, so that every animal down there has a shot at you. Can you live with these conditions?"

He agreed. What else could he do? Fifteen minutes later, when he was selecting new stock, we got in a terrific argument about boxes. He said he didn't see why he had to pay a nickel a box on each scatter pin set. I told him it was because I paid four cents a box myself and that when you threw in the shipping charges I wasn't making any profit on the boxes myself.

"No shit, Shmuel," he said. "You should get a bigger mark-up." I nearly threw him out of the joint.

One day in the spring I took a cab down to Maxwell Street to check up on him. The street had changed a good deal since I had last been down there—what was it, maybe fifteen years ago. A new freeway had taken out a good chunk of it. A few of the old clothing stores were still in business, their salesmen trying to pull in customers off the street. There were two or three fortunetellers. An old black man was selling used-auto parts which he had lined up on the sidewalk. The smell of frying food, onions and Polish sausage most strongly, was in the air. Mostly black and Mexican were on the street.

In the middle of it was Schlifkin and his card table with my stock displayed on it. He was waiting on three Mexican girls. I hovered over at the side. When he saw me, he said: "Shmuel, you! To what do I owe the honor?"

"I'm checking up on you, Schlifkin. In a manner of speaking you're my partner, you know. Or at least I have an investment in you."

"Shmuel, you want a cup of coffee or a sandwich maybe?" He had a little black kid working with him, a gofer, no more than eight or nine years old.

"A sandwich down here? Schlifkin, are you trying to kill me so you can get off my books?"

"Shmuel, let me finish up with these ladies, I'll be with you in a second."

"Schlifkin," I said, when the girls had left, "you are breaking my heart with these prices. These expansion bands, you're paying me fourteen-forty a dozen, at a buck and a half a piece you're not making out. You should be asking—and getting—at least two-fifty. The Elvis neckchains you're giving away at ninety-eight cents. The Zippo-type lighters everyone gets at least two bucks. You're letting them go at a buck and a quarter. Schlifkin, the prices you're charging are giving me ulcers."

At this point a hillbilly couple came up to the card table, four or five black high school girls were looking at I.D. bracelets, and what looked like an older Polish woman priced lighters. Schlifkin was in his element, busy, doing business. He was a happy man.

"Shmuel," he said, "I got to take care of these people. I'll be in on Thursday. Save the hot items for me, willya?"

Schlifkin was Schlifkin; Schlifkin would always be Schlifkin. I had about as much chance of changing him as a snowball in hell. Yet something made me want to protect him. From what? From himself, I guess. Fat chance! Still, you had to ask, What was the point of a Schlifkin, a man who broke his back working for nothing, a man who asked nothing but to be allowed to do a little business. It didn't seem like a lot to ask. Not that for a minute I wished to be one myself, but there were worse things in life to be than a Schlifkin. When you came right down to it, what did it matter that I carried him on my books, a permanent entry, Schlifkin, Louis—$500.

"Shmuel, another five hundred and I can stock the place the way it should be stocked. I'll pay you back two hundred a week. Five weeks and I'm off your books. It can't miss."

Schlifkin had found a vacant store on the rim of the Loop. They were willing to let him rent it for the Christmas rush at a $100 a week, heat but not lights included. It already had fixtures, counters, and shelving. All it needed, according to Schlifkin, was stock.

"What do you think I'm running here, Schlifkin, a charitable foundation?"

"Shmuel, this time it'll be different. I've got a woman working for me. She knows the business. I don't have to sign no lease. I go in the week after Thanksgiving and I'm out after New Year's. It's a chance for me to make a small pile. It can't miss."

"At your prices, you can miss."

"Shmuel, I'll let you come in and price everything yourself. Shmuel, I need this. Give me a break, Shmuel."

"Stop with the Shmuel, goddamnit, Schlifkin."

"Every Friday I'll come in here, I'll give you two hundred. I'll give you my note."

"What'll you write it on, toilet paper? Because that's about what it'll be worth."

"Screw yourself, then. I'm talking to you one businessman to another. You want to be insulting. O.K. Fuck you." He was wearing my overcoat. By now Good Will wouldn't touch it with a ten-foot pole. One button was left of the original four. There was a rip at the breast pocket. He must have slept in it.

"Hold your horses, Schlifkin. I didn't say I wasn't going to work a deal with you. I'm not going in for a full five hundred, though. I'll go four hundred. Again with conditions: I set all prices, I help you choose the stock, you pay cash for all additional stock while you're in the store. Take it or leave it, Schlifkin."

"Shmuel, you're a *mensch*."

"Call me Shmuel once more and the deal's off."

Whenever we sent merchandise over to Schlifkin's shop I marked both the price he was paying for an item and the price he ought to get for it on the box. Sometimes Schlifkin came in to pick it up himself; a couple of times a rough-looking character, a drifter of the type you see around carnivals who was the brother of the woman Schlifkin had working for him, came to pick up merchandise. Like Schlifkin under our agreed-upon arrangement, he paid on the spot. No money, no merchandise. Once, to check up on Schlifkin, I sent a spy, my nephew Norman, to see if he was actually getting the prices I told him he ought to get. Amazingly, according to Norman, he was.

"One other thing, Uncle, and this you're not going to believe."

"What aren't I going to believe?"

"Crazie Louie has a girl friend."

"You mean the woman who works for him?"

"Yep. A hillbilly. Her name's Vera. She has a tattoo on her forearm. You ready for this, Uncle—she calls Crazy Louis 'darling.' "

"That's Schlifkin's business. How's the store look? They getting any traffic in there?"

The next time Schlifkin came in he gave me the details himself. Not about his lady friend but about the store. After he had deducted his rent and the money he paid his help, he was clearing somewhere between four and five hundred dollars a day—and there were still two weeks to go until Christmas. The woman who worked for him, this Vera, made a bank deposit at the end of each day, or so Schlifkin said. Meanwhile, he was using two or three hundred dollars of my merchandise every day. He was also paying off his debt to me.

"I got a little gold mine there, Shmuel, a goddamn little gold mine," Schlifkin said.

It didn't take much figuring. After five or six weeks in the store Schlifkin could walk away with a nice piece of change—maybe twelve or fifteen grand. Schlifkin was flying. His happiness was so obvious you could almost touch it. He had even taken fifteen minutes off to buy a pair of shoes—plain-toed black, Army surplus they looked like. Some days he wore a necktie over one of my shirts. Schlifkin was becoming a respectable businessman.

Then after New Year's, he didn't come in for a week, then two, then three weeks. I was still carrying him on my books for $178. Where could he have gone? Maybe he had taken his little pile of dough and returned to Cleveland, where he could face his family, now that he had made a mild success. Maybe he had taken his lady friend down to Florida. Schlifkin didn't seem the vacationing type, but you never knew. I once heard a story about a man who ran a restaurant on Roosevelt Road who worked three-hundred-and-sixty-five days a year; once, just once, he took a weekend off to go to South Haven—and he never returned. He didn't know about this thing called leisure, and once he had a small taste of it, he was through with work. Could something similar have happened with Schlifkin? It seemed unlikely.

One afternoon I walked over to his room on Milwaukee Avenue, but the card with his name was no longer there; some poor soul named Mendoza lived in that rat's nest now. I called Schlifkin's sister, Mrs. Rabin, but she knew nothing of his whereabouts either. Eventually, I supposed, he would turn up. If he didn't, he did me out of a lousy $178. Big deal. Still, I wondered where the hell he had flown to.

Then one day, about a week later, Schlifkin was on the phone.

"Schlifkin," I said, "where the hell are you?"

"I'm in a flop on Madison, Shmuel."

"What's going on, Schlifkin?"

"You're not going to believe this, Shmuel, but that broad took me for every penny I had."

"Vera?"

"Yeah, goddamn Vera. The day after New Year's I sent her over for a last bank deposit, and she withdrew everything from the account—everything. She took off with her brother, if that bastard really was her brother. I've looked all over the city for them, but they must be in Tennessee or Alabama or some goddamn red-neck place. I feel like a real schmuck, you know what I mean? I'm out of gas, Shmuel. I'm through, finished, done for!"

"Don't talk that way, Schlifkin. You'll come in, we'll talk about it, I'll put you on the books for another few hundred, you'll start up again."

"No, Shmuel, I've had it. It's over."

"Schlifkin," I said . . . but he had hung up.

I got in my car and drove up and down Madison Street looking for him among the bums, but no luck. I tried again the next day and the day after that. No luck. On the fourth day I received the telephone call from Officer Levine that Schlifkin's corpse, in my overcoat, had been dragged from an icy Lake Michigan.

The next day I called Schlifkin's sister. She flew in to Chicago to identify the body and had it flown back to Cleveland for burial in the family plot. I thought about flying in for the funeral, but decided against it. Dead was dead.

Last week our accountant came in to close out our books at the end of our fiscal year. Among other details, I learned that the $178 Schlifkin owed was a write-off in the category of a bad debt. Schlifkin was finally off my books. For the first time I spoke to the accountant about retirement and what would be involved in turning the business over to my nephew. I must be feeling my age. I'm thinking seriously about getting out. I think maybe I've had enough.

Marshall Wexler's
Brilliant Career

■

*I*n 1963 I was twenty-eight years old, a newly-minted Ph.D. in political philosophy from the University of Chicago, and spending the year as a visiting assistant professor at Harvard. Harvard was having a look at me for a tenure-track appointment in the department of government, and I was having a close look at Harvard, and was rather amazed at what I saw. I had passed my entire educational life in Chicago, in Hyde Park between 57th and 59th Streets, going as a kid to the University's Lab School, thence to the College, and then on to graduate school in the philosophy department. Intellectually, the University of Chicago was competitive and international—peppered with German refugee scholars and, as I would only later realize, not quite first-class Englishmen—but socially it didn't exist. So I was surprised at what I discovered at Harvard, where the social element, or so it seemed to me, was quite strong if not absolutely central.

This was evident throughout the university, but nowhere more so than among undergraduates, those little demons of sophistication. How different they seemed from the earnest, often rather dour, usually somewhat neurotic undergraduates at Chicago, their heavily underlined Modern Library copies of Plato and Aristotle under their arms, always ready for yet another discussion of what constitutes the Good Life. At Harvard, it struck me, undergraduates did not need to discuss the Good Life because, without anyone having to tell them about it, they knew they were already living it. What went on in the classrooms at Harvard, at least in non-scientific subjects like my own, seemed of less than primary interest to the students. At Harvard a teacher was expected to be brilliant, but above all to be fresh and entertaining, rather like a bright, charming movie. The main point is that what went on in the classroom could not have held much importance, because the most important thing in these students' lives had already happened—namely, they had been accepted at Harvard.

One of the two courses I taught during my second semester that year was Theories of Government, which met Monday, Wednesday, and Friday, from 9:00 to 10:00 A.M., in Emerson Hall. Some fifty-odd students were enrolled, most of them upper-classmen. I did the standard thing—I remember smiling at a *New Yorker* cartoon that appeared around this time, showing a small bald man at a lectern above the caption, "Teacher greets students on opening day of class with pleasantries"—that is, I announced the intentions of the course, passed out the syllabus of readings, explained that along with a mid-term and final examinations a twenty-page paper would be required. When I had done with details I asked if there were any questions. There appeared to be none. As I was gathering up my papers and was about to dismiss the class a pudgy kid with thinning hair raised his hand.

"Excuse me, sir," he said, and there was something about that "sir" that wasn't quite convincing, "but I was wondering: on the paper and the exams, do you want us to report back your own ideas and opinions, or do you prefer us to attempt to think independently and strive for originality?"

"May I ask your name?"

"Marshall Wexler," he said.

"Mr. Wexler," I said, "I don't know if you're going to believe this or not, but I do prefer that my students think independently and strive for originality, difficult as either of those conditions is to achieve. But in your case I am going to make an exception. I want you to take very careful notes recording everything I say in this class, and I want you to bring them to me in my office every Friday afternoon, so that I can make certain you never stray onto the path of independent or original thought. If there are no other questions, then class dismissed."

For three weeks running, slipped under the door awaiting me in my office at Robinson Hall on Friday afternoon I found a cleanly typed set of notes summarizing everything I had said in Theories of Government during the past week. What impressed me was the quality of these notes. Marshall Wexler not only caught precisely what I was attempting to say in my lectures and in class discussion, but frequently, I felt, said it rather better than I. He wrote in short sentences—always lucid, always correct. His powers of formulation were striking; he could render a thorny conception smooth, restate a subtle, sometimes tangled notion in language straight and simple without any loss of complexity. Real evidence here, I recall thinking at the time, of a superior intelligence.

I shouldn't have minded having a set of Marshall Wexler notes for the entire course. Were I ever to give it again, these notes would probably have improved it. But after three weeks the punishment had gone on long enough, and so the following Monday before class I told Wexler that he needn't worry any longer about supplying me with notes. That afternoon, during my regular office hour, he knocked on the door and asked if I could spare him a few minutes.

"I want to apologize for my opening-day performance in your class," he said. "I don't know why I did what I did—senior-year fatigue maybe—but it was stupid and I regret it. Please forgive me."

"It's forgiven and forgotten," I said.

He was about to leave when I invited him to chat for a moment. He sat in the chair opposite my desk, let his green bookbag drop to the floor, and, crossing one leg over the other, loosed a very winning smile. This, I thought, is not a charmless kid.

"I think we're from the same city," he said.

"You grew up in Chicago, too?"

"Northside," he said. "We live at 3400 on the Drive. I went to Francis Parker. My father's idea. Most of the guys I grew up with went to Senn, a few to Lake View. But Parker was the surer route to Harvard."

"Did your father go to Harvard?"

"My father never finished high school," he said. "He came here from Poland—from Bialystok, actually—in 1933, when he was seventeen. He's done extremely well. Somewhere along the line he'd heard that Harvard was the best school in America, and so he decided that he wanted his son—I'm an only child—to go there. I think it would've broken his heart if I hadn't. Anyhow, here I am."

"How do you like it?" I asked.

"It's all right. Lots of bright kids. Everyone's got some odd distinction or other—either he's a math whiz or a state oboe champ or his great-great-grandfather was one of the founders of the Somerset Club. The great thing about going to a school with a hot reputation is that you find out how little there is behind it. It lends perspective. Also, you don't have to spend the rest of your life brooding about how much better everything would have been if only you'd gone to Harvard."

"What're you studying? What's your major?"

"I'm in history and literature," he said. "But do you know the Lionel Trilling joke about majors?"

"I don't think I do," I said.

"It's in the story 'Of This Time, of That Place.' A student, who's a kind of bully boy, describes himself to the professor who's the main character in the novel as 'a former English major.' To which the professor asks him, 'In what regiment?' Not bad, eh?"

Marshall Wexler went on to tell me that he was one of the principal editors of the *Crimson*. He had also been working on a special research project with David Riesman. The year before, as a junior, he had read Proust in an independent tutorial with Harry Levin. For the most part, at my prodding, he talked about himself. Apart from the fact that I was sitting behind the desk, if a stranger had walked into the office at that moment he might have had a difficult time deciding who was the teacher and who the student, so much more in command did Marshall Wexler seem than I. Twenty or so minutes later when he left my office, he asked if I minded calling him Marsh. I said that I didn't, but I now wonder if he expected me to ask him to call me Ben, which I certainly did not do.

Back in Chicago early in August, I received an invitation from a Mr. Max Wexler to attend a party in honor of his son Marshall's having been awarded a Mellon Fellowship to Balliol College, Oxford, where he would be studying Politics, Philosophy, and Economics. I was a bit surprised, less by the announcement of the fellowship than at receiving the invitation. After that single session in my office Marshall Wexler and I had had no further private meetings at Harvard. He did well on both my exams and wrote a strong paper on Hobbes's *Leviathan,* all of which earned him an easy A in the course, one of three I gave that semester. But when the course was over there was no further word from him, no mention of our perhaps one day meeting in Chicago, nothing of the sort.

I'm not sure why I decided to go to the party. I was still unmarried, and my schedule was freer than it later became. Perhaps I was curious to see the Wexler kid in his own habitat. Perhaps I had nothing better to do. In any case, on a sunny Sunday afternoon I drove down from Hyde Park—I had a yellow Volkswagen bug in those days—along the Drive, past Soldiers Field, the Aquarium, the Field Museum, the lovely panorama of brightly colored sailboats tied to buoys on Lake Michigan that always struck me as awaiting painting by Raoul Dufy, over the S-curve, past the Drake Hotel and Lincoln Park, the lake a calm pellucid blue on my right all the way. I turned off at Belmont, found a parking space on Aldine, and walked over to the Wexler's apartment at 3400 Lake Shore Drive.

It was one of the grander buildings along the Drive, a building of formidable dignity and gray elegance built around the turn of the century that would not have seemed out of place in a fashionable neighborhood in Paris or Rome. The lobby had a burnished marble floor and walls paneled in deep walnut. There was no doorman but a tall white-haired man in the muted livery of a dark maroon jacket and black clip-on bow tie sat behind a high desk near the bank of elevators, where he had a good view of everyone entering. I told him I was here for the Wexlers, and he directed me to the ninth floor. As the elevator opened a very black woman in a nurse's uniform pushed forth in a wheelchair a small, hairless, vacantly staring little man in a light camel's-hair coat and a brown velour hat that, resting slightly askew on his head, he didn't appear to have put on himself. As I stepped in and the door began to close, I heard the man behind the desk ask the woman, "Mr. Bernstein O.K. today, Emma?"

There were two apartments on each floor. When I rang the Wexler bell a maid in black dress and white apron came to the door and informed me that the guests were in the living room down the hall and to my right. I walked along a lengthy hall, passing what felt like eight or nine doors, one of which was open and gave off into another long hall. This was one of those old Chicago apartments whose size one couldn't begin to estimate or rooms number. It was built during the days when the wealthy kept staffs of live-in servants, and so had maids' rooms, special pantries, a breakfast room, endless closets, four or five bathrooms, who knew what else. The size of the place threw me a bit, and it was only when I entered the vast living room, with its large windows looking outward to the south over Belmont Harbor, a room now holding perhaps fifty or so people, not counting five or six Scandinavian-looking women in uniform with trays of drinks and canapés, that I had a chance to grasp its extraordinary decor.

I am a son of the lower-middle class—my father owned and ran a dry-cleaning shop, we ate in the kitchen, left our shoes in the front hall in winter, and the rest of it—and so am normally not very sensitive to my environment, but this room demanded notice. A great lavenderish deep shag rug ran wall to wall; champagne-colored flocked wallpaper supplied background for a number of sizable paintings in heavy gilt frames of the fake-masterpiece kind that used to hang in the lobbies of the Balaban & Katz movie palaces in downtown Chicago when I was a kid. The furniture, of which there seemed a large quantity, so that you had the feeling of being in a showroom, was upholstered in heavy fabrics but in pastel colors; the lamps were especially ambitious. An enormous fireplace, surrounded by a dark marble mantel, was filled with a life-size brass peacock, its tail fanning out in a multiplicity of colors.

On the level of taste, this, I remember thinking, had a long way to go to get to vulgar, when someone tapped me on the shoulder from behind and I turned to find Marshall Wexler standing along-side a small, red-faced man, bald, wearing an expensive-looking dark gray suit and red silk necktie which was badly knotted and in which he did not look quite comfortable. Marshall was in standard Ivy League get-up of seersucker suit, foulard tie, button-down shirt, and plain-toed cordovan shoes, none of which seemed to go with this room.

"Professor Kaufman," he said, "may I present my father, Mr. Max Wexler? Dad, this is Professor Benjamin Kaufman, who was one of my teachers at Harvard and who now teaches at the University of Chicago."

Mr. Wexler and I shook hands. His grip was firm, his skin rough. Below the French-cuffs of his white-on-white shirt and large gold cufflinks, his hand had what looked to be a permanent grime; the nails were clipped very short; the thumbs were slightly bent back and seemed, somehow, brutal. I glanced quickly at his son's hands, which were soft and rather pudgy, though the thumbs—peasant thumbs, I thought—were similar.

"It is always a pleasure to meet one of my son Marshall's teachers," he said. He had been in this country for some thirty years but he still spoke with the accent of a greenhorn. He pronounced his son's name "Ma-shul." He was stocky, maybe 5'3" or 5'4", four or five inches shorter than his son, of whom he was obviously very proud.

"It's good to meet you, too, sir," I said. "You must be very pleased about your son's winning a scholarship to Oxford."

"Very proud," he said. "But then Ma-shul has always brought his father reasons to be proud." He squeezed his son's upper arm and looked over at him admiringly.

A heavy-set man came up, in powder blue trousers, a pink shirt with long pointy collars, and a yellow sports jacket of complicated texture. He had a cigar in one hand, a drink in the other. "So how's the young genius?" he bellowed, inserting the cigar into his mouth and slipping an arm around Marshall.

"Pretty good, Mr. Mutchnik," said Marshall. "Mr. Mutchnik, this is a former teacher of mine at Harvard, Benjamin Kaufman.

Professor Kaufman, this is Morrie Mutchnik, a business associate of my father's and an old family friend."

"Oh," said Mutchnik, rolling his eyes behind thick-lensed black-framed glasses, "a Haaavahd professor. I'm tremendously impressed."

"Actually, I teach at Chicago," I said.

"That ain't exactly bush-league, either," he said, removing the moist cigar from his lips. "Never went to college myself, though I had one daughter downstate and another at Rollins in Florida."

Marshall and his father excused themselves to greet other guests. Marshall said that he would appreciate a word with me—he had some questions about Oxford—before I left.

"So tell me," Mutchnik said, "has the kid really got it? Is he really brilliant or what?"

"Near as I can tell," I replied, "he has a very good mind."

"The old man, I think, maybe truly is some kinda genius," Morrie Mutchnik said. "He came here from Poland in the early 30's, just in time to save his ass from the Nazis, a kid, alone, speaks no English, knows no one, without a pot to piss in, you should pardon my French, professor. Today he is one of the giants of our industry."

"What industry is that, Mr. Mutchnik?"

"Call me Mutsy," he said "everybody does. The scrap-iron industry, formerly and less elegantly known as the junk business. In the Depression Maxie Wexler worked for an old guy on the West Side name Warshovsky. He worked the alleys of Chicago in a wagon pulled by a horse. He hauled radiators from abandoned buildings, ripped the copper tubing from basement plumbing. Nights Maxie doubled as a watchman, sleeping in the shack in Warshovsky's junk-yard. He kept his eyes open, saved a few pennies. When Warshovsky died he bought the yard, wagon, broken-down horse and all from the widow. Whatta I have to tell a smart guy like you, professor? One thing leads to another, junk leads to real estate to second mort-gages to a car-insurance business to savings-and-loans to by now who the hell knows what else Maxie Wexler is into."

"Much diversified, as they say in the business section."

"Diversified? I hafta laugh. Did you know that Maxie Wexler

owns the cemetery where my parents, rest in peace, are buried and where I myself, may I too rest in peace, will one day be buried? Which means that my descendants will one day be paying Maxie's descendants rent for room for my corpse."

"You're in the scrap-iron business yourself?" I asked.

"Almost but not quite. I own the industry trade journal. *Scrap Iron Age* it's called. What can I tell ya? It's a good living. It's also how come I've got the lowdown on Maxie Wexler and the other large-scale operators."

"Is there a Mrs. Wexler?"

"Rose Wexler died seven, maybe eight years ago. Bone cancer. Not a nice death. Now it's just Max and the kid. Ma-shul, you'll notice he calls him. The *shul* part is right. He is Max's *shul*. He comes to the kid to worship, if you know what I mean. Ma-shul is someday going to be a very rich man. I wonder if he has any of his old man's talent."

"That kind of thing can be pretty hard to measure."

"I was only thinking that Maxie Wexler's native shrewdness with Haavahd and Oxford behind it could be a really dangerous combination, if you know what I mean, professor."

Just then a small, slender man with heavily pomaded thick black hair slapped Morrie Mutchnik on the back. "Mutsy, you old putz," he said, "where'd you get that jacket, at a dead maharaja's estate sale?" Mutchnik introduced him to me as Earl Schneider, also in the industry. They began to talk, and I slipped away. I finished my drink and, figuring it was time to leave, began to look for Marshall. He was still with his father. When I told him that I had to be off, he said he would walk me to the door.

As we made our way down the long hall, Marshall asked if I had any advice for him about Oxford. I replied I hadn't any, except not to let himself be turned into an Englishman. Probably he already knew the same names in philosophy in England that I did—Isaiah Berlin, A. J. Ayer, Stuart Hampshire, a younger man named Bernard Williams—though I shouldn't be surprised if he discovered that the best teachers turned out to be people neither of us had heard of. He asked whether I would mind if he wrote to me from Oxford, and I said that I would be pleased to hear from him, though I was myself not the world's greatest correspondent. We shook hands as the elevator arrived, and glancing down quickly at his hand clasping mine, I felt the pressure of the thumb that so resembled his father's and for some reason I felt I understood this extraordinary young man a little better.

I never really expected Marshall Wexler to write from England, and so was a bit surprised when his letters began to arrive not long after his arrival at Oxford. They were, I thought, strangely intimate, given that we scarcely knew each other and had only the background scenery of the city of Chicago in common. They read like nothing quite so much as entries in a journal, but a journal that he, Marshall, for some reason chose to pass along to me to comment upon if I wished. They were well written, filled with information and gossip about English intellectual life. Much talk about "Isaiah" and "Freddy" Ayer, stories of witty put-downs delivered by Maurice Bowra and John Sparrow, a few Spoonerisms ("I remember your name, all right, it's merely your face I cannot recall")—slightly stale crumbs from high table, or so I concluded, as they were picked up at the lower tables at which Marshall sat as a student at Balliol.

But the real subject of these letters, it began slowly to emerge, was what I should today call Marshall Wexler's brilliant career. At this stage, of course, the subject was more precisely what Marshall Wexler should do to make a brilliant career.

I'm not at all sure Marshall wanted my advice, or needed it. Instead he appeared merely to want someone before whom to sound out his ideas, someone who appeared to have more experience of the world than he. There was, in fact, six years' difference in our ages, not enough for me to play at being fatherly or even avuncular. So I just listened, or rather read, as Marshall set out his plans, and when I commented upon them at all I did so in a neutral sort of way.

Early in his correspondence, Marshall wrote that he had decided the academic life was not for him, even though he thought he had some talent for it. He recognized, he claimed, the grandeur of real scholarship practiced at the highest level—at the level of an Erich

Auerbach or a Gershom Scholem or a Ronald Syme, such were the names he invoked—but the academic world was populated by much lesser men, was, he felt, in fact dominated by them (present company excepted, he tactfully added), and didn't offer anything like the scope of possibility or richness of environment he required. He had thought about the law, but the time of apprenticeship before he could hope to be able to do anything significant seemed to him altogether too long. Business, where his father had succeeded so handsomely, held no interest; and with his father's fortune and generosity, money, he knew, was not going to be his great problem. He had thought about government, possibly diplomacy, but then he knew that things were not easy for Jews in the State Department and saw no point in wasting time blazing trails. He regretted not having cultivated the scientific side of his education, for science was both serious and offered a chance for life in the great world (he mentioned C. P. Snow, at that time a great figure in England), but suspected that he might not have the aptitude for doing science at the top level, or it would have shown itself by now.

Almost by elimination, then, that left journalism. In one of his letters, Marshall mentioned his fascination with the career of Walter Lippmann, whose early books he had been reading and who, like himself, was the son of a rich man and had been a Jew at Harvard. Walter Lippmann's was a career of a kind to which he, Marshall, aspired. He thought, he said in this letter, that he might write to Lippmann—the year was 1964 and Lippmann was then a very active sixty-five—to see if he would be willing to offer advice. My guess is that Marshall must have written such a letter, though I don't known for certain. I base this on the fact that Marshall's first job after completing his second year at Oxford was at *Newsweek,* where Walter Lippmann himself in those days had a column. I base it, too, on the knowledge I was soon to acquire of Marshall's habit of writing flattering letters to the intellectually illustrious.

One day while I was lunching at the Quadrangle Club at the university, Samuel Garskov, a famously gruff character in the history department who had recently was a Pulitzer for his two-volume biography of James Madison, interrupted my conversation with a colleague to ask if I knew a kid named Marshall Wexler. When I said I did, Garskov removed from the breast pocket of his jacket a crumpled letter, typed on light blue stationery under a Balliol letterhead. I don't recall all that the letter contained but its main point was to thank Professor Garskov for his fine Madison volumes, which put all of American history for the first time in clear perspective, at least for his correspondent, who also felt that the work would have a very long life. In a few economical paragraphs Marshall managed to convey that he was young, intellectually penetrating, a fellow Jew, and immensely admiring of the historiographical genius of Samuel H. Garskov. In a postscript Marshall asked that Garskov say hello to me, his former teacher at Harvard.

"So, Kaufman," said Sam, not bothering to apologize for breaking into the conversation, "who is this kid? Is he some kind of bullshit artist, or is he on the level?"

"I don't know, Sam," I replied, "but you have to admire his taste in historians."

"Up yours," he said.

Over the next few years, I discovered that Marshall had written similar letters to Hannah Arendt, Saul Bellow, Edward Shils, Milton Friedman (setting out mild disagreement but expressing "enormous admiration" for Friedman's intellectual rigor), and a number of other luminaries at Chicago. Did Marshall, I wonder, send similar epistolary corsages to people at Princeton, Yale, Berkeley, and Stanford (he had earlier had a chance to canvas Harvard in person)? I don't know how well these Marshall-grams, as I began to think of them, went down elsewhere, but for the most part they succeeded at Chicago. And why not? To be told that one's work is indispensable by someone young, highly intelligent, and obviously on his way up in the world is not something that tends to invite skepticism. Unlike Sam Garskov, at least two other recipients of Marshall-grams remarked to me, in the same thoughtful tone of voice, "He seems an interesting young man."

Marshall Wexler was an interesting young man, though they didn't know the half of it, and I myself had only begun to know maybe 55 percent. Marshall had telephoned me once or twice from his father's apartment when he was home from Oxford on holiday. Once we were going to meet for lunch at the Standard Club, where he had a junior membership, but owing to complications of one sort or another the lunch never came off. But his letters, written at irregular intervals, continued to arrive.

After Oxford, Marshall began his job at *Newsweek*. He was one of fifteen or so associate editors and worked on what they called there "the front of the book," specifically on national news. This was in the days before the newsmagazines permitted bylines, so it was impossible to tell what bits and pieces were his. He continued to write to me from New York, perhaps a letter every few months. He had taken to New York right off—he had an apartment on East 61st Street, just off Madison—and felt that he hadn't made a mistake in going into journalism. He said that he didn't expect to remain any longer than necessary at *Newsweek*, though for now he was still learning enough about the inner workings of journalism to make staying on worth his while. Not the least interesting to him were the struggles for power among the editors near the top of the minutely small-type masthead. Around this time, I published a small book, with Yale University Press, on *The Meno*, a copy of which I thought of sending to him but in the end decided not to.

It was in the summer of 1967 that I next heard from Marshall. He was, he told me over the telephone, in town for his father's funeral, which had taken place three days earlier. I offered condolences and apologized for not knowing; I didn't read the Chicago papers and so missed the obituary. Max Wexler was fifty-two—Marshall was himself twenty-six that summer. He had died in the elevator of the 3400 building, of a heart attack, on his way to work. Marshall wanted to know if we could have our too-long-delayed lunch, perhaps the next day, at noon, at the Standard Club. It would be good to see me again, he said. I told him it would be good to see him, too, and wondered, fleetingly, if I meant it.

It was one of those steamy Chicago summer days, and after walking over from the Illinois Central Station to the Standard Club

I felt as if I could use a change of shirt, if not of skin. But once inside that anonymous gray building on Plymouth Court across from the John Marshall Law School, all seemed shady and cool. I sat on a maroon leather couch, enjoying the air conditioning and watching older Jewish men, expensively but not flashily tailored, most of them in gray suits and earnest neckties, greeting one another with confident handshakes. The only discordant note was a Filipino nurse attempting to crash through the deafness of an older man, also in an expensive gray suit, seated at a small table near the door; she was yelling at him not to worry, his son and daughter-in-law would be here soon.

Marshall arrived five minutes late, in a blue blazer, gray trousers, black loafers, a blue tie with yellow stripes not quite pulled all the way up to his collar button. The pudginess of his Harvard days had solidified into adult weight. His already thinning hair had receded further, but he now wore it combed over his ears and long in the back, a concession to the style of the day.

"Ben," he said, "what a pleasure after all this time." In his letters he had always addressed me as Professor Kaufman, but I was going to tell him to call me by my first name anyhow. We shook hands, and he touched my elbow, steering me over to the bank of elevators.

He had reserved a table in the men's grill. It was a comfortable room, where we were seated by a mulatto maître d', served by an Italian waiter, and had our dishes cleared by Mexican busboys. A certain quantity of smoke drifted to the ceiling, but it was the smoke of very good cigars.

Once more I offered condolences on his father's death.

"He was a remarkable man, my father," Marshall said. "He knew what he wanted, and through concentrated effort he got it." He reached out for a roll, which he broke in half with those same short strong thumbs of his father.

"You know, my father's death has taken me out of the financial wars for good" he said. "He arranged things so that I shouldn't have to worry about money for the rest of my life. It's an interesting position to be in."

"I should think it would be," I said. I was myself sweating out tenure at that time, and it looked to be no sure thing.

"I realize most people dream about being in my situation," he said, buttering the half roll, "but in a curious way not having to earn money makes it more pressing to figure out what you do with your life. For most of the men in this room, you know that isn't a very serious question. For them what you do with your life is you make money, you invest money, you give some of your money to good causes, you arrange to pass your money on to your children in an orderly way. It's a lot simpler."

Marshall ordered a bowl of vegetable soup, a steak sandwich, very rare, with grilled onions and fried potatoes, and asked for a double order of coleslaw. He drank two martinis before lunch and sipped at a third with his meal. He must have smoked eight or ten cigarettes with his coffee, during which he devoured the small plate of brownies and cookies that the Standard Club, famous in Chicago for its food, set out at the end of a meal. Through lunch Marshall told me about the current power struggle at *Newsweek*, laying it out in considerable detail, adding that he had sided with the right party, which meant that he soon figured to be promoted to senior editor, the youngest in the history of the magazine. He would have the opportunity, if he wished, of becoming Paris bureau chief or covering the war in Vietnam, which was then heating up tremendously. Marshall was a man with alternatives, a man rich in possibilities.

"You know, Ben," he said, looking at me earnestly, "this country is going to be up for grabs, and before too long. The blacks, the universities, maybe even the white working class are going to cause terrific disruption. And our war in Vietnam is going to make it all wilder. A big shake-up is in store. A man has to position himself for what lies ahead."

"My own position remains the same," I replied. "I'm just another guy trying to get his work done. I'm not for disruption, and I hope you're wrong in your predictions. I only want the conditions that will allow me to write my books, teach my students, raise my family—did I tell you that my wife is pregnant?—maybe get a little smarter about the world."

"You have no desire to be in on the action, to be part of the life of your time?"

"I suppose not," I replied, "at least not in the way I sense you do. My interests are scholarly and so are my instincts. I don't mind standing well off to the sidelines and watching other people making history."

"Maybe it's the difference between our work," he said. "Journalism excites the appetite for action and influence. To go into it for any other reason would be pretty stupid, wouldn't it? I mean, it isn't complex enough to devote your life to practicing it the way you would an art; and nothing that comes out of it lasts for more than a week or two. No, the big attraction is the chance it provides to have a hand in directing the action. That, anyhow, is what I want."

Back on the steamy Loop streets, after we had shaken hands and gone our separate ways, I thought about Marshall Wexler's unusual freedom. He was intelligent and talented—and his talent and intelligence, combined with his high yet not inaccurate estimate of himself, kept him from making the silly mistake of starting at the bottom. And now he was rich, very rich, "out of the financial wars," as he put it at lunch. There was great hunger in him, and not only for drink and rare steaks and cigarettes, which I took to be the outward manifestations of a deep inward craving. There was also, I sensed, something missing, though I couldn't just now say what it was. Marshall could, I supposed, go a long way. It would be interesting to see how far.

A year or so later I had a call from Marshall in New York. He was coming to Chicago as part of *Newsweek*'s team covering the 1968 Democratic convention. We agreed to meet at the magazine's suite at the Conrad Hilton. Marshall mentioned over the phone that he expected it to be a wild convention. And in fact the night before the opening there were wild doings in Lincoln Park. Allen Ginsberg was chanting for peace, Abbie Hoffman was full of hijinks, the police chased people who were lighting bonfires.

When I saw Marshall the next day these events appeared greatly to have stimulated him. At the *Newsweek* suite he seemed suddenly no longer a former student but a commanding, rather worldly, figure. The door was left open and people drifted in and out, some to chat, some to help themselves to coffee or a drink. A tall man with a droopy mustache and floppy hairdo wandered in and Marshall introduced him to me as Kurt Vonnegut. Later Norman Mailer and William Styron dropped by. Terry Southern came around and so did a local character named Studs Terkel. Marshall knew them all and they all knew Marshall.

"They can smell blood," Marshall said, when we sat down to eat the sandwiches he had ordered up from room service. "This convention is going to be a writer's bonanza. It's made for hot copy. You've got Mayor Daley, Chicago cops, hippies, crazies, freaks of every kind, and more journalists than politicians. In short, all the makings for a magnificent carnival of the highest unreality."

After eating, we walked over to the windows. From this, the eighteenth floor of the Conrad Hilton, we looked out over Grant Park, where a vast rally was in progress. Policemen were lined up at the edge. While we were standing at the window something we couldn't make out happened, for suddenly there was a cloud of smoke that must have been from tear gas. The police had put on their masks and were now cutting a swath with their billy clubs through the crowd of scattering protesters. From the window of this probably $1,500-a-day suite it looked as if a war was going on.

"Journalism wasn't a mistake, Ben," Marshall said, gazing out and speaking with that particular earnestness of tone he reserved for his own career. "It's where the action is, and where it's going to be for a long time. No one any longer knows what the hell's going on in the world, or even what's going on under his nose, until a journalist tells him. Journalists are going to call the tune, Ben, there's no question about it."

That same afternoon Marshall told me of his plan to leave *Newsweek* and start a political and cultural magazine of his own, to be called *New Horizon.* The title derived from Cyril Connolly's *Horizon;* it was to be a monthly; left-wing but, as I remember Marshall putting it, in a "distinctly uptown way"; and it was going to be published in Chicago. He planned to make use of his Oxford connections as contributors. He had hired as his managing editor a middle-aged woman, a former editor at *Vogue,* who was now living with her third husband in Chicago and had very good social connections with various Lowells, Auchinclosses, Plimptons. He was prepared to risk a million dollars of his own money on the venture.

New Horizon was to begin publication in the autumn of 1969. Marshall planned to move back into the apartment at 3400 Lake Shore Drive, which he still owned. Publishing a magazine in Chicago was risky, but New York didn't need another magazine and the West Coast, though filled with political tumult just then, was almost always death on any kind of intellectual enterprise, or so Marshall said. He asked me if I wanted any part of the action. I wasn't sure whether he meant as an investor or as an intellectual contributor of some sort. But since I had neither the money for the first nor the talent or temperament for the second, I told him I would be content to settle for being a regular subscriber.

"Would you mind if from time to time I ask you how I'm doing?"

"Of course not," I said, "but you'll have to let me judge how much truth I think you can take. Or how much I'm willing to tell you."

"I hope it's a fair amount," Marshall said. "You're all I've got, you know."

I failed to ask him what he meant by that remark, though in later years I thought a good deal about it. Had Marshall, who so far as I knew now had no family, come to think of me as family—an older brother, perhaps, or a youngish uncle—simply because I went back to his college days? Or was it that he continued, in some odd way, to think of me as his teacher, with all the obligations that involved in initiating students into the truth, generally in as kindly a way as possible? Maybe it was a bit of both, with other elements mixed in that I never discovered. If Marshall decided to use me as an occasional confidant, that was all right with me, for I had now begun to take a genuine interest in his life. But I remember his managing editor, not long before she left *New Horizon* after only slightly longer than a year in the job, saying to me, "That little son-of-a-bitch eventually uses everybody."

It was at one of Marshall's many parties in his refurbished Lake Shore Drive apartment that she said this. It occurs to me that I do not know the precise meaning of the word "refurbished," and so I'm not quite sure it covers what Marshall had had done to the place. His parents, certainly, would never have recognized it. All the rooms were now painted starkly white. The fireplace in the living room, once the habitat of the great brass peacock, had been sealed up, the mantel above it removed. Track lights designed in Milan had replaced the rococo lamps. The few couches and chairs in the room were modern, leather, black, spare. A glass cabinet containing stereo equipment was along the same wall as a bar with four high stools of black tubular metal. Mounted but unframed paintings and drawings, most of the former in black and white, including a few entirely black Ad Reinhardt canvases, and all of them originals, were placed along the walls of the long hall leading into the living room. An enormous Jackson Pollock drip painting—it, too, in black and white—hung on the wall where the fireplace used to be and was the only such decoration in this austere room.

I wondered when modern art had become an interest of Marshall's, and one evening I asked him. He smiled and asked if I remembered the famous John Adams remark about his studying politics and war so that his sons would have the liberty to study mathematics and philosophy so that their sons could study painting, poetry, music, and the rest of it. I did indeed remember it, but why did he ask?

"Well," he said, "in the Wexler family, if my father were still alive, he would have been able to say, 'I collect junk so that my son may put junk, at great expense, on his walls.' "

I didn't attend probably even a third of the various parties, fundraisers, and quasi-public meetings that took place at Marshall's apartment after he became publisher and editor-in-chief of *New Horizon,* though his secretary must have called to invite me to most of them.

But the roster of celebrities I saw there—especially during the trial of the Chicago Seven, when the spotlight of radical political action was on our city—was fairly impressive. The attorney William Kunstler, glasses atop his head, long unruly sideburns framing his large face, was a regular during the trial. The cartoonist Jules Feiffer was there on several different evenings. Under the Jackson Pollock one night, Jane Fonda and Susan Sontag compared notes on Hanoi. I heard James Baldwin, recently returned from Turkey, proclaiming, with Marshall's canapés in his mouth and a scotch and cigarette in his hand, that America was a soulless lost country. "Don't mind Jimmy," a famously malicious homosexual novelist said to me, "he just wants to be Martin Luther Queen." On another night, Leonard Bernstein, trailing cigarette ash on Marshall's parquet floor, told Tom Hayden and Huey Newton, in a hoarse and exuberant voice, that for the first time in his life the country seemed to him on the edge of real revolution. At a party for Cesar Chavez, a dozen or so dancers from the New York City Ballet, in town that week for three performances at the Auditorium, leavened a group of middle-aged labor leaders, civil-rights activists, and the usual crowd of liberal women, free-loaders, and hangers-on. On another night, an albino-like Andy Warhol offered me $400 for my wristwatch, an old Longines that had belonged to my father.

Marshall Wexler, who not so long before had asked if as a teacher I encouraged originality, moved easily among these people. Through his own magazine and through his pieces elsewhere—the *New York Review of Books, Ramparts,* the *New Statesman*—he had begun to be a mildly famous figure in his own right.

Over the seven-year life of *New Horizon,* my former student instructed the leaders of the civil-rights movement that in America morality grew out of the barrel of a gun; approved the race riots in Chicago, Detroit, and Newark as acts of racial justice and on the admittedly Leninist grounds that the worse was the better; wrote a pamphlet on nuclear weapons that ended in a call for unilateral disarmament; accused Lyndon Johnson of war crimes and asked for his imprisonment; perversely agreed with the domino theory in South-east Asia but maintained that we ought to be prepared to let the Communists have Thailand; demanded reparations for every black in the United States; and much else besides.

Marshall later stitched these various pieces together, with a lengthy introductory chapter and an epilogue, into a book he titled *The Culture of Disaffection*, which turned out to be a modest best-seller. In it I am acknowledged as one of the "formative influences" on his thought, though so far as I know I influenced nothing. I found his left-wing views less interesting than the audaciousness with which he put them forth. Although I am by trade a political philosopher and a teacher of government, truth to tell, in my view since the fourth century B.C.E. in Athens things have been pretty much downhill all the way. Rightly or wrongly, I like to think of myself as viewing politics from above the rather cramped perspective of right- and left-wing.

The Culture of Disaffection began a strong publicity run for Marshall. It was the middle 1970's, when authors filled the chairs on all the talk shows; and Marshall turned out to be very effective on television. A local station offered him a thrice-weekly editorial spot on its five o'clock news. He was asked quite often to appear on one or the other of the Sunday morning network political discussion shows. His plain style, clear point of view, and willingness to make extreme statements served him well on television. Whenever a boldly leftist opinion was needed, Marshall Wexler could be relied upon to supply it without either hesitation or qualification.

It was a busy life, and no one ever commented on Marshall's living it without a wife, or even a regular woman during these years. It occurred to me once to consider that perhaps he was homosexual, but there was no evidence of that, either. I thought of him as too interested in his career to have much time for sex, art, or anything else.

Well, I had to think otherwise when my wife called my attention to an item in the Tempo section of the *Tribune*. Marshall Wexler was engaged to Renee Phillips, a tall, elegant black anchorwoman on the Chicago ABC affiliate. She had been a civil-rights worker, one of the first females admitted to Yale, and a woman obviously on her way up in the world. Among people who worked with her in Chicago, I later learned, she was known as the Media Medea. For Renee Phillips, Chicago would be no more than a stopover en route to a key job on network television in New York or Washington.

The next day I was at the State of Illinois Building, in the Loop, to renew my driver's license. Standing in the long line of people awaiting an eye test, I was tapped on the shoulder by Morrie Mutchnik. Excusing himself, he asked if we hadn't met some place before. He apologized for not remembering my name. He was unforgettable, done up today in lime trousers, a black shirt open three buttons down from the neck, showing an ornate mezuzah on the matted black and gray hair of his chest, and a peach-colored jacket. On his thick and hairy wrist he wore a large but wafer-thin gold watch with a black face. I reminded him we had met at the Wexler apartment several years back.

"Refresh my memory," he said. "Tell me again. What's your connection?"

I reminded him that I was a former teacher of Marshall Wexler's and he arched an eyebrow over his black-rimmed glasses.

"Ah," he said, "Ma-shul. I see he is about to wed, or so the papers say. Do you know the broad, by any chance? I've only seen her on television. Cold as ice she looks to me. I assume," he added, with the heavy smile of a man not accustomed to irony, "that she's not Jewish."

I asked if he had been following Marshall's career.

"Yeah," he said. "I see him on the television. I'm even a charter subscriber to his magazine, which if you ask me is a real piece of crap, but from a professional point of view nicely done, if you know what I mean."

I recalled that he was himself the publisher of a magazine.

"You don't suppose he believes all that *meshugass* he writes and publishes, do you?"

He didn't wait for my answer.

"I can't believe that Max Wexler's kid would be that dumb. His old man knew the score when he was seventeen. I think this kid knows it, too. He can't believe any of this political horseshit. He may think he believes it, but not very deep down he's gotta know it's a hustle."

"You think he's that cynical?"

"What's cynical got to do with it? I think this kid is so hungry for power he can taste it. He's got a big appetite and he's doing the best he can to feed it is all. Nothing cynical about that."

"What do you suppose he wants?"

"Look, professor," he said, pronouncing "professor" with an inflection better suited to the word dummy or schmuck, "this is a kid who's burning up with ambition. He probably goes to sleep at night dreaming of someday masterminding somebody's campaign for the presidency, so that he can be Harry Hopkins or what's that guy's name with Woodrow Wilson? House. Colonel House. He dreams about it and just as he's about to enter the Oval Office to tell the President what to do he has to get up and change the sheets. I could be wrong about this, but I don't think so. Our Ma-shul is a kid on fire, if you want my opinion."

For Morrie Mutchnik there was no great complication. Marshall Wexler was an operator, pure and simple, in a world of operators neither pure nor simple. The only real question was how successful was the operation. By Mutchnik's standard Marshall was doing pretty damn well. But Mutsy Mutchnik's standard was not mine. In my world—academic, with pretensions to being philosophical—questions of belief and intention entered in, causing things to become complicated rather quickly. Did Marshall believe in all that *meshugass*? Did it matter? The more I thought about it the more it became evident that the question of what, precisely, Marshall believed was less interesting than whether he believed in anything at all.

Whether Marshall was a man of the Left or of the Right didn't seem important to me. What did was the utter authority with which he was able to write about matters—nuclear weapons, foreign policy, welfare programs, race—on which he could have known no more than what he had read. Marshall was smart and quick, with a genuine talent for lucid expression. But lots of people had such gifts. None that I knew had Marshall's authority, his easy confidence in his own rightness, in his own ability to see through the tangle of complexity of any subject and emerge with the only sensible, intelligent, and correct view possible—his.

Any subject, that is, but the Jews. Until now, so far as I knew, Marshall had never written about things Jewish. So far as I knew, too, he had no special education or training beyond what I myself had had: rudimentary Hebrew-school instruction ending at bar mitzvah. But now he decided that United States policy toward Israel was a great and heinous mistake, the "linchpin," as he described it, in a vast American structure of disaster around the world. He attacked it with the full force of the not inconsiderable talent at his command. He attacked it, moreover, as a Jew speaking chiefly to Jews. No, that is not quite right: he attacked it as a Jew speaking for the Jews. All of us.

In writing about Israel and U.S. foreign policy, both in his own magazine and elsewhere, Marshall had somehow appropriated the Holocaust—made it into an event whose true meaning had eluded everyone else and whose enormity only he was large-hearted enough to comprehend. If you didn't know who Marshall Wexler was and where he came from, and you read him on the Israeli failure to understand the "lesson" (as he called it) of the Holocaust, you would have thought Marshall was himself a survivor of Dachau or Auschwitz. A note of high moralism crept into the writing. When Marshall wrote about the Jews, he slipped easily into the first-person plural. Whenever he used that "we," speaking of all Jews, I found myself shuddering slightly. Now, for the first time, Marshall became something more than a talented young man who appeared to be winning through. No, now I found Marshall Wexler slightly repulsive.

I remembered his request, when he first began *New Horizon,* that I tell him from time to time how he was doing, and I decided to take him up on it. I called to suggest lunch at the Quadrangle Club. He asked if I minded the Standard Club instead, since his schedule was a bit crowded just now and he would be grateful not to have to make the trip out to Hyde Park.

Seated in the men's grill, after we had ordered our lunch, I began by congratulating him on his engagement.

"She's an interesting woman, Renee," he said. "Not quite what my father would have had in mind for a daughter-in-law, I suspect."

"As we say in psychoanalysis," I said, "say a little more please."

"My father never used any other word than *shvartze*. My marriage would have been a real test for him."

"Would he have passed it?"

"Probably, my guess is. He wouldn't have done anything to lose his son. You know, Ben," he said with a smile, "in me you see a perfect case of a child who grew up with too much love in the home."

After the food arrived, Marshall asked what was on my mind.

"I'd like you to stop being Moses," I said.

"What's that supposed to mean?"

"You know," I said, "leader of all the Jews."

"What're you talking about?"

"I have to tell you, Marshall, it depresses me profoundly when you write as if you knew what was best for the Jews—all of them. There're lots of Jews out there, friend, and most of them don't share your views at all, myself included."

"It doesn't work?"

"It disgusts, if you want to know," I said, beginning to warm to the subject. "I find myself really offended by your moralizing about the Jews and instructing Israel to handle itself more like Marshall Wexler. I think you ought to lay off the Holocaust. It's just too serious for your kind of journalism. And I'd be obliged if you'd drop that goddamn 'we.' I'm no part of your 'we' and don't want to be, ever. I think you ought to knock it off—all of it."

"Ben," he said, his voice filled with conciliation, "what are we talking about here, the Jews or the first-person plural?"

"We're talking about you, Marshall. About the state of your beliefs, and how far you're ready to go to get what you want. What the hell do you want, Marshall?"

"I want to be a player, Ben. I want a seat at one of the main tables. Is that so much to ask?"

"And what'll you do if you get one?"

"I'll worry about it then. First let me get it."

I felt I had gone as far as I could. I had questioned his motives, which seemed to me going pretty far indeed, especially since I was his guest. There was no point in taking things a step further and telling him off—if in fact I hadn't already done so. Somehow we got through the rest of the lunch. When the waiter asked if we wanted coffee, Marshall looked at me and I read in that look that we would do better not to linger.

"Ben," Marshall said, shaking my hand as we stood outside the Standard Club, the racket of street repairs making conversation difficult, "I'm grateful for your candor. I'm not sure what I can do with it, but it's good to know that I can count on an old friend to tell me the truth as he sees it." He squeezed my hand a final time, released it, then turned back into the club.

If Marshall held a grudge, I never discovered it. Two weeks later I had a call from his secretary inviting me to yet another party at 3400 Lake Shore Drive, this one for Arthur Miller, who was having a play done in revival at the Goodman Theater. I decided not to go.

Then, some three weeks after, watching the ten o'clock Sunday-night news, I heard that Renee Phillips and her fiancé, driving back from Green Lake, Wisconsin, where they had spent the weekend, had been killed in an automobile accident. As reporters put the story together, Miss Phillips's black Porsche convertible apparently spun out of control, jumped the median on the expressway north of Milwaukee, and flew into the grill of a moving van headed in the opposite direction. Whirling police and ambulance lights flickered on the screen, which showed the gnarled black Porsche and beefy Wisconsin state troopers lifting two body bags into the back of an ambulance. "Miss Phillips," said the weekend anchorman, with great solemnity, "leaves the scene at the outset of a brilliant career."

Marshall received roughly five inches of obituary in the New York *Times,* chiefly given over to snippets from reviews of *The Culture of Disaffection.* There were no survivors, immediate or distant, and his estate was divided among various liberal good causes. The *New Horizon* struggled on for four or five issues, but without its owner's energy and ambition, it quietly folded. How far Marshall would have gone had he lived a full span of years, no one can say; and it's pointless to conjecture what he might have been like at seventy. When I think of him, of his talent and his desire, it all seems to me less sad than wasteful. Morrie Mutchnik was at least wrong about one thing: his descendants wouldn't have to pay rent to Max Wexler's descendants for his own ample corpse.

Paula, Dinky, and the Shark

■

The morning Paula Melnick read in the *Trib* about the murder of Jimmy Kogan—his body, riddled with bullets, found in the trunk of his own white Jaguar, the car left in the parking lot of the Edgebrook Lutheran Church—she was neither shocked nor even surprised, yet somehow sadder than she expected to be. The wonder was, she felt, that he had made it to the age of fifty-seven. To Paula, who had known him since childhood, he was always Jimmy Kogan. To the newspapers he was James ("The Shark") Kogan, generally described as the Mob's man in charge of gambling and prostitution in Chicago. It occurred to Paula that morning that Jimmy Kogan was one of the few Jewish boys she had grown up with who had gone into his father's business—and had not become, like most, a physician, lawyer, dentist, CPA (like David, her own husband), or professor—and had actually surpassed his father in the same line of work.

Paula (then Cohen) grew up three doors down from the Kogans on Lunt between Francisco and Sacramento. Lou Kogan, Jimmy's father, was notable among fathers on the block in never seeming to go to work. He played golf from April through October at Twin Orchards Country Club; from October through April, with occasional breaks for trips to Miami, Phoenix, or Palm Springs, he played high-stakes gin rummy with cronies at the Covenant Club in the

Loop. A small man (5′2″ or 5′3″), bald, with a carefully tended mustache, Lou Kogan was four or five inches shorter than his wife Mary, whose maiden name was Doyle and who was said to have been a dancer—a chorus girl, actually, one of the old Chez Paree Adorables—when young in the 1930s. She was still beautiful in her late forties, Mary Kogan, good-natured, kindly, yet somehow, Paula sensed, not very significant.

Lou Kogan smiled a lot, was always joking, but, owing perhaps to his reputation, there was something slightly menacing about him, or so it seemed to Paula. Whenever Paula saw Lou and Mary Kogan together, little Lou and his statuesque wife Mary, she, Paula, couldn't resist thinking about a dopey coin she had once seen, which on one side showed a small man in tails standing next to a much taller woman in an evening gown, and on its other side showed the same couple from the back but with the man's hand under the woman's skirt, resting on her exposed and well-shaped behind.

As for Lou Kogan's reputation, it began with his older brother Harry, who through the Prohibition years was a Bugsy Siegel lieutenant, a head-knocker, a real tough guy. "One of those guys who bends your knees—the wrong way," Paula's father had once put it. Lou was Harry's little brother, roughly ten years younger and someone Harry was supposed to have always looked after and to have doted upon. One of the stories about Lou Kogan was that, because of deals his brother had worked out during the War, he, Lou, was still collecting a dollar a month on every cigarette vending machine in the city of Chicago. "It adds up to a nice piece of change," Paula's father said, "a damn nice piece of change."

Maury Cohen, Paula's father, considered himself something of an expert on the subject of the Mob in Chicago. And with some reason. He owned two saloons, one in the Loop, the other on West Madison Street, and he had been dealing with the "boys," as he called them, for a great many years. From the Teamsters who delivered his beer to the dapper Sal Musalloni who sold him paper napkins, detergents, and his towel service, he had done business with the boys from way back when. He figured it must have cost him in the neighborhood of two to three hundred a month to use their various services, but then their services weren't entirely restricted to beer and napkins, either. When a greedy cop sent in a mature-looking girl for a drink and then pretended to nab Maury Cohen's bartender for serving a minor, or a health inspector put the screws on for more than the standard *schmear*, a call to the boys would quickly put things to rights. What over the years Maury Cohen had contributed to the boys added up to another damn nice piece of change. But if you wanted to do business in Chicago, especially in the liquor business, you really didn't have much choice.

Paula loved her father, who, as far back as she could remember, always treated her as if she had good sense and was able to grasp anything he told her. Once, when she was fourteen, he told her he regretted that she wasn't a boy, because if she were she would have been a terrific businessman, a much better one, he thought, than her brother Jerome was ever likely to be. Paula and her father even looked alike, which was no bargain for her. Like her father, Paula was short and stocky—she would have to watch her weight all her life—with a slightly yellowish, not very good skin whose defects could not quite be covered up with make-up. Her hair was a color she used to describe as "dishwater brown," straight and rather thin, and as a girl she wore it in bangs over her somewhat too broad forehead. Her brother Jerry meanwhile had inherited their mother's dark good looks and slender frame. Paula felt that she could have put them to better use, but there was nothing to be done about it. One of the things Paula had learned from her father was to accept things as they were, play the hand dealt to you, take the game as it was.

And as it was, as near as Paula could then determine, it was a pretty good game, all things considered. Her daddy was rich, as the Gershwin song had it, and her ma was good lookin'. She was conscious of having a good mind, though conscious, too, that it was a pitilessly humorous one. At some point in life, Paula told herself the morning she read of Jimmy Kogan's death, recalling the youthful good looks of Jimmy and his sister Diane, a person realizes that it is better to have a strong clear mind like her own than it is to be beautiful, with natural elegance and physical ease. I am now fifty-five years old, Paula thought, looking down at her thick ankles and back at her heavy calves, and apparently I still haven't reached that point yet.

At a fairly early age—perhaps even before she was ten years old—Paula began to see things from a humorous standpoint. Perhaps this was owing to her being so plain looking, so that she could never regard herself as an object of romance, couldn't hope to please anyone through physical charms, couldn't in some sense take herself altogether seriously. Whatever the case, the comic element in life tended to shine forth before her. The whole dating bit, the dance of courtship that began late in grammar school, had from the start seemed to Paula chiefly funny, another occasion for laughter and irony. Although she didn't then know what the word irony meant, nor that it had already become her method for dealing with the world, she did know that it made other people, and especially men, uncomfortable. When she was a sophomore in high school, a pudgy and perspiring boy named Nathan Levin—when it came to dates, Paula didn't have much choice—attempted clumsily to remove her bra in the front seat of his father's Buick at a drive-in movie, she heard herself say, "Maybe you need testing for basic motor skills, Nathan." Less than a minute later, the poor flustered boy had started up his father's Roadmaster and was driving Paula home. Women, Paula learned, were supposed to appreciate humor—not initiate it.

Lou Kogan, who was no ironist, used to call Paula "Beautiful." "How are ya today, Beautiful?" he would say when she came over to visit his daughter Diane, known to everyone as "Dinky" because of her size—she was not quite five feet tall when an adult—and natural delicacy. The Kogans moved onto the block when Paula was eleven. She and Dinky Kogan were the same age; Jimmy Kogan was a year and a half older than his sister, the same age and grade in school as Paula's brother Jerry, though Jimmy Kogan and Jerry Cohen never became close friends in the way that Dinky and Paula did.

"How are ya, Beautiful?" Lou Kogan would say, when Dinky and Paula returned from school to do their homework together in Dinky's room. "And you, Princess," he would say, talking now to his daughter, "doesn't your old man deserve a kiss?" He was almost always at home, often sitting in the kitchen, or sometimes out on the front lawn of his ranch house, built of costly limestone on a triple lot, practicing his golf swing by hitting cotton or plastic golf balls. For a while Paula resented that "Beautiful" business; she had a fairly good idea of just how beautiful she was. "I'm all right," she would think to herself when he greeted her. "How are things with you, Pee Wee?" But then she decided not to take it personally. "Beautiful" was probably the way Lou Kogan addressed waitresses and secretaries and his manicurist. He no doubt thought it was charming. He was not a man other people were likely to correct—not on this point or any other. He was allowed to live comfortably with the delusion that he was a charmer.

Paula and Dinky and Jimmy were driven to grammar school and picked up afterward by a man Dinky called Uncle Mickey, though, as she explained to Paula, he really wasn't her uncle. He was a nice enough man, with unruly hair, missing two bottom front teeth, and in warmer weather, when he wore short-sleeve shirts, his right forearm showed a tattoo of a sword plunged into a heart surrounded by a wreath of tiny roses. Uncle Mickey drove them to school in an Oldsmobile, of which the Kogans had three, two Ninety-Eights and a white convertible for Mrs. Kogan. Once, when Jimmy was fifteen minutes late returning to the car after school, Uncle Mickey became very nervous, locking Paula and Dinky in the car and telling them not to open the doors or even the windows for anyone, no matter who. It turned out that Jimmy was being kept after school for some classroom mischief, and when he finally returned to the car Uncle Mickey was clearly enormously relieved. Uncle Mickey, as Paula's father would later tell her, was a bodyguard assigned to watch the Kogan kids.

Lunt, Coyle, Greenleaf, the shady streets west of California Avenue with their pleasant, often opulent homes, most of them built since the War, were inhabited by a number of families whose money came from odd, not always licit dealings. There were families such as the Coopermans, who lived directly across the street from the Cohens. Sam Cooperman was a liquor distributor, but he was said to have had powerful Canadian connections that paid off handsomely during Prohibition years. The Coopermans' son Arthur was a fat boy and a considerable sissy. There was Irv Singer, the bookie, whose daughter Sandy had had her nose, cheeks, and chin redone by a locally famous plastic surgeon named Brent (originally Brodsky). There was Bernie Becker, who had made a ton of money selling Buicks, then blew it all by buying prizefighters and getting in serious trouble by fixing fights, so that at one time both the boys and the FBI were in pursuit of him. There was Sid Goldin, the fix-it attorney, whose name was always popping up in Kup's column in the *Sun-Times* and who was into God alone knew what.

But even among these people the Kogans seemed pretty exotic to Paula. They took no part in the life of the neighborhood. The canasta games among the women, membership in Ner Tamid the conservative synagogue on Rosemont, the PTA meetings at Boone School, the Kogans had nothing to do with any of these things. Although Lou Kogan golfed at Twin Orchards Country Club, where Paula's parents were members, neither his wife nor kids ever spent any time there. Paula had no recollection of the Kogans ever entertaining or having cousins over for holidays or of hearing her friend Dinky mention visiting family or friends. Lou Kogan had his golf pals at Twin Orchards and his gin rummy cronies at the Covenant Club, and of course there was the mystery of his work, to which he seemed never to go and which seemed somehow to take care of itself. Friendly enough on the surface, the Kogans kept to themselves.

Lou Kogan had his own ideas about raising his children. He was very strict with his daughter. In high school Dinky was kept on a much tighter rein than all her other friends. She could have had a date every night of the week had Lou Kogan permitted it. But in fact she could not go out at night during the middle of the week past nine o'clock, could not go out on dates at all until her junior year, and then had to be home no later than eleven thirty, at which time her father or Uncle Mickey could dependably be found awaiting her, generally standing in one of the large living-room windows.

What made this complicated was that Dinky Kogan was one of the most sought-after girls in Senn High School. She was small, bosomy, large-eyed, with dark good looks, cute—immensely, intensely cute, which was, as Paula well remembered, the ideal of the day.

Paula, Dinky, and the Shark

Beyond this, Dinky seemed so nice, so genuinely good, which was to say kind, considerate, without snobbery or rivalry or meanness of any kind. Girls adored her, and she was asked to join the best clubs in the school. Boys were mad about her, attracted by her good looks, and further drawn in by her sweetness. Most boys felt protective about Dinky; Paula herself felt something of this same protectiveness when near her. Nothing bad, she could remember thinking, must be allowed to happen to Dinky.

Dinky did well enough in school, was appreciative of intelligence in others (she was a great audience for Paula's jokes and sharp comments), and not exactly unintelligent herself, but, Paula sensed, strangely incurious. Dinky seemed not much interested in penetrating beneath the surface of things. Perhaps this was owing to her being Lou Kogan's daughter. With such a father, who knew what prodding beneath the surface might turn up? Dinky, so far as Paula could make out, did not exactly fear her father, yet at the same time her obedience to him was complete. Lou Kogan believed, for instance, that college was no place for girls; and so Dinky did not go to college but never, at least in Paula's hearing, complained about it.

As strict as Lou Kogan was with his daughter, just that loose was he with his son. When Jimmy Kogan turned sixteen, his father gave him a brand-new Olds, a Delta 88 hardtop convertible with a lush two-tone blue and white paint job. Paula's brother Jerry told her that Jimmy Kogan drove out with friends to the cathouses of Kankakee and Braidwood, Illinois, on weekends. Jimmy always seemed to have plenty of money; he usually carried a couple of hundred dollars on him, which was a serious sum for a boy in his junior year in high school in 1951. There was a rumor that he played in a high-stakes poker game that met weekly in a suite at the Somerset Hotel on Argyle and Sheridan. There was an even better rumor—again reported to Paula by her brother—that once, in the Saxony Hotel in Miami Beach, for a thousand dollars put up by a few of his father's friends, Jimmy Kogan "mixed it up" (as Jerry put it) with two prostitutes while Lou Kogan's pals looked on. Were these stories true? Who knew? What Paula did know, from Dinky, was that Jimmy came and went as he pleased, keeping his own hours, doing much as he wished, living like the son of a powerful medieval baron, which, in a sense, was what he was.

Jimmy Kogan was not as good looking as his sister, but there was something very appealing about him, or so Paula felt. He had come into some of his mother's height, and was 5'10" or so, which was tall for a Kogan. He was dark, and had begun shaving every day by the age of fifteen. An out-of-the-ordinary quality of tidiness, even fastidiousness, was evident in his appearance. His pants were always freshly pressed—he never wore Levis or tan washpants like the other boys at school—his dark hair carefully brushed. He somehow managed always to look as if he had stepped out of a shower only a half hour or so before. His nails were manicured. He looked like neither his father nor his mother, neither Jewish nor gentile, though he had—Paula could think of no other way to describe them—very Jewish eyes.

Jimmy Kogan made quite good grades without ever appearing to study. Dinky claimed that she never saw him crack a book while at home. He appeared to manage his already fairly complicated young life with a nonchalant mastery. As Lou Kogan lived in the neighborhood without really having much to do with it, so Jimmy went to Senn High School without really having much to do with it. Sports, dating, and the rest of it seemed to hold no interest for him. He had considerable charm, of a salesmanly kind, which meant that he could make all but the most suspicious people like him; and doubtless he could have had his pick of the school's best clubs and fraternities if he had been interested. But, again, he simply wasn't interested. His range of operations was already much wider.

It wasn't easy to get anything like a clear reading on Dinky and Jimmy Kogan's feelings for each other. Dinky didn't talk all that much about her brother, at least not to Paula, though when she did mention him it was always respectfully, for she had been brought up to respect the men in her family. Paula doubted that Jimmy talked about Dinky to anyone. He tended to treat her, as everyone else did, protectively, even a in a proprietary way; after all, she was a Kogan woman, and as such part of the family holdings. Jimmy called his sister "Dinker," which no one else did and which must have been a childhood name; it implied an intimacy that was not otherwise permitted to show itself. Sometimes, when he didn't have business elsewhere, Jimmy gave his sister and Paula rides home from school in the hardtop Olds. He generally said little during the drive, and Dinky and Paula did all the talking.

The summer between their sophomore and junior years in high school, Paula and Dinky went out for an evening on the town, escorted by Jimmy Kogan, to celebrate Dinky's sixteenth birthday. Lou Kogan and his wife were away for a few days on business, and he had apparently told his son to show his sister a nice time on her birthday. Jimmy had himself just graduated from high school, and was going to the University of Michigan in the fall (where he dropped out after a year, considering it—no doubt rightly—a waste of his time).

They drove in Lou Kogan's midnight-blue Olds Ninety-Eight, Jimmy and Dinky up front, Paula alone in the back. The Edgewater Beach Hotel was still standing, marvellously impressive in its cream-colored stucco, lanterns hung out back for dancing under the stars. The night was warm, the sky clear. Dinky and Paula wore summer dresses and high heels. Jimmy wore white trousers and a powder blue blazer with a dark blue knit tie. A light breeze blew upon Paula sitting alone in the back of the cavernous Olds. The lights from oncoming cars gliding northward on the Outer Drive blinked beguilingly. Life, thought Paula, does have its lovely moments.

Jimmy began the evening by taking them to dinner at the Empire Room at the Palmer House. He had booked a table, but the maitre d', a man with black marcelled hair and a thin mustache in the French style, seemed to know him and didn't even bother to check his reservations book. After he had seated them at a very good table, Jimmy shook his hand into which, Paula noted, he slipped a ten-dollar bill. They ate pinkish prime rib and a light salad, and for dessert Jimmy had ordered baked Alaska in honor of Dinky's birthday. "Happy birthday, beautiful sister," he said when it arrived.

After dinner they walked over to The Blue Note, where they listened to a young Sarah Vaughan. Being underage, Paula and Dinky drank Cokes; Jimmy, who was also underage, nevertheless ordered a scotch and water, which he scarcely touched. Later they dropped into The Black Orchid, where a new, dazzlingly handsome singer named Harry Belafonte performed. Farther north on Rush Street, they stopped at Mister Kelly's, where they listened to a comedian whose name Paula could no longer remember.

What she did remember, most distinctly, was that back in the car—it was around one thirty in the morning—Jimmy said that he had to make a little pickup on Fulton Street. They drove into the dark Fulton Street neighborhood—it was one of the food marketing centers in town—past a great many loading docks and large doors bolted with weighty locks. Jimmy stopped the Olds at a dark corner. "Keep the doors locked," he said, as he left the car. "I'll be back in a minute." He climbed the stairs to the dock above which a sign read Pachetti Produce. From the back seat of the car, Paula could see him kick noisily at a steel-shuttered door. After a short while, it swung back, and a large black man with blood-shot eyes came out. He and Jimmy exchanged a few words. Then the black man went back, returning thirty or so seconds later with a paper bag, which he handed to Jimmy, who shook hands with him and then returned to the car.

Jimmy tossed the bag in the back seat, started the car, and turned it in the direction of the Drive. "Paula," he said, "do me a favor. There's some money in that bag. Count it and let me know how much you get." Paula removed eighteen packets of greasy bills from the bag, each packet bound by a rubber band, and in the glint of the street lights counted every one as the Olds whisked northward on the Drive toward home while a disc jockey named Jay Andres played light classics on the car radio. The total came to nine thousand dollars. When Paula reported this to Jimmy, he said merely, "Good. Thanks." It was quite a night.

It was on another Saturday night, two weeks later, when Paula went over to the Kogan house to borrow some tennis balls from Dinky, who was out for the evening with her parents, that she next saw Jimmy. He answered the door in a white terry-cloth robe and dark blue pajama bottoms held up by a drawstring at his small waist. His hair was still wet, though brushed back off his face. When Paula told him what she wanted, he invited her to come in while he looked around for a can of balls. She waited in the living room. It always seemed to her that there was something oddly unlived-in about the Kogans's house. The furniture always seemed too new, and there was usually nothing on the walls: no paintings, no prints, no family pictures. It was as if the family that owned the place hadn't yet moved in.

Jimmy returned with an unopened can of Wilson balls, which he handed over to Paula.

"Where're you playing?" he asked.

"Just at the park, Indian Boundary," she said. "Tomorrow morning, with Lenore Fink."

"It's a tough game, tennis, at least without lessons," he said. "Nobody ever learns to play it very well on their own."

And as they continued talking, Paula sensed from Jimmy Kogan's sudden interest in her that he was going to attempt to seduce her. She decided, on the spot, right then and there, that if he tried, she would let him. And he did try—and she let him.

It took place in the Kogans' basement, on a Naugahyde couch, among knotty-pine walls, with a slot machine over in a far corner. Paula regretted the heaviness of her legs. She felt slightly unclean next to Jimmy Kogan. The act itself seemed awkward and inelegant. She was glad it was over with quickly. Ah sweet mystery of life, she thought to herself, I still haven't found you. Jimmy Kogan's lean and hard body lay resting on top of hers, he breathing more heavily than she, finished before she had even begun. He acted grateful afterwards, and also a trifle guilty. Nothing was said about their ever going out together, or perhaps her traveling up to Ann Arbor to meet him for a weekend at college. Paula thought that maybe Jimmy was a little ashamed of himself, acting under the impulse of what the boys at school called horniness. After all, Lou Kogan's son ought to be able to do better than his little sister's girl friend—and, Paula would have been the first to say, her none-too-pretty girl friend.

If she was right about this, at least she didn't have to worry about his telling anyone about his easy conquest. Apparently he never did. Certainly, Dinky never mentioned it or acted any differently toward her. Three weeks later, Jimmy went off to college. Whenever Paula saw him afterwards, though he was friendly, he acted as if nothing had happened between them. Years later, after Paula herself had married, at a pre-nuptial dinner for her brother she felt herself inwardly blushing when her father, with a drink too many in him, said that he could remember worrying, when his daughter was sixteen, that she wasn't a virgin and that his son was. The line got a big laugh.

Paula and Dinky remained good friends through high school, even double-dating the night of the senior prom, when Dinky's father let her stay out until two o'clock in the morning. Since Lou Kogan didn't believe in girls going to college, Dinky, sadly but not grudgingly, stayed in Chicago, working as a bookkeeper for a cousin who sold uniforms to municipal employees—policemen, firemen, transit authority workers—on Roosevelt Road. Paula went to the University of Illinois, where she got her elementary schoolteacher's certificate and met her future husband. David Melnick was at Illinois to study accounting. He was a Phi Sig Delt, Paula an SDT. He was plumpish, wore glasses, was already beginning to lose his hair, but was solid, kind, with an appreciative sense of humor. David adored her, Paula felt it from the first. Here was a man she could trust, with whom she could say exactly what she thought, who didn't seem to mind the possibility that she just might be more intelligent than he.

Paula and David didn't marry until two years after his graduation. His family owned a neighborhood dry cleaners, and didn't do all that well, and David didn't want to start out married life taking help from Paula's parents. He passed his CPA exams the year after his graduation, the same year that Paula, who was a year behind him in school, graduated. She had begun teaching at Joyce Kilmer School, living at home, and the following year they married and moved into a one-bedroom apartment in Skokie.

Dinky Kogan had married two years before, the first of her three marriages, to a salesman ten years older named Herbie Miller. He was tall, good looking, and had the successful salesman's easy flow of cheerful talk. The wedding was a spectacular event. Dinner for four hundred and fifty at the Ambassador West. "Only a man who has no real friends could throw such a large wedding for his daughter," was Paula's father's comment. He and his wife were invited to the wedding and so was nearly everyone else on the block. Paula was one of the bride's maids.

"An extravaganza," said Paula, describing the Kogan wedding plans to her mother, "a true Cecil B. DeMille production. A twenty-two-piece orchestra has been hired; there'll be elaborate ice sculptures, an eight-course dinner, champagne fountains—the works."

What Paula chiefly remembered about the wedding was the noise. The clash of cutlery and the buzz of conversation with Lou Breese's orchestra going at it relentlessly while photographers hopped about crying for attention and smiles to get imperishable shots of each of the sixty tables as waiters dodged with heavily laden trays—all this made for an impressive din. Paula looked around the room to see if she could spot any famous gangsters. No shortage of suspicious-looking characters in the room, she thought, but the only one she could recognize was a man named Jake ("The Barber") Factor, who had supposedly once been kidnapped by a man named Roger Touhy, who went to prison for the alleged kidnapping and, not long after being paroled, was murdered in the Chicago streets. Jake the Barber, Paula thought, didn't look all that kidnappable. His nickname derived from the darkness of his beard, which had the texture of tree bark; he looked as if he could use a fresh shave every fifteen minutes or so.

Paula noted Jimmy Kogan, who was, like herself, a member of the wedding party. Her "deflowerer," as she jokingly thought of him, had grown thicker and come to look more authoritative over the past five years. He was, as always, cordial to her and, again as always, gave no hint of their fling in his family's finished basement. Even now Paula could not help asking why she had allowed herself that brief business with Jimmy Kogan when she had. She knew that some women were stimulated by worthlessness in men, but she also knew that she wasn't one of them; not she, who planned to marry an accountant. No, the more she thought about it, the more she felt that the attraction was danger. Jimmy Kogan, even as a kid of eighteen, lived close to danger. Paula would never forget that rumpled brown paper bag with its nine thousand dollars. What did the money come from? Gambling? Prostitution? Pay-offs of one sort or another? And why was it given to Jimmy Kogan? From whom did it come?

To whom was it going? Rich stuff, danger, and, Paula, that most commonsensical of young women, had to admit, sexy stuff, too. But an atmosphere of danger had its limitations. Living outside the law might make a man seem more interesting, but, if Lou Kogan was any example, it didn't much add to his refinement. The one moment from the wedding that Paula would never forget was when Dinky, looking even more beautiful than brides are supposed to look, in her dazzling wedding gown, approached her father, who was drinking with Jake the Barber at one of the three bars set up in the room for the wedding.

"Daddy," Dinky said, "I just wanted to thank you for making this, the happiest night of my life, possible. Thank you, Daddy—for everything."

"You better smile, baby," Lou Kogan said, a bit drunk, his hand on Jake the Barber's hulking shoulder, "you cost me a shit-load."

Herbie Miller, Dinky's husband, happened to be a drunk, a fact that he was able to keep hidden from Dinky throughout their court-ship and nearly the entire first year of their marriage. He was able to bring this off because he wasn't an everyday drinker but a man who went in for binges, taking off days at a time to devote to his drinking. Usually he did this under the guise of being on the road selling—Dinky wasn't one to question his whereabouts—but once he didn't show up at home for four straight days, when there had been no word about his having to leave town. Jimmy Kogan, at Dinky's urg-ing, found him, unconscious, with a roomful of empty bourbon bot-tles, at the Del Prado Hotel on the South Side. The Kogan family sent him to a sanitarium to dry out, put him in treatment, even at one point threatened to kill him if he didn't quit drinking (Mob therapy, Paula called it, when she later heard about it), but it was no go: a drunk remained a drunk, and an unfit husband for Lou Kogan's daughter. Dinky divorced Herbie Miller, charging mental cruelty, the same year that Paula graduated from the University of Illinois.

Larry Katz, Dinky's second husband, was in the advertising business. Dinky and Larry, Paula and David double-dated three or four times. He, too, was good looking, but small and dapper, a man who wore Italian loafers, smoked French cigarettes, and elegantly fingered a gold Dunhill lighter. Paula found him amusing, noted that he had no interest in boozing, and thought him dedicated to Dinky, which he was. The problem turned out to be that he was also dedicated to a number of other women. Three years into their marriage Dinky learned that Larry was a compulsive chaser. A girl who looked to be eighteen or nineteen, a secretary at Larry's office, showed up at their house in Lincolnwood one gray autumn afternoon to plead with Dinky to give Larry his freedom so that he could marry her. It was the first she had heard about her husband's needing his freedom; and soon she would discover that he had in any case been taking it without asking for years. Women began to call the house, ask for Larry, and when told he was not at home left no messages. Her brother once spotted him in a Loop restaurant with another woman, and when he reported it to Paula, she lied so that Jimmy wouldn't have him roughed up, and said that it was probably his, Larry's, cousin. Dinky never told her father or her brother about her husband's carryings on. She would have left him long before she did, which was after five years of marriage, but she had had two children with him—a boy Richard, a girl Karen—and tried to hold things together as long as she could. "I'd rather be married to a drunk," she once told Paula, "you get fewer late night phone calls."

Dinky was living alone with her two kids in the house in Lincolnwood when Lou Kogan, at seventy-two, died, alone, in bed watching television, of a heart attack. He was found the following morning by the maid, who let herself into the Lunt Avenue house at eight o'clock. Mary Kogan was in Phoenix, visiting her sister. Jimmy handled the funeral details. A small-type obituary appeared in the *Trib* and in the *Sun-Times*. Lou Kogan, unlike his son, was never considered newsworthy. Paula went to the funeral at Piser-Weinstein Chapel on Peterson Avenue. A rabbi, who never knew Lou Kogan, spoke of his love for his family and joked about his passion for golf. All quite hollow, Paula thought, from her seat six or seven rows behind Dinky and her children and Jimmy Kogan and his wife (the daughter of a lawyer with powerful First Ward connections) and their two daughters. As the rabbi rattled on about the importance of memory in reconciling us to death, Paula let her mind contemplate the cool injustice of the world. Her father was currently wandering the halls of the Northwest Home for the Jewish Aged with Alzheimer's disease, a contemporary with whom she and Dinky had gone to high school had recently died after a prolonged struggle with multiple sclerosis, her mother had been suffering for the past four years with shingles (not to speak of her diabetes)—and Lou Kogan, a man who so far as anyone knew never did anything for anyone, Lou Kogan gets to slip gently off while watching the "Johnny Carson Show." He got away with it one last time.

Dinky got away with nothing. Shortly after her third marriage, at forty-three, to a nice guy (at last) named Arnie Ashen, who was in the drapery business, she had her first mastectomy. She broke down when she told Paula about it, in Paula's kitchen, and Paula, holding her friend in her arms, wept, too. Poor Dinky, whom everyone wanted to protect but whom no one could—not from bad marriages, not from cancer, not from anything serious. She had her second mastectomy two years later, and cancer next showed up eighteen months after that in the form of leukemia. Along with other of Dinky's friends, Paula gave blood, when vast quantities of it were needed toward the end. Odd ties, thought Paula; she had now exchanged blood and semen with the Kogan family.

Paula and David went together to the funeral service for Dinky at Piser-Weinstein. But, it being a Wednesday and less than a month before tax-filing time, David returned to his office and Paula drove out alone to Westlawn Cemetery, following the small funeral procession in her car. There, under a grey Chicago sky, a rabbi intoning the Kaddish in a baritone voice with a European accent, Diane Kogan, forty-seven, mother of two, was slowly cranked down into the earth in a grave next to her father's. A cold March wind lashed Paula's face, and her tears felt as if they froze on her cheeks.

Family and friends were invited back to Dinky's mother's house after the funeral. Mary Kogan still lived in the ranch house on Lunt. After twenty-five years, the once-lovely old neighborhood looked much diminished. Many of the houses originally built on double and triple lots had sold off their extra land, and newer, less grand houses had been build next to them. The older houses seemed a touch shabby; on a number of them the trim on windows and doors needed paint; everywhere the landscaping seemed less luxurious. Two Filipino children emerged from the front door of the Georgian house Paula and her brother had grown up in. The Cooperman house, which had once seemed to Paula a mansion, with the land surrounding it having been sold off and built on, now seemed merely too big, even slightly vulgar.

The Kogan house, too, looked a little the worse for wear. Its limestone did not weather well, and the grey day didn't do much to bring out its highlights. Inside it had the same slightly unlived-in Kogan feel that Paula remembered from her girlhood. Dinky's son Richard, who was fourteen and wearing a mourner's black ribbon on the lapel of his grey suit, met Paula at the front door. She hugged the boy, kissing him lightly on the cheek. He told her that there was coffee and food set out in the dining room. Paula wasn't at all hungry. She wanted to wander off to Dinky's old room, where they used to do homework together, and made a mental note to do so before she left. Instead she walked down to the basement through the door off the kitchen. It was unchanged: the bar ("wet bar," they used to call it in the real-estate ads of the day) in one corner, the now almost antique slot machine in another corner, a table set up for a card game, a University of Michigan pennant in blue and gold on one wall, the old Naugahyde couch.

Paula heard footsteps on the stairs and looked up from her seat on the couch to see Jimmy Kogan walking down into the basement. She recognized him more from newspaper photographs and television news shots than from their days growing up together. It was no longer possible to discover the boy in the man. Jimmy had grown thicker, looked padded. He had more gravity than his father had had. He wore a black suit with a shirt with dark stripes and a black knit tie; as a member of the immediate family of the deceased, he, too, had a black ribbon on his lapel. Paula thought she detected something a bit hard around his mouth. He wore glasses, aviator type, slightly tinted, which made it difficult to look into his eyes. Those eyes, Paula knew, must have seen a lot. Had Jimmy Kogan ever ordered a man killed? Had he ever killed a man himself? In an unwelcome fugitive thought, it occurred to her that it would be much more interesting to sleep with him now than when they were both kids.

"Paula Cohen," he said, with a broad smile, "if it weren't for the solemnity of the occasion, I'd suggest a quickie."

"It couldn't be quicker than the last time," she answered, deciding on the spot not to be daunted by him. "And by the way, my married name is Melnick."

"Ah," he said, "you're cruel, Mrs. Melnick."

"It takes a shark to get a shark," she said.

"How about that 'shark' business. I bet all those years you had no idea you were living a few doors down from a shark."

"Listen, you could have done a lot worse. You could have been James 'Greasy Thumb' Kogan or James 'Teats' Kogan or who knows what else. Thank the Lord for small favors."

"How has life treated you, Paula?" he asked, an earnest note in his voice.

"Decently, I suppose. I'm happy in my marriage. I have two sons. I've not had anything besides the standard misfortune. It's been a quiet life, I guess, but I have no great complaints."

"We get the kind of life we choose," Jimmy said authoritatively.

"Really?" Paula said. "I'm not sure Dinky chose hers."

"I got news for you. Life is pretty much winners and losers, with a few people choosing not to play and so they get to watch the game from the sidelines, like yourself. But no matter which role you play, there's a price to pay, and everyone pays it, even eventually winners, now or later."

"And your life?" Paula asked. "Did you choose it?"

"I did," he said, "and young, though sometimes I think it chose me. Where my love of action came from I don't know. Probably from the same place that Dinky's lousy taste in husbands came from. Still, the action has given me what pleasure and success I have had in life, and it will no doubt bring me down in the end. All I know is that you have to roll the dice when you have 'em, or you get the hell away from the table. I've always preferred it at the table."

Paula thought but said nothing about the activities that had brought him to the table and kept him there. In the atmosphere in which they had been brought up, it wouldn't make much sense to drag in conventional morality anyway.

"The death of someone like my sister, who never harmed anyone, kind of makes you wonder who's calling the shots. But I'm conning you. I think I knew very early in life—a lot earlier than most people—that no one is calling them. It's all arbitrary. It's every man for himself, with real pity reserved for those suckers who think that the whole thing makes sense. It don't. You have my word on it."

"So what's the point of it?"

"Don't let it get you down, Paula, but there isn't any. There's only carrying on your business, doing what you do best, enjoying those things that give you pleasure, and waiting till the call comes telling you it's all over. Don't worry about that call, by the way. It'll come."

Years later, reading about Jimmy Kogan's body being found in the trunk of his car in the quiet suburb of Edgebrook, Paula recalled this, her final conversation with him, with great clarity. She wondered if, when his call came, Jimmy was as ready for it as, the day of his sister's funeral, he appeared to be. She wondered if he was able to face what must have been a gruesome death with courage. She wondered, too, if he was right in what he said about the real suckers in life being those who thought the world could be shown to make sense. His own death, given the way he lived, certainly made perfect sense. What didn't quite make sense was how desolate it left Paula Melnick.

Another Rare Visit with Noah Danzig

■

I am writing this with a five-for-a-dollar Bic ballpoint on lined notebook paper, both purchased for me in the hospital gift shop by a black orderly named André with a bebop walk and the hairdo known, I believe, as the Drippy. For someone who has always been quite sniffy about the materials of his craft—stationery by Balfour, pens by Mont Blanc—these are damned poor tools. But then I shouldn't be complaining. That the staff in the small psychiatric ward here at Louis A. Weiss Memorial Hospital allows me to have a pen or anything with a sharp point at all is a concession, a victory, a great leap forward in my recovery. Seven weeks ago, on the night I was dragged in here by the police, in a hammerlock, a cop's meaty hand over my mouth, through the emergency-room entrance on Clarendon Avenue, they made the mistake of leaving my watch on my wrist. When I woke from the first strong sedative, I smashed the crystal and tried to eat the glass; or so they tell me. I guess I broke down in a big way, really flipped, cracked up in italics.

Life's bitter little ironies, both my parents died at Louis A. Weiss Memorial. Louie Weiss was a big-time liquor distributor, from which, as we say in Chicago, you can draw your own conclusions. I can remember when the hospital was first built, on Marine Drive with views of the lake, in the 1950's. It seemed a grand place. Forgive the literary allusion, but whenever I thought of Louis A. Weiss Memorial Hospital I always remembered a passage from a Karl Shapiro poem which runs:

This is the Oxford of all sicknesses.
Kings have lain here and fabulous small Jews
And actresses whose legs were always news.

About the kings and actresses I am not prepared to say, but there was never, at least in the old days, a serious shortage of fabulous small Jews at Louis A. Weiss Memorial: little men with marcelled hair, manicures, and impressive cuff links. But the neighborhood changed. The new generation of well-to-do Jews moved out to the northern suburbs. Uptown, on the edge of which the hospital was situated, became Appalachian (or "billy," as we say in Chicago). Mexicans moved in along the streets west of Sheridan Road, Vietnamese took over Argyle Street, and Blacks were everywhere. The Jews once again became a minority, even at Louis A. Weiss, which used to seem for all intents and purposes a Jewish institution. As I roam these halls in my blue terry-cloth robe, now that I have been given the run of the floor, I occasionally come upon some old guy with a goatee in peach-colored slacks and a Madras jacket, looking slightly dazed, as if he had checked into a once grand hotel in Miami Beach—the Fontainebleau, say, or the Eden Roc—only to find that the action and the old clientele had gone elsewhere.

I am, as you may have gathered from the snippet of verse quoted above, a literary man. Specifically I am a literary biographer, or, more precisely, a biographer of writers. I have written studies of Alexander Herzen, the Goncourt Brothers, Bronson Alcott, and Louise Bogan. Secondary characters, I suppose most of them might be called. But then I have never thought of myself as writing about particular men and women so much as about particular instances of the old and unsolved problem of the relation between the writer and his writing, the manifold connections between life and work—and especially the almost inevitable clash between decent behavior and the production of stellar art, the choice that all writers at a certain level of seriousness seem sooner or later to have to make between greater imperfection of the life or of the work. As a biographer and literary man, this, for me, has been the all-absorbing, the only really interesting question.

I don't for a moment expect that you have read any of my little studies, all of which were brought out by university presses and are rather specialized. What you may have read, or at any rate heard about, is my essay on Noah Danzig. It ran about eighteen months ago in the *New Yorker*, at a length of some 80-odd columns, under the rubric "Reflections" and the title "Imperfection of the Life and the Work." Noah had been dead a little more than a year when it appeared. My editor at the *New Yorker*, a woman in her seventies who keeps two standard poodles in a one-bedroom apartment in the Village and has been working for more than thirty years on a translation of Prevost, when she called to inform me of the essay's acceptance said, in a sibilant whisper, "It's devastating, you know, absolutely devastating." She went on to remark that Noah Danzig's reputation would never survive my "little piece of handiwork." "You have quite finished him off," she hissed. "After your essay appears, he will be done for." I cannot say that I was displeased to hear her say it.

I first met the novelist Noah Danzig roughly twenty-six years ago, through the New York *Times*. I had written a few pieces for that newspaper's Sunday book-review section, and one day an editor there telephoned to ask, with some trepidation, if I would care to do an interview with Danzig. I say with some trepidation because a few months earlier the same editor had asked if I would care to do a similar piece on a Chicago poet for whom I hadn't the least regard. "No," I remembered replying, "but if she would care to do an interview with me, I suppose I would be willing to consider it."

But Noah Danzig was different. He was a writer I hugely, all but unstintingly, admired. Then on the edge of winning all the international recognition and prizes that would be his, he already had a select and intensely devoted following. A Noah Danzig novel had about it an unexplainable, quite magical feeling of intimacy. Its author seemed to be saying what you thought and felt, only better—more penetratingly, with fuller understanding, richer humor, much more elegantly formulated. Around this time, I recall, someone wrote a rather tender short story about two graduate students living together in Berkeley; at night they would get into bed and read Noah Danzig aloud to each other before making love. Their choice was meant to suggest their high intelligence and sensitivity, soulfulness, depth.

"Sure," I told the editor at the *Times Book Review,* "I wouldn't mind doing a piece on Noah Danzig. Fill me in on the details."

The editor obtained Noah's unlisted number in Chicago, and when I called we agreed to meet at the Whitehall Club in the Whitehall Hotel, just west of Michigan Avenue on Delaware. From gossip I had understood that Noah Danzig could be as touchy as a fresh burn, as suspicious as a rich widow, and as mean as a slum rat. He was at the time coming off a painful divorce, which couldn't have increased his cheerfulness. Everything I had heard about him warned me to tread lightly. He was said, moreover, truly to dislike giving interviews, but for some reason he agreed to make an exception in my case. (In my *New Yorker* essay I bring up Noah's tremendous hunger for attention of any kind, all pursued under the guise of despising the vulgar glare of publicity. He would turn up, for example, at some suburban department store to sign copies of a new novel long after he was beyond needing the money, or speak to thirty or so older Jewish women who had a reading group in Skokie. "A Rare Visit with Noah Danzig," the *Times Book Review* titled my piece; all told, as I note in my *New Yorker* essay, over the years there were to be no fewer than 235 such "rare visits" in print.) I was, then, a bit nervous about this meeting with a writer who somehow made it seem that he was a much-put-upon man trying to get a job of work done, and to whom I, in my immense admiration for him, did not want to seem just another of the world's many nuisances.

From scores of photographs of him that I had seen, Noah Danzig was unmistakably himself walking into the quiet lobby of the Whitehall. He was tall and sinewy, yet seemed somehow fragile. He had penetrating blue eyes, yet was otherwise dark. He was quite bald, yet, owing to the bushiness of his eyebrows, the thick black hair on the backs of his hands and wrists, and a beard that must have required shaving twice daily, he gave the impression of hairiness. Every feature of his face bore its own odd complexity. His scalp, for example, was furrowed and mottled. His eyes were hooded. One of his front teeth was slightly longer than the other. And Gogol would have greatly enjoyed describing his thin, high-bridged nose with its large and dark nostrils, faintly quivering, as if taking the scent of something vaguely disgusting. The general effect, which would intensify as he grew into old age, was like some prehistoric version of a Jewish eagle. It was a face that from every tissue and cell proclaimed: I am of abnormal sensitivity; I am long-suffering and great-souled; I am (to quote Henry James, whom Noah, by the way, never thought much of) "that queer monster, the artist, an obstinate finality, an inexhaustible sensibility."

Noah Danzig had a cold, and, as was plain from the expression on his face as he entered the lobby, he expected the world to be ready with plenty of Kleenex and sympathy. His great quivering, bony, black-holed nose was dark red at its tip. It was nearly the same color as the maroon of his tie and matching socks. He was wearing a checked suit, with sharply cut lapels and small, high pockets cut into the trousers. The effect was lavish but somehow resembled the combination of a best man at a lower-middle-class wedding and a racetrack tout. I walked up to introduce myself.

"As you can see," he said, "I have this lousy cold. I may have to break things off in the middle of lunch." He shook my hand absent-mindedly, rather weakly; no evidence on his part of enthusiasm or even mild curiosity. His cold seemed to absorb all his energy and interest. He was then in his mid-fifties, I in my early thirties.

Given this dreary beginning, the lunch itself went rather better than I expected. I told him right off that I greatly admired his novels, that they had the power of changing the way I looked at the world. When I mentioned other contemporary novelists, he was very forthcoming in his putdowns. The chunky Jewish novelist who threatened to bring about a revolution in the consciousness of our time was, according to Noah, a perfect little *clichémeister*. In answer to my query about two brothers who were critics and editors in New York, he replied, "Oh, you mean Frank and Jessie?" An ambitious Southern novelist he described as a discount-house Faulkner trying to live out a pathetic Scott Fitzgerald scenario. The young writer who had just produced an enormous *succès de scandale* with a book about masturbation was no more than "a bright boy" who at least in this case showed "hands-on experience." So it went. I set up the pins, Noah bowled 'em over.

Somehow, without his having to say so, it was understood that none of these harsh opinions was for publication. "We seem to have an immediate sense of *rappaport*," he joked, establishing our Jewish connection. "By keeping my mouth closed, by saying nothing, it looks like I may yet wind up winning the public-relations derby for novelists." I took this remark to have the collateral meaning that he rather counted on me not to write anything that would damage the general view of him as well above the petty traffic of literary reputation and interested only in the large questions of the human spirit.

As we were leaving the Whitehall, weaving our way across its crowded floor, Noah ran into a man he knew but who didn't seem to know him.

"You don't remember me?" he said, astonished. "We had dinner here, in this same room, with your daughter not more than six weeks ago." The man looked puzzled. "You've blocked it out," Noah said, laughing. "Amazing!"

Out on Delaware, walking toward Michigan, Noah explained that he had met the man at a party given by a couple connected with the Lyric Opera. "I have this weakness for people who speak lots of foreign languages," he said, "and this guy speaks four or five of them rather well. Anyhow, he tells me that his daughter, who's a senior at Radcliffe and a big admirer of mine, would love to meet me. So we set up a date for dinner for the three of us at the Whitehall. We're having drinks before dinner arrives, and he begins to tell me how interesting Shakespeare is in German—how much more interesting, in fact, than in English. He goes on and on about it. For fifteen, maybe twenty minutes worth. Finally, I'd had enough. 'Look,' I said to him. 'I'm sorry to have to say this with your daughter at the table, but I don't think I can take any more of this German-Jewish bullshit right now, so why don't you just knock it off?' "

"What did you do then? Walk out?"

"No," said Noah. "Why should I? He invites me to dinner, why should I leave just because he proves a bore? But I have to admit that what I said did put a bit of chill on the wine." He smiled his expansive, long-toothed smile.

I do not have a copy of the piece I wrote for the *Times Book Review*, but I recall it as being close to the kind of piece Noah Danzig might have written about himself, if he could have done so under a disguised name. It made him out to be an immensely winning man, charming and brilliant, a writer working quietly but persistently against the shoddy grain of his age, a soul struggling on behalf of all of us to rediscover the permanence of meaning in a world that has slipped its moorings—or some such overblown nonsense. The *Times* bought it, and I suppose a number of people who read it did, too.

The week after my elegant puffery appeared in print, Noah called to ask if I were free for dinner on Thursday, two nights hence. There was a Greek restaurant he was partial to, the Greek Islands it was called, and he had a friend, a woman, who, having read my piece, wanted to meet me. I said Thursday was fine.

"Do you mind dining Chicago style?" he asked.

"Chicago style?"

"At six o'clock," he said, a smile in his voice.

"Fine with me," I said. "I take it that it's bring your own sleeve-less undershirt and peach edition of the *Herald-Examiner*."

He laughed. I remember feeling gratified at being able to make Noah Danzig, himself no mean comedian, laugh.

I met Noah and his friend Sally Nussdorf in the dark and dinful Greek Islands.

"Oh," she said, putting out a hand, "I expected a much older man." Then she laughed. "God, what a line! From what terrible old movie do you suppose I picked it up?"

I liked her right off. She was dark, stocky, with fierce, almost savage, probably dyed red hair growing low on her forehead and the thick features of the Eastern European Jewish working class. To put it in Chicago parlance, if Sally had been a man, she would have played third base in softball and been a helluva handball player. Yet she carried herself as if she were a great beauty. And, strange to report, before long one began to take her at her own valuation, at least while the lights were down and the room shadowy. Sally was able to bring this off, I decided, through sheer energy and intellectual vivacity.

When the waiter brought our steaming food—thick rib lamb chops for Sally, an enormous plate of roast chicken for Noah, an impressive shish kebab for me—Noah, surveying all this grub, remarked, "They certainly don't spare the horses here."

"Dear me," Sally said, "let's hope they do."

Perhaps I was obtuse, but it was not immediately clear to me that she and Noah were lovers. I am still not certain that during this time they were. He treated her with kindly good humor, but also with a certain careful distance. Although Sally was nearer my own age than Noah's, there was, I sensed, no attempt at matchmaking on anyone's part. It was, moreover, plain that she adored him. How he felt about her was what was difficult to fathom. As I subsequently learned, they had indeed once been lovers, though over the past three years Sally Nussdorf had had bad bouts of cancer of the breast and of the cervix.

One of the recurring complaints made by critics of Noah Danzig's fiction was that he wasn't very good with women characters. Here the work and the life fused nicely. It wasn't that he didn't care. He was sexually prideful. He once told me that a young lesbian approached him to propose that he father the child she and her lover wanted to raise, the two having decided they admired his genetic endowment. Another time he mentioned that his physician told him his prostate was in remarkably good repair for a man of fifty-seven. Fame, especially artistic fame, can be a splendid aphrodisiac, and Noah seemed to want to take advantage of his resources in this line whenever possible. But I was often surprised to discover how ultimately unambitious he was on this front, despite a persistent flirtatiousness. He just didn't seem to get, at least in my view, dollar value. His fame ought to have brought him dazzling and fascinating women, but among the seven or eight he coupled with during the time I knew him, all had rather emphatic flaws: they were hopelessly neurotic or shy or witless or idiotically subservient to him. He seemed to be searching for uncritical adoration, but was unable to find even that. No wonder Noah Danzig couldn't create convincing women— he knew so few.

But I wasn't interested in Noah because of his power or ineptness with women. I was interested in him because in those days I thought him a great writer—easily the best writer of his day in the most important literary form of the century. All the heroes of his novels were plainly himself, got up in various wigs, false noses and glasses, taped-on mustaches, and other easily penetrated disguises; and people who knew Noah from the old days claimed they could point out a real-life counterpart for nearly every one of his subordinate characters: the smarmy lawyer of *Tigerman's Fallacy* was based on a local show-business lawyer who had his office at One North LaSalle Street; the emasculating blonde in *Lapidus & Sons* was in fact married to an administrator at Northwestern University; the corrupt cop in *Mr. Horowitz Takes a Holiday* was someone he was later to introduce me to; and so forth. And if he invented no characters, his plots, where they could be said to exist at all, were absurd. Yet despite all this, there was an extraordinary virtuosity in his fiction. A virtuoso, I had come to conclude, is what Noah Danzig really was, a kind of Jascha Heifetz of literature. When one went to hear Heifetz play Beethoven, after all, it was more for the Heifetz than for the Beethoven. Similarly, one read a Danzig novel less for the normal pleasures of fiction than to watch Noah perform on the page.

His greatest invention was of course the character of Noah Danzig, amusing, sensitive, comic, gallant, questing, self-abasing, deep, charming, generous, bumbling, and by the end of each novel somehow a little wiser than when he set out. It was through this character, putatively the author himself, that Noah was able to develop the intimacy with his readers that his fiction seemed so often to call forth. Like the writer famously referred to in *The Catcher in the Rye,* Noah Danzig established himself as someone you wished to telephone after finishing one of his books.

Now, in my case, there was the added pleasure that Noah Danzig began frequently to telephone me. I lived in Hyde Park in those days, he on Cedar, off Rush Street. He would pick me up in the afternoons—he wrote in the mornings, as I did, too—and we would tool around town in his powder-blue, humpbacked Volvo, visiting the haunts of his boyhood and young manhood. Despite what at times seemed his world-weariness, a large part of him remained a Chicago wiseguy, the drugstore cowboy from Marshall High School. This part could emerge at any time. Once, while we were riding down from his apartment, the elevator stopped for a young man with shoulder-length black hair, dark beard, and dark eyes. "Ah, Rasputin," said Noah, who clearly had never seen him before, "what do you hear from the Tsarina?" Another time, driving along in the Volvo near Maxwell Street, he honked at a young black boy on a bike who refused to leave the middle of the street; he honked again, then a third and a fourth time. When the boy finally pulled over, Noah, rolling down his window, called out, "What's a matter, son? Don'tcha believe in death?" I remember asking him if he wanted to go with me to see an Ingmar Bergman film. "No thanks, kid," he said, "I prefer my Kierkegaard straight." At the Art Institute, passing a large painting of Judith carrying the severed head of the Assyrian general Holofernes, he stopped, pointed didactically, and looking at me with sternness said, "Let that be a lesson to you, son. Don't ever screw around with a Jewish girl."

Not everything was jokey. Noah could be very touching about old friends who had been taken out of the game by death. (I later came to think that the only way to earn his permanent regard was to die, rather a high price to pay.) He could cut through much non-sense with admirable economy. I once told him about some outrageous act on the part of a writer we both knew, and remarked that such behavior bespoke an astonishing insecurity. "Why say 'insecurity'?" he replied. "Why not choose a good old-fashioned word like 'cowardice' or 'swinishness'? 'Insecurity' implies that such crummy behavior has an excuse, when it really doesn't. Let us call a spade a spade, a schmuck a schmuck." One windy afternoon we were walking along the Grant Park side of Michigan Avenue when Noah told me, quite without provocation or even transition, that he regretted not having put more time and energy into his private life—he had

had two failed marriages—into family and friendships, but he had early learned that such time and energy as were available to him were entirely consumed by the work on his novels. I felt honored to hear that confession.

Around this time Noah began reading to me from *Hochfelder's Revenge,* his novel then in progress. Usually he would do so at dusk, seated on a green leather couch before the windows in the small living room of his Cedar Street apartment. The crepuscular light streamed over his shoulder, his half-glasses rested on his complicated nose ("one of the chosen noses," he called it), his face was intensely, even beautifully, concentrated on the typescript pages in his long and bony fingers. The best readers not only see but hear the words, said Robert Frost, and so, too, naturally, do the best writers. Part of Noah's magic was that you couldn't read him without also hearing him, even had you never met him, so distinct was the sound of his prose.

I was much impressed by the patience with which he worked on this book, adding and throwing out large chunks. Here was the serious care of the genuine artist, tireless at getting things exactly right. As I sat there, drinking in Noah's well-made sentences, hilarious physical descriptions, happy formulations of subtle emotional states, I again felt honored—honored and privileged to be in this room listening to this man. How was it that Baudelaire described his relationship with Delacroix: respect on my side, kindness on his? Now, when I read that I feel that only a young man as drunk on literature as I could have been so stupid.

We were sitting at Gene & Georgetti's, a locally famous steak joint on Franklin Street, amid the tumult of lawyers, commodities-market guys, and ad-agency characters dining, in high Chicago fashion, on red meat in the company of tan women. Neither Noah nor I had a tan woman, but two very serious planks of medium-rare strip steak lay on our plates. We were chatting amiably, speculating on the spiritual lives of the people sitting near us. At one point a dark and heavyset man, who looked as if he had to shave every portion of his face but his teeth and eyeballs, walked past gripping the arm of a rather striking redhead.

"Women," said Noah, his mouth filled with steak, "are amazing. They will do anything. You saw that guy who just walked out? If I were a woman, I'd as lief lie down with a grizzly bear."

As we carved and chewed away at our steaks, I mentioned that I had run into Sally Nussdorf at Marshall Field's earlier in the week.

"Ah," said Noah, extracting a metal toothpick from a small leather packet, and, covering his mouth with his left hand, digging away at some bit of steak. "Ah, Sally, the working-class queen."

I said that I liked her. She seemed to me full of wit and energy.

"And depression," Noah added. He went on to tell me that Sally had apparently expected him to marry her, which he thought was quite nuts. Everything in the air nowadays worked against marriage, women had come unhinged, sex was hanging everywhere, like salamis in a delicatessen, a man had to be bonkers even to consider marrying. "Besides," he said, a cold glint in his eye, "I would never marry a woman who has lived so near death."

I puzzled over that remark for a long while afterward.

I don't want to give the impression that Noah Danzig and I were constant companions. When he was in Chicago I usually saw him once, sometimes twice a week. But there were long stretches when he was out of the country. His growing fame regularly brought him invitations to spend three or four weeks in this cultural institute in Seville, or that center in Jerusalem, or another institute in Bellagio, or he would be off to a conference on modern literature in Kyoto, or be part of a writers' delegation to the Soviet Union. In all these places he offered minor variations on the same theme—that the artist in modern society had been made into an utterly dispensable figure, irrelevant, a mere clown and jester, of no importance, with no place to rest his head. I once heard him do this turn in Chicago, at a luncheon, to which he managed to have me invited, for bankers, real-estate developers, and high-level corporation executives. Noah was picked up in a limousine, fed smoked salmon and filet mignon, and paid a speaker's fee of five grand, for which he told his audience that in a bustling commercial city such as Chicago the artist, yea, verily, had no place to rest his head. Afterward, Noah rested his, and

I mine alongside his, on the soft leather seats of the Mercedes limo that took us back to his apartment.

Like a number of contemporary writers I have known, Noah was not much for correspondence. When he was abroad, I would occasionally bat off a note to him containing a bit of literary gossip or comedy about our fair city. Sometimes, if I read something that really impressed me, I would make mention of it or, if it were brief, send along a copy with my letter. In this line I recall sending him a remarkable memoir by Nathan Asch about Asch's painful relationship with his father, the international best-selling novelist Sholem Asch. It was an immensely moving, I thought quite wrenching piece of writing about the unmitigable absence of understanding, despite much love, between a father and son, and the heavy psychological burden of growing up under a famous father. Sadder still, I learned that Nathan Asch had died shortly after this memoir was published—making it seem as if he had had to fire off this last shot, bellow this final *cri de coeur*, before departing the earth.

Perhaps it was a mistake to send the memoir to Noah. He had, I knew, two daughters from a marriage made in his twenties. These girls had grown up in Los Angeles with their mother, who had soon remarried. My sense was that Noah did not see much of his daughters, both of whom were past thirty, not now, not ever. Between them they had four children of their own, which made Noah a grandfather, a *zaydeh*. Yet the idea must have been slightly appalling to him. No one seemed less grandfatherly than Noah, who carried himself as if he were a perpetual forty-two, old enough to be well seasoned but not yet fatigued.

Perhaps, though, the Nathan Asch memoir rubbed his own sense of guilt as a failed Jewish father. In any case, he wrote back that he quite understood the motives and situation of the old man, while the son, Nathan, was like everyone else nowadays—a man with a case. Specifically, Nathan Asch wished to take his case, which was against his father, who after all only wanted to get his work done as best he was able, into that most severe of tribunals, children's court, where all parents are adjudged guilty and damned. No, Noah's heart went out to Sholem Asch, who at least didn't write essays about what a miserable ingrate his son was. The son's whining, Noah thought, though impressive, was far from original.

I thought Noah's reading of this memoir itself highly original, especially given his own long-standing interest in family life. In his early novels, Noah wrote about these half-savage Chicago Jewish families, coarsened by corruption, driven mad by money, sprung loose by pretension and foul ideas in later generations, but who through it all retained some rugged, unbreakable link with family feeling, which ran so deep among some of them that it gave them their own, almost primordial depth and density. They knew their duty; they knew why they were here; they knew, despite a zillion distractions, what life was supposed to be about. But did their creator? Did Noah Danzig, pen out of his hand, know what life was supposed to be about?

How could he not have known and yet have written so convincingly about those who did? It seemed a naive question to ask. Yet the more I thought about Noah, the more insistent it became. It remained the chief question about Tolstoy, who wrote so beautifully about the sweetness of family life among the Rostovs and the Levins, all the while driving everyone in his own family at Yasnaya Polyana nuts with his harebrained notions of education, property, chastity, diet. At a vastly reduced level, there was Noah, writing so touchingly about West Side Chicago paterfamiliases' love for their undeserving children, while this same man, a *zaydeh* no less, makes a jackass out of himself trying to get the attention of a woman thirty years younger than he—with knockout legs—on a Michigan Avenue bus.

For a long while I fought the idea that it was all a fake, a trick, a piece of hypocrisy available only to artists. I worked hard to square this central contradiction. A Noah Danzig, I would tell myself, while portraying true family feeling was in fact expressing his own deep inward yearning. To make such yearnings real was one of the things that artists did; what they couldn't have, they could at least on paper create. Perhaps if they had such things in their own lives, there would be no need to create them in the first place. Art grew out of deprivation, which was itself one of the miracles of art. Or so I told myself. What a chump!

A chump I should have been perfectly content to remain, discovering subtler and subtler causes for the central contradictions between the behavior and ideals of certain artists, espousing evermore elaborate ideas of artistic creation, had not I, some sixteen or so months later, in the finished pages of *Hochfelder's Revenge,* come across a man of apparently endless ambition eating very rare steak with his bare hands in a Chicago steak joint. Permit me to quote from the pages of that novel:

> His chin awash in grease from steak and sauteed mushrooms, bits of red meat adhering to the spaces between his small, sharp front teeth, Feldman, unsatiated still, now picked up the large T-shaped bone with both fists and began to gnaw. He gave off a low hum as he chomped, moist fists adapting their grasp as if playing some primitive, slightly bloody harmonica. His upper lip glistened with juice, his small teeth working systematically up and down, intent, it would appear, on marrow. Feldman was pure carnivore, a meat-eater and, one was prepared to believe, a man-eater, too. One felt one was watching a scene from a film entitled *One Million B.C.* done in modern dress; one felt, even so late in the game, rather sorry for the poor dead steer; one felt, finally, here was a dangerous young beast, determined to devour whatever lay astride his path.

Funny, somehow Noah had neglected to read that passage to me in the dusk at his Cedar Street apartment. Could it have anything to do with the fact that I was, as I learned the further I got into the novel, meant to be the model for Morty Feldman? My own teeth, to be sure, are large and rather square, and I do not pick up steak bones in public places; but there were other identifying marks, too minute, boring, unmistakable, and painful to go into here, all pointing to a portrait of me as something of an updated Sammy Glick, a man who, taking no prisoners, leaving no hostages to sentiment, will do anything to get ahead. And by anything let me hasten to mention that Noah included walking away from a vivacious working-class woman who has had a horrendous bout with cancer after he—not Noah Danzig, you understand, but this lowlife Morty Feldman—has been her lover, used her badly, and then has refused to make any permanent connection with her. In the signed copy of *Hochfelder's Revenge* that Noah sent to me, he wrote, "Not everything in this book is, I know, going to be to your liking, but please believe it is the best that an old general practitioner can do."

Maybe twenty or thirty people in the world would ever know that I was the model for Morty Feldman in *Hochfelder's Revenge*. True, to me these were twenty or thirty important people, but I could get over that. What I couldn't get over so easily was the sense of betrayal. A wretched little hustler, a blind fool on the make, a full-out creep, was this what Noah Danzig thought of me during the many (I had until now thought) comradely afternoons we had spent in each other's company? Or was I ever in his company in any real sense at all?

Why did Noah do it? He worked from life, everyone knew that about him, but I had supposed I would be an exception, a friend he wouldn't use for fodder. I believed in the authenticity of his intimacy; I believed our friendship meant enough to him not to sacrifice it so cheaply on a secondary character in a less than first-rate novel. I was wrong to believe all these things. You can't play with a dangerous cat and expect to come away unscathed.

Noah was away when *Hochfelder's Revenge* appeared—in the south of France, if memory serves, living in the house of a Chicago wholesale car leaser—and I was just as glad he was and I didn't have to worry about running into him. Instead I wrote a carefully composed, rather brief letter, telling him how disappointed I was to find myself a particularly unpleasant character in one of his novels, that I thought our friendship might have meant more than it apparently did to him, and that I found the entire business depressing in the extreme. Some four weeks later I received a postcard from France telling me not to take it so hard and that, who knew, somewhere down the road I might have a chance to get my own back at him, signed "As ever—Noah."

We never met again. I watched his career henceforth from far back in the stands, not wishing him one bit well. In his sixties, Noah continued to garner prizes, both here and in Europe, so many that he began to seem a bit posthumous, even though he continued to produce at the same slow and steady rate of a novel every four or five years. When a new book appeared, front pages of the book reviews were set aside and reviewers lined up to praise him. There was a continuing flow of "rare" visits by journalists. Although his novels never became quite booming best-sellers—they were too cerebral, a touch too difficult and self-indulgent for that—they were often taught in universities and he was widely translated. Money, I assume, was never a serious problem.

And yet despite what appeared to be the even flow of Noah Danzig's success—the perfect portrait of the author ascending gracefully into old age and mature wisdom—one sensed that something was beginning to go slightly wrong. The praise was still there, but it began to feel rather perfunctory. When younger critics wrote about the current literary scene, the name Noah Danzig no longer came up. He had ceased to speak to the age, in the way he once seemed to have done—his obsessions seeming to be ours as well. Nor could he be said to speak to the ages. The once reliable virtues of the old virtuoso were not much in demand. Approaching seventy, Noah published *Freifeld's Fiasco,* a work clearly meant to be his magnum opus on old age and death. It was vastly disappointing; in it one discovered that all Noah Danzig had to say was that he hated growing older and was terrified of death. The whining was impressive, as he might have said, but nothing very original here.

On three or four occasions, I was asked to write about Noah, but of course I refused. Two academics, each doing studies of him, approached me for information. I told them that I hadn't any, adding that I had stopped reading him years ago. I was patient. I waited. My time would arrive.

I was reading in bed, listening to music on WFMT, the chief

classical-music station in Chicago, when at the ten o'clock news break, the station announced the death, in London, of a heart attack, of the novelist Noah Danzig at age seventy-nine. The next day's New York *Times* carried an obituary on its front page. I read it slowly with my coffee, poured myself another cup, then went into my small study, where I began writing "Imperfection of the Life and the Work."

Normally, I write in longhand, later transferring what I have written into typed copy. But this time my mind was working too fast for my pen. Links, connections, comparisons, analogies, metaphors came at me with a tornado-like whoosh. I composed directly on the typewriter. I didn't stop for lunch. Working from eight that morning till five-thirty that evening, I produced 10,000 words, very few of which later needed any serious revision. That night my sleep was fitful. My mind was crowded with fresh observations, insights, angles of approach. Seven or eight different times I had to leave my bed to take notes; twice I had to get up to walk off my excitement.

In writing this essay, I began for the first time to feel that I understood the means by which art was created. It was created, I sensed, in one of two ways: through the force of great character, which made it authentic; or through the imitation of great character, which, however grand and glittering it might for a while seem, made it always and ultimately a cheat. I cannot rewrite my entire essay here, but what I chiefly did in it was to expand upon Van Wyck Brook's notion that literature was a Great Man Writing, except that I enlarged considerably the notion of what constituted a Great Man beyond Brooks's rather straight-laced one. The Great Man might be neurotic (Proust, Kafka, Joyce), or chaotic (Tolstoy, Dostoevsky, Balzac), and on occasion even orderly and obvious in his good character (Goethe, Henry James, Chekhov), but always there was a largeness that never cheapened itself, never asked for special dispensation for being an artist, never viewed life as being useful above all for the creation of art. It was not difficult to go on to demonstrate that, by these criteria, Noah Danzig, being no great man, produced something a good deal less than great art. Art, I claimed in my essay, had its own morality, its own severe tests, and Noah, I proved by deft quotation and neatly formulated assertion, failed them all.

JOSEPH EPSTEIN

The completed essay ran to 26,000 words. I wrote and revised the entire piece in five days, on intellectual fire the full time. It all went smoothly, pure sailing on ice. Quotations from the novels seemed to be at my fingertips. Arguments that had never even dimly occurred to me before now arose exactly where and when I required them. During these five days of composition, I resented having to take time out for meals or sleep; normal hygiene seemed an irritating distraction. I rose each morning and went directly to my desk. It was as if the words were waiting for me—and had been waiting for nearly twenty years. Late on the afternoon of the fifth day—a day on which, in my passion to be done, I neither showered nor shaved—I typed out the famous lines from Yeats's "The Choice" ("The intellect of man is forced to choose / Perfection of the life, or of the work"), then wrote that Noah Danzig, having too early chosen the latter, completely spoiled the former, which in turn made achieving the latter impossible, thus rendering both his life and his work sadly, perishably trivial. I pushed my chair back from my typing table. "There, Noah," I said aloud, "after all these years we are even at last."

Vengeance, the Italians say, is a dish best served cold. After my Noah Danzig article appeared in the *New Yorker*, I received something like a hundred and thirty letters about it, all but two or three agreeing with my general line of argument. Some people wrote to say that they had never understood all the fuss about Noah's obviously self-glorifying fiction in the first place. A critic who was an exact contemporary of Noah's wrote to say that what he found so troubling about the later novels was their repeated and boring insistence on his, Noah's, own virtue and spirituality; as my essay "masterfully" (his own word) showed, Noah had to insist on his virtue and spirituality because he himself in fact possessed neither. A friend in New York wrote to say that my essay was causing a tremendous stir in intellectual circles there. "The general consensus is that you have finished the old boy off for good."

It was time now to get back to other work. I had been reading for a little book on the politics of André Gide, and now intended to return to it. Certainly I had no intention of making a career out of

~*216*~

attacking Noah Danzig. In writing my essay on him, I felt I was telling the truth as I knew it, saying an interesting thing or two about the sources of serious literary art, and along the way putting paid to a little debt that had been building in me for a number of years. It was over, done, and time now to move on.

It was in Paris, where I had gone to do further research for my Gide book, that I had my first Noah dream. Dream, which implies story or bits of plot, is perhaps too grand a word. What occurred was that in the middle of otherwise quite normal sleep, Noah Danzig's face appeared, his luminous blue eyes staring out coldly at me. It happened again, on the flight back from Paris to Chicago, only this time Noah's head was shaking slowly, remorselessly, admonishingly. I must have cried out, for a stewardess, gently touching my arm to wake me, asked if I were all right.

Back in Chicago Noah's face, the asymmetrical teeth, the complicated nose with the dark nostrils, the mottled and furrowed scalp, and always the cold blue-eyed stare, was appearing almost nightly in my sleep. The head never spoke. I read its look to mean that it had been done a serious injury, felt it had been foully wronged.

I must have reread my *New Yorker* essay ten or twelve times to determine if I had been unfair to Noah. It was strong stuff, no question about that; no one would ever say that it was in any sense "balanced," yet in writing it "balance" was hardly what I was after. I began with a sense of personal injury, true enough, but that injury I took to be an objective sign of bad character in an author that led me to discover the effects of bad character running throughout his work. My purpose was to show the connection between character and art, to prove the point that without largeness of character there could be no authenticity of art. I was correct about all this. I had no regrets.

Yet why did Noah's face, his forbidding, disapproving, injured face, continue to appear in my sleep? It did so nightly now, causing me to get up for good, no matter what the hour. Insomnia gave me more time to dwell on the puzzle: what did Noah want? Had he not himself suggested, after I had accused him of the worst possible faith in using me so badly, that I would doubtless one day have a chance to get even? Was he telling me that I had gotten more than even, that I had gone too far? This was all quite nuts, of course. I realized that. But the realization did not help me to find sleep; it didn't keep Noah's cold blue eyes from haunting my dreams. What's the good of knowing you're crazy even if, with this self-knowledge, you remain crazy?

Work on my Gide book was out of the question. Such literary journalism as came my way went undone, not helping my reputation for reliability. (Fortunately, I had my large fee from the *New Yorker* to live on.) I lined up Noah's nine novels and three collections of stories alongside the chair in my living room in which I did most of my reading, and, bleary-eyed from lack of sleep, I would riffle through them at all hours, looking for some passage that would explain what was going on and perhaps free me from this craziness. I was drinking lots of Cokes and coffee; most days I didn't bother to get dressed. After eighteen years away from them, I began to smoke cigarettes again.

I never found the secret passage. What I did decide, though, through the blear of sleeplessness, the caffeine, the nicotine of more than sixty cigarettes a day, and the stink of my own unkempt body, was that I had badly misjudged Noah Danzig. I took him for a man, when he was instead that quite different thing, an artist—less than a great one, to be sure, but psychologically a perfect type. For such a man there are no ethics, only aesthetics. The complete artist was like the complete politician—interested only in the omelette, not the eggs that had to be broken to make it. But the larger point, I began to see, was that the more complete the artist the less complete the man. Men didn't come much more incomplete than Noah. I shouldn't have been angry at being ill-used by him; my mistake was obviously in assuming him capable of friendship to begin with. My mistake was in assuming that Noah Danzig was fully human.

I was on to something here. It was a bit of a blur, a touch hazy, but worth pursuing. I urgently felt the need to talk this over with someone, and as soon as possible. I needed to lay it all out, to check my thoughts in the company of someone more objective than I to see if my conclusions made any sense. I hadn't been out of the apartment in weeks, except to buy groceries and cigarettes. I had been brooding on this alone for much too long.

Next thing I knew I was sitting on a stool in a sports bar on Addison Avenue. The bartender, a brawny fellow with weight-lifter's arms and wearing a basketball ref's shirt, asked if he could help me.

"A plain glass of vodka with a little ice," I said. "And by the way, do you read many novels?"

"Not many," he said, setting the vodka before me. Television sets played all around the room, different games in flow. Backboards with baskets were on the walls; also lots of college pennants and photographs of athletes. A heavy punching bag was set up in a far corner.

"Ever hear of a guy who writes novels named Noah Danzig?" I asked.

"Can't say as I have," he said. "But look, old buddy, can you excuse me for a minute?" He picked up a phone behind the bar and tapped out a number. I sipped my vodka, and in my fatigue my shaking hands caused me to spill a little. Jesus, I thought, looking down, what am I doing here in my bathrobe? Then I noted that under it I had on pajamas, and was also wearing house slippers whose bent backs caused me a momentary stab of shame. Strange, I thought.

"Anyhow, old buddy," said the bartender, now returned, "you were about to tell me about reading novels or something."

"Ever read a story called 'Tonio Kröger'?" I asked.

"Can't say as I have," he repeated.

"Too bad. It would tell you nearly everything you need to know about Noah," I said.

"Would it really?" he said.

I felt vaguely that he was humoring me, but I had to be careful. I knew I was in a shaky condition here. Mustn't make snap judgments. Besides, the main thing was to set out what I thought I had now discovered and where, exactly, I had gone wrong.

"This guy I'm talking about has been dead for a while, but he keeps showing up in my dreams. It's made hell of my life, I can tell you. I haven't had a good night's sleep in months. But that's not the important thing. What is. . . ." And just as I was going into my rather elaborate explanation, two young policemen, one white with a thick mustache, the other a black man, were standing on either side of my stool.

"How're you doin', pal?" the cop with the mustache said.

"A little tired, but otherwise pretty good," I said. "How about yourself, officer?"

"Why don't you let us take you where you can get a little rest?" said the other cop.

"Sure," I said, conscious that in these clothes I had better go easy with these guys, "but has either of you ever heard of a fellow named Danzig?"

"Played second base for the old St. Louis Browns?" the cop with the mustache asked.

"Not exactly."

"Look," said the other, the black cop. "Why don't we get out of here. Go someplace where we can talk?"

As the three of us left the bar, my slippers made a flapping sound against the floor. Odd that I hadn't noticed it when I came in. Each of the cops grasped me firmly by the upper arms. In the car, the black cop drove, the cop with the mustache sat with me in the back.

"God," I said, "I forgot to pay for my drink."

"Don't worry, pal," the cop with the mustache said, "We took care of it for you. Why don't you tell me more about this guy Danson from the old St. Louis Browns you mentioned?"

"Not Danson," I said, "Danzig. He wasn't a ballplayer. He was a novelist. And do you mind not calling me 'pal'?"

"Kinda touchy, ain't ya, friend?"

"Go to hell," I said, and then—it must have been the caffeine, the nicotine, the vodka, the lack of sleep—I did this ridiculous, stupid thing: I slapped him. Not punched, you understand, but slapped. It felt damned effeminate. Who did I think I was? Adolphe Menjou? Clifton Webb?

I recall the cop's rather yellowish teeth smiling out from under his thick black mustache, as if to say, "Ah, well, at least this night's not going to be a total loss." The next thing I felt was a tremendous shot to the stomach. I threw up all over him.

"Son of a bitch," he said, clapping me in a hammerlock. "They'll fit you up with a nice snug jacket in a little while now, pal."

And so we drove the few remaining blocks to Louis A. Weiss Memorial Hospital, where, beaten, exhausted, dappled in my own vomit, in a hammerlock, and now missing a slipper, I was bum's-rushed through the emergency room, forced to swallow a pill, and strapped to a gurney on which I was wheeled off to the loony ward.

"Well, Noah, old friend," I recall thinking just before the sedative did its quick work, "I guess we're even again."